THE AGGRESSIVELY
SUBMISSIVE HITCH-HIKER

THE AGGRESSIVELY SUBMISSIVE HITCH-HIKER

Because No Good Deed Goes Unpunished

JAKE NIKOLI

authorHOUSE®

AuthorHouse™ LLC
1663 Liberty Drive
Bloomington, IN 47403
www.authorhouse.com
Phone: 1-800-839-8640

Published by AuthorHouse   02/05/2014

ISBN: 978-1-4918-5873-8 (sc)
ISBN: 978-1-4918-5874-5 (e)

Library of Congress Control Number: 2014902013

Any people depicted in stock imagery provided by Thinkstock are models, and such images are being used for illustrative purposes only. Certain stock imagery © Thinkstock.

This book is printed on acid-free paper.

Because of the dynamic nature of the Internet, any web addresses or links contained in this book may have changed since publication and may no longer be valid. The views expressed in this work are solely those of the author and do not necessarily reflect the views of the publisher, and the publisher hereby disclaims any responsibility for them.

Contents

Chapter   Title   Page

01:    White Shark 1

02:    The Mimes 19

03:    Cast Into the Fire 35

04:    Snagged Like the Whip Caught Gandalf 46

05:    Where ever I go They'll find me 55

06:    Snagged My Heart Again 64

07:    If You Say So 75

08:    Another Response 91

09:    Someone New 103

10:    The eco box 116

11:    Can't make Apple Cider with Lemons 132

12:    My personal Voyeur 142

13:    Yeah, like they'd stop 155

14:    New Neighbors 168

About the Author 185

I started writing with the idea I'd name this "No Good Deed Goes Unpunished" after the statement came true for me when I found my stalker having dinner with my parents at Le Mesa.

01: White Shark
November 2010

As I approached the Harrison/Giles off ramp a blurry silver blob which was parked on the shoulder of the exit slowly came into view (engine failures happen on occasion right?). At first I assumed it was benign, just another dud, a vehicle with some defect forcing the operator to ditch it and call for a ride. Considering there are some four hundred and fifteen thousand people living in the metro, it's not at all uncommon to see one or even a couple within the same mile.

My timing on the other hand was not quite as typical. Just after the vehicle a feminine silhouette quickly turned into a white blur. As if the words were falling out of my mouth I muttered to myself "Holy crap, she's gorgeous" before jamming on the brakes hard enough it's surprising I didn't skid right off the ramp into a ditch. Naturally I glanced up in the rear-view mirror to find her fluorescent white jacket about two hundred meters back. She kept staggering back and forth across the white line marking the inside of my lane as she proceeded. Far enough even it's lucky I didn't accidentally clip her as I passed. The wind was rampant that night, every couple of seconds a tuft of snow would whip up into the air and blow across the road from either side. A little of which made it through the crack in my window and melted on my face. At times it'd be so dense the road in front of me would disappear.

It was an odd predicament at three-thirty in the morning. So I glanced back up in the mirror, a little confused as to whether or not I wanted to spend the time. If it weren't for the chill bead of water dripping down my shirt I probably would have been half way home already. Again she stumbled across that line and quickly back onto the pavement. Our globe was tossing her around enough however I couldn't find it in my heart to drive off. It had to be miserable out there, she even pulled her hood over her face with her left hand to mask herself from the wind.

It was well below zero too, after I'd set my thermostat on full blast it just barely kept me from shivering so violently I'd lose control of the vehicle. I can only imagine the sensation I just created, a chilly burst of winter air bellowing across the skin as my car blazes past at some sixty miles an hour, displacing enough air molecules it probably knocked her right back into a foot and a half of snow.

Normally I like to make excuses for the bad habits I've picked up over my short years, like the cancer sticks, or the reason for my open window. So I snatched the air freshener from the pocket behind my passenger seat and squeezed twice. As I prefer to at least claim I'm a considerate smoker, I didn't want to smell offensive. I never should have started in the first place. It's an aroma that no one except he whom inhales enjoys . . . for as long as he can manage to avoid the health complications it causes that is, and naturally I was embarrassed to smell like my grandfather's office after forty years.

She still looked like a little stick figure in my mirror, as far as I could tell she may be kind of cute. It finally occurred to me as I was contemplating her predictable rating on the hotness scale, our ecosystem sent some more snow bursting through my window like a hammer atop a wack-a-mole's noggin. After she staggered off into the snow and back onto the road I quickly realized I should let the machine do her walking instead of watching her freeze for another minute or so.

I stuck the transmission into reverse and started backing my way down the off ramp, stopping again some five or ten feet shy so I wouldn't accidentally squish her of course. Seems to me that would be a bit rude, her day had probably been crappy enough already just landing in her predicament.

I glanced back toward the car's blind spot as she walked up to my passenger side window and stuck my finger on the button to lower it. When she got close she started to bend over and look inside. Surprisingly enough she didn't start running the other way the moment she saw my little beige Hyundai Elantra and the dent in its passenger door. She just gazed inside and amused me with her face as her jaw nearly hit the ground. I almost couldn't keep myself from giggling (the view through my window just screamed damsel in distress.

I could just barely see her so I had to lean over a smidgen, just enough to gaze around the frame between the two passenger windows. I'd guess she was trying to be cautious, keeping enough distance to ensure she could run the other way if I were out to be a loon. She didn't say a word for almost ten seconds, I had to inquire, "Need a ride?"

Her voice squeaked ever so slightly as she responded, "Yeah . . . I ran out of gas and had to pull over" with her thumb turned back toward the silver scrap metal before she paused again.

Her eyes slowly widened like the Grand Canyon whence I plucked the lock open and I tried to coax her in, "There's a gas station just down the road, hop in."

She didn't hesitate a wink; just yanked my door open and plopped down next to me. She started in as soon as she tucked her purse up by her feet, "I really didn't expect anyone to stop"

"Yeah there aren't many cars on the road this late."

Now that she was in my car, I was able to get a better look at her. I started scanning for reasons to kick her out. Her feet were stuck in some knee high furry black boots, her pants were designed with a black on white leopard pattern, her fluffy white jacket looked pretty warm, and her long black hair was tied up into a ponytail. While I couldn't see much more than the outline of her fluffy jacket and purse, nothing visible indicated cannibalistic tendencies . . . .

I didn't quite know what else to say so I offered my hand, "I'm Jake?"

After shaking my hand she cocked her head to the side and prompted, "Wow! I could have met a lot of really creepy guys tonight!?"

As she offered her name in return I started searching for words. I'm sure I could have said something amusingly romantic or condescending like, "Yeah, its mighty late for a pretty little lady like you to be walking around these parts!" as I wink like a hungry hillbilly. I don't really make a habit out of picking up hitch hikers however, so I didn't antagonize her much. I just mustered up a quick word, "They don't roll so well without anything in the tank do they?" as I gestured back toward her car.

She chuckled as I started forward, "No they kind of don't?" and pulled the bungee out of her hair to let it down, "After I pulled over I realized my phone was dead so I couldn't call anyone for a ride either!?"

"Well that sucks." I nodded a little and shoved the tranny back up into third.

She cast her hands toward the sky in exasperation as she continued, "I was in town visiting family, and borrowed my Aunt's car to go to this sorority reunion before I got stuck here" She didn't even take her eyes off of me, "When I got there my sorority sister started chewing me out because I showed up late, she just went on and on about how we need to be on time to these events, if we join a sorority we need to be diligent about it, we need to have each other's backs! After she came up to nag me later in the night to ask if I'd show up on time to the next one I just got fed up and left!" she threw her hands forward as if she wanted to smack the bitch. "Don't you just hate people like that!?" and she turned back toward me.

"They ain't my favorite." I was a little discontent with the polarization and changed the subject, "Which school?"

"It wasn't like any one would lose a quart if I were late to a freak'in party!? . . . oh UNO!?" she drew her torso back into her seat and pointed back toward the road behind us, "and then I got stuck back . . . ." She looked back, left, right and toward me again.

We were already out west on Harrison, I glanced over toward her and her eyes were as wide as the grand canyon, but this time the sides of her mouth were drooping down toward the floor as I spoke, "Really, what's your major?"

The look of terror on her face disappeared almost instantaneously as she jolted forward and smiled, "Oh! I'm a . . . a surgeon . . . from Ashton!"

"Heheh, a quart" I chuckled a bit under my breath and inquired, "So do you hold the fat flaps, or are you the one actually sewing people up?"

"I do most of my own stiches." She finally took her eyes off me and chuckled a little bit.

"Sounds righteous though, saving lives for a living?"

"It is, but it's really hard to feel bad for people who smoke sometimes, at a pack a day they have to spend several thousand every year on something that can only kill, that money not only could have paid for most of the operations in claims, but is usually the reason they need work done in the first place. Some of them shouldn't get the operation. Many can't pay their medical bills, several won't even listen to me, and they always keep killing their selves with it."

". . . well yeah, its kinda common knowledge they're bad for pretty much everything in one's life . . ." Apparently the air freshener wasn't fooling anyone.

The car was quiet for a few seconds before she barked, "Do you believe in god."

After she'd put money higher on her list of priorities than her patients' lives I wanted to say, "Yeah he's driving a beige Elantra." But could only expel, "I'm more . . ."

"What!? I can barely hear you!?" She rolled up the window and turned the music down. "Do you go to church?"

"Well no . . . . I'm more spiritual than religious, but I can't entirely discredit the possibility either."

"The possibility of what?" she turned her head to the side a little as she asked.

"God existing and all" I had to pause for a second and think "It's been years since the noun "god" has even come across my mind."

"What is spiritual?" She cocked her head to the side as she spoke again, "If you don't go to church what do you do?"

"I don't know whether or not to believe, but respect those who do, I just try to follow my gut I guess, try to live a moral life."

"Oh, that's cool . . . Do you need directions?"

The words came out in a belch, "Nah, we'll get there", as I turned onto 132nd. "I take it you do believe in god?"

"Yeah we go to church, and do this thing with the food drive! I mentor a couple of girls in foster homes, and we give to charities all the time."

"Kewl" I didn't really know how to respond so I nodded a little, volunteering for stuff like that is pretty honorable.

She was silent for a couple of seconds before asking, "So what else do you do? Are you in school?"

"I'm looking into on line colleges, so I can do the work any time of the day. I'm kind of a night owl. Plus it would maintain an open availability for me to continue working"

"That's cool, I was working all through college too. Usually a local University is ideal but . . . its tuff I guess . . ." she turned back toward me again, "it'll be worth it right?"

I muffled my voice the way I'd imagine the stereotypical Hick to sound, "Definitely, dats da pOnt of an erduKaton aren't it?" I was more focused on the freedom to research whatever I wanted than the "character" I'd build in a structured environment anyways, with an ever changing world I don't think it matters so much if I get a little more done one day a little less the other, so long as it gets done.

"Wow, this is really good music to calm me down."

"Ya like it? It's one of my favorite prog-rock bands, El Ten Eleven." I had their signature album playing at the time.

"What do you want to go into?"

"I'm leaning toward Electrical Mechanical Engineering, I think, well I don't know I think I'll start off with general ed credits and go somewhere else, but I keep finding this stuff Tesla did back in the day and it's kind of fun . . ."

"What stuff from Tesla?"

"Oh he released a bunch of patents and improvements for different electromechanical motors and transmitters, I want to run a couple of tests on basic physical attributes for the motor and see if I can't make an alternative fuel practical.

"So you want to develop a more efficient engine?"

"Yep. That's why I'm on this planet."

After taking our last right I pulled up to the first gas station I could find and gawked over at her like a cat bringing home a mouse.

She giggled at me with a finger pointed toward the unlighted convenient store, "I think their closed."

"Oh yeah . . . a can to put your gas in would be useful huh . . ."

She continued to chuckle as we pulled away from the pump. Luckily the QT not but a block east was open, so I pulled right up to the door.

I was dangerously close to E myself so I tried to explain, "Ok well . . ." as I jerked back up to face her.

She propped the door open lunged out onto the concrete swiveled round and cut me off though, "I'm sure there's a pay-phone inside, I can call for a ride!?" as she bent over again to face me.

"You don't have to, I can give you a ride back . . ."

I couldn't get a word in however by the time my tongue started flapping around she barked, "Ok!" and slammed my door.

She was already in the convenient store as I started mumbling to myself and I backed up toward one of the pumps, "I was just going to tell you my cars going to move." I didn't want her to think I'd ditch her there.

When I got out the night's air crawled up my spine despite the jacket I had on over my uniform, it was making me shiver yet again so I wanted to make it quick. After plucking the hatch lever I unscrewed my gas cap stuck the nozzle in and turned around to stick my debit card in.

After entering my pin the screen coded out and claimed to decline my card. I tried it again in hopes it was just a bad entry, but had no such luck. Naturally I was frustrated . . . . the words "what the fuck, there's a grand in that account" slipped from my mouth. I wanted to curl up in bed already so bad it was tempting to just kick the machine until something falls out. I started playing back the last week in my head and dug up my answer. I bought a TV the night before and my bank likes to block all transactions postdating large purchases. So I propped open up my wallet and found three twenties, a ten, two fives, and eight ones; surely enough to make it home! So I made my way toward the store.

She caught me just inside the door and blocked my path to the clerk, "What are you doing!?"

"I was just going to get gas? I'm riding near E. It'll be kind of a pain if we both run out."

"I'll get it." She cut in as she spun around toward the clerk to hand him her card, as she cast her hand to the side, she bellowed out, "Put this on his pump, what-ever it costs!"

I tried to cut in but the clerk was already tapping away at the register, "OK . . . thanks?" I was a little bewildered as I turned back out the door and she walked the other way back into the store. So I started trotting back to my pump and glanced back into the convenient store. I couldn't help feeling a bit guilty as I yanked the lever on the pump. The meter started climbing . . . just as it approached 3 gallons that stupid voice in my head starting going rampant, I didn't stop so I could extort her. I cut off the feed at 3.23 gallons and mumbled to myself, "that's a hundred enough-ish miles." After hanging up the nozzle I started looking both ways like a shoplifter on the look-out, but she was somewhere deep inside the store . . . The wind kicked up again and blew some more snow my way so I flopped back into the driver's seat for shelter.

I was getting tired . . . and a bit impatient as I started looking back into the store for her. Unfortunately she was just out of view and I let my tongue roll again, "she must be looking for the gas can still . . . or something . . ." before the last song in the album ended. After flicking it along to the next one I closed my eyes and sat back to wait.

A couple of minutes later she came stomping past my door, chuckling as she beckoned, "Why'd you only get three gallons?"

She startled me a little bit and I replied as I jolted back to life, "You don't need to buy me gas." as she continued past my window to the pump and started filling the little lunch box sized gas can she just acquired I shut my eyes again.

As if hours had passed I glanced in my side mirror; wondering how it'd take so long to fill that tiny thing, curious how long it'd be before I could pass out again. Low and behold my timing was stereotypical yet once more, she was bent over the can with her ass aimed back at me . . . So I snickered to myself and closed my eyes again, apparently that little can was deeper than I'd thought. She had a nice ass for an old lady though . . . .

After a couple of minutes my passenger door unlatched and screeched open so she could flop back in next to me. "Ugh, I still need to fix that."

"Huh?"

"Nothing, that doors just been squeaking ever since I was unlucky enough to graze a deer on the highway and had to limp my car home"

"I didn't even notice?" she glanced over toward the hinge and back to me, "How bad was it?"

"It was lying there . . . and I had to replace half of the accessories up front, the radiator, and bend out the frame just to get the piece of scrap metal to roll again without overheating."

"Wow that sounds like a pain."

"Kinda, I had to tie a rope between the radiator support and the back of my brother's car to pull it back into shape enough to close the hood . . ."

"Nice." She chuckled and looked back toward the hood, "It doesn't look bad from here."

"Thanks." I couldn't wait to sleep again so I started down Q.

"So what got you stuck on alternative energy?"

"When I was little my dad's friend, a chiropractor, was showing me this stuff that Nikola Tesla did about a hundred and fifty some odd years ago. One of the most interesting was his magnifying transmitter."

She squinted with her left brow as she spoke, "Like a radio transmitter?"

"Well one version was used as a radio; supposedly another emitted a scalar wave formation instead of the digital signal coming from a modern transmitter. An adaption he made allowed him to wirelessly power this little car he'd drive around town out by Warren Cliff." I merged into the left most lane by mistake, as I turned left two cars in the right lane boxed me in so I was unable to merge out of the left one, I tried to fall back but a flood of them closed in on me from behind.

"Are you sure you don't need directions?"

"Nah, we'll miss that ramp, but I got it." I paused as I merged right, "I'd like to reproduce one but the trouble is finding the right documents on the circuitry, supposedly most of his stuff was either ditched when J.P. Morgan decided he couldn't make money off of something so difficult to meter as wireless energy and cut funding, or burned when the Warren cliff tower was suspected for use by German spies." She sat up in her seat again as I turned north to follow the interstate back an exit further away from her car so we'd still end up on the correct side of the interstate. "There is a lot of potential in all of his unfinished works, like the radiant receiver he discovered when he was working on his Warren-Cliff tower. One of the modifications he made to it actually sent more of a surge back to the power-plant than what was being provided by it, and he blew a bunch of generators." She started to look around franticly, and sat up a little further in her seat again. The detour must have unnerved her, but I had just made it back to the on-ramp heading west so it wouldn't take much longer. She still looked like she was going to have a panic attack, glancing at every car, every sign, and back at me. "I want to continue his research on radiant receivers. Hopefully I can utilize them as a standalone power-source for rural locations. It'd aid our eminent transition off of fossil fuels, if possible I'd like to energize a car like the Tesla Roadster either wirelessly or with a reciever."

She didn't take her eyes off of me, but she started to scoot away toward the door like she was expecting me to bite her or something. "Don't you just plug them in overnight like a phone?"

"Well yeah, but it only has a range of some three-hundred odd miles, at sixty that is a maximum of a five hour drive, if someone wants to say go on a vacation and drive from here to Denver Colorado, a nine hour drive, they would have to stop for about 7 hours to charge the battery, plus the weight of all their cargo would reduce the range even further, possibly requiring them to stop twice and nearly tripling the time required for the commute. Limited drive times for electric vehicles are going to be a major roadblock in utilizing those motors for a reliable economic system, as the average drive time for a semi trucker is at least eight hours, and they are typically traveling at around seventy five miles an hour on larger interstates, not to mention their cargo."

Her back was almost against the passenger door, and her hand in her purse. "That could be just the kind of thing we need."

Her posture made me wonder what exactly was in her purse, probably pepper spray, but luckily I could see her Aunt's car up on the off ramp. "Hopefully, I'd kinda prefer to fight my way into a growing field instead of a dead end."

She finally looked back toward the road, and jumped a bit when she saw that I wasn't some freak job Axe murderer quack, the switch between personas was almost instantaneous as she started gasping, "OK! Well if I have any trouble, I'll just . . . give you the Derka-Derka distress call!" She ripped her seat belt off and shifted back toward me. I didn't know exactly what to say so I gave her a blank look, and she prompted again, "Have you ever seen Team America: World Police?"

I didn't even know it existed so I shook my head and mumbled, "Nope . . . ?" as she lit up again.

"Oh, well . . . it's a hilarious movie, you should watch it." She looked between her car and me as we came to a stop, "If I can't get it in the tank, I'll do this!" Naturally she hit the roof with her elbow when she started to flail her arms above her head looked up and snickered. Without a hitch in her movement she hopped out of the door and ran a little ways to hers. Not but a moment later she came running back, gesturing toward her car through the driver's window, she beckoned, "I can't figure out how to get the gas tank open . . . it's my aunts car." So as she stepped away from my car a little bit, I pulled the key to hop out and follow her up. We walked up a ways without a retort until she professed, "I swear I'm not an idiot, it's my Aunt's car" but I was too sleepy to care . . . I just shrugged when she made eye contact.

After we made it up to the driver's door my first impulse was to search for a latch, I scoped the lower frame and the center console for a lever, a button, anything with a gas oriented symbol on it other than the fuel gauge which was riding on E just like I'd expected. So I asked her, "Still have the manual?" and she ran around to the passenger door to start rifling through the glove box. Flipping back to the index was but a quick chore, and then she found some other page before I leaned over to peer over her shoulder, all of a sudden she dropped the manual and darted back around to the gas tank. There wasn't a latch, she just plucked the door open . . . but when she twisted on the gas cap, it didn't budge. So I snatched the manual and walked back toward her.

She snatched it out of my hand and flipped back to the same page before calling out, "It says it's a locking gas cap." she tried to open it as she handed me the manual, twitching it back and forth like a master lock's dial.

After two tries it wouldn't open so I read it aloud, "Says, three clicks clockwise, two to the left, four right, and then turning it counter-clockwise should open it up . . ." she rattled it around again and finally it started turning right out of the inlet. After letting the gas cap swing and flop against the body panels she picked up the gas can and tried to pour it in. I took the opportunity to stretch both hands up toward the sky rolling onto my tippy toes, and looked back down at my watch before I started mumbling to myself, "Jesus, its four twenty three."

She'd been fumbling around with the can before jumping up a little bit and turning back toward me again, with the gas can in hand she professed once more, "I swear I'm not an idiot, but it won't . . . it won't pour?" she handed me the can and I looked down at it, there was this little lever on the base of the spout where it screws on to the can.

As I pushed down on the switch and dumped it into her tank I chuckled and let my tongue flap around, "I guess they're putting child safety stuff on gas cans these days."

She flailed her hands up with bent elbows again as she began to implore, "I swear I'm not an idiot."

My only response was to shrug and reassure her, "I never said you were, it's not like you gave someone too much morphine and killed them? Crap happens . . ." She was silent, "Machines break down all the time . . ." as I glanced up toward her and cocked my right brow up a bit I prodded, "You haven't over dosed a patient have you?"

She stomped her left foot against the ground as she answered me, "NO!!" so I chuckled and pulled the can's nozzle out to hand it back. She gestured at me with the gas can, holding it up to my face as she rolled up onto the balls of her feet. "Oh . . . well . . . do you want a gas can?"

I wasn't sure how to respond again, "Nah, we have enough crap at home. One for 2cycle oil, one for the mower, and the snow blower" but shrugging was becoming a habit in this situation.

"One for the snow blower?"

"Yeah . . . it was used so we had to get it running at first, who-ever had it before us must have forgot to put oil in the gas . . . it works pretty well for the crappy winters like this one though."

"How did you get it running?"

"I don't know, my dad did it before I could remember anything."

She stared at me for a few seconds, and then down at her left hand with the can in it, "Well . . . thanks!? I really didn't expect anyone to stop."

"I'm just glad I found ya instead of some creep." Most guys I know are actually pretty decent but she may have more experience with the other side of their personalities, being a woman and all . . . .

As her face lit up she leaned back a little and poked my left shoulder, "Well . . . thank you, it was really sweet!"

My eyes drifted toward my car, "Don't worry about it . . . ." I shrugged again, "Mine was still running . . ." there was a bed just two miles away I could curl up in.

Just before my eyes closed themselves she lunged forward and gave me a hug as she hollered, "Aww come here." I could smell the wine on her breath now, after staggering backward she gazed back at me again.

"Ight . . . well take care." She kept staring at me for another moment. "Ya don't need directions do ya"

She slowly shook her head and smiled, "You take care too! I know my way back."

As I walked back to my car I started fumbling around in my pockets for keys, the tips of my fingers were starting to go numb already and it was hard to feel the difference between a flash drive and keys, a couple of feet shy I had to stop and dig around before I could actually pluck them out and hop in.

I dashed straight for the tunes and tossed up some more prog-rock. Her tail lights flashed a couple of times, usually when a car runs dry like that it takes a little bit of effort for the fuel pump to force the last bits of fire water through what used to be an empty tube. Apparently she got it to ignite as her car rolled forward, so I sparked the T.D.C. cylinder and stuck the shift lever into first so I could start my ascent back up the off ramp. The light at the top of the hill was green. She turned left onto Giles into the left most lane just before I made the turn with her in her blind spot. We continued down the road until the next light, it was red so we came to a stop.

I'm assuming she was aiming for the gas station just off the road as she was in the turn lane; it was a new one that went up within the last two years. I would have gone there but they hadn't been getting enough business yet and always close at two in the morning. When I pulled up and stopped next to her I glanced her way and found her waving good bye, the light turned green signaling her to turn so I flashed a peace sign and let the clutch out a bit. I'm kind corny so I started mumbling to myself as the Eco box began rolling home, "Safe travels M-Lady."

The road started curving not but some thirty degrees left through the next light, and I was getting really sleepy. I couldn't help but to yawn and cover my gullet with my fist as I'd strain to keep my eyes open and on the road. Mid yawn a calico cat dashed from the right shoulder into my path; forcing me to drop the shifter down from third, let out the clutch, hit the brake pedal, and yank my E-Brake, I was barely able to stop shy of the critter as he dashed across the opposing traffic's lane and down into the Oasis.

I felt kind of silly rambling to myself, "Lucky no-one's awake at five little road-pie. I'd rather squish ya than get rear ended" there wasn't a single vehicle in view so I slapped the shifter back up into first again and continued down the road.

When I finally pulled up to my street, there was a blue hue leaking through the living room window. Eager yet, I scurried up to the door and unlatched the deadbolt. My older brother barked down at me as I broke through the threshold, "You're finally home!? I thought you only worked until two or three?"

"We got out late and I got side tracked. Wha-cha up to?"

As I climbed to the top of the stairs he followed up, "Just finishing up my last load of laundry before I head back to my place." He was loafing on the couch and playing browser games on his laptop while he was waiting. "What took so long this time?"

I flopped down in the armchair by the front window and started in, "Oh five minutes before close we had a sixty three dollar order, my closer wanted help finishing off a bowl after work, we had to go explore this new CD he got, then I found this surgeon on the side of the road and gave her a ride to go get gas."

He scoffed and looked back toward his game, "Yeah you found a surgeon, at what, five twenty?"

"Yep!"

"There's always a good excuse eh!?" He gazed back at the screen disapprovingly and continued building his little defender towers. "So what were you really doing? Drinking again?"

"No . . . Just that . . ."

He nodded and frowned, "Uh-Huh"

He never likes to listen to my excuses so I got up and stumbled off to bed, making sure to grumble along the way, "I'm-a hit the hay" just as I'd passed him I. Figuring I'd prod at his massive ego I rambled again, "She was actually pretty nice for an MD too" and continued staggering off to my room. I was still wearing my uniform when I flopped face first into the pillow, and the world around me disappeared pretty quickly.

When I was only six or seven my family took a vacation to Silver Dollar City. My mother was looking for things to do one morning and found a cave nearby with a regular tour running through it. Everyone seemed to like the crystals, stagnations, or the bats most of all. My favorite however was when the whole group was led into the deepest part of the cave, with a room just barely big enough for all of us to fit in. They explained to that usually in higher spots daylight would always reflects off walls and finds its way to ruin the effect, but down there one could find perfect darkness. They asked everyone to turn off their phones and flashlights, and shut off their lanterns. It was perfect, I couldn't even see my hand touching my nose, I wanted to lay down right there and take a nap.

My dad and his high-school friend (The Stench) have always kept our families close, since before I can remember his son and I would trade off houses to sleep over and play video games until the elders woke up which we took as our cue to go to bed. Their family came with us, and I'm glad they did. As The Stench decided to pinch his wife's behind, some forty of us filled the room with a bellowing laughter as she yelped. It was one of the most amusing noises I have ever heard as both the yelp and a crowd of jackals refracted off every wall in that tiny cave, and echoed yet again down both paths.

I've always had two layers of drapes just to keep my room the way I like, as close as I can make it to that cave after everyone shut down the lights, not just dark as if the room lacks any light sources, but as if the walls consume the rest.

Even with those two layers this becomes pretty difficult above ground level, especially at ten in the morning when the sun is high in the sky. It always finds a way to leech through a seam in the window and scorch my retinas, waking me from my nirvana. The room was already well lit as light squirmed through the edges of my window, making it impossible to doze off again. So I threw my pillow over my face, hoping to catch maybe just fifteen more minutes. It's hard to put a snooze button on the sun though.

The night just fore started to replay in my head as I returned to consciousness.

I always tend to wonder if I'd left any holes in a day's work, or if there was anything I needed to call in and have retrieved before the next manager finds out it's out of stock and doesn't have time any longer to pick it up. Through all the mindless orders, the cash drawers, bank, dining room, kitchen, and log books I couldn't recall missing any product or even any tasks we hadn't time to attend to that night which would still need attention. I was home free, and I had the day off for once.

Soon the bowl crossed my mind, after work a buddy and I reviewed a couple of different perspectives from which to evaluate Stephen Hawking's theory on black holes. He insisted it may someday be possible to utilize a worm hole and transport goods across the country. He was off of his Micho Kaku kick for a bit but we always seem to ramble over some sort of uncreated technology like that.

I had a problem with whether it'd be safe to chuck an organism through one as even if it were possible to bypass the issue that one is unlikely to survive after having every atom disassembled and reconstructed. I had to figure it likely the memory of whoever stepped through would be wiped clean, like a hard drive or cassette tape going through the x-ray machine at the airport. Food and other nonperishables would be the only likely objects we could warp; all the vitamins, minerals, and other sustenance in food would still be essentially the same so long as the chemical structure is unaltered, making it safe enough to consume.

He's usually pretty reckless though, and elected himself as the first to hop on through . . . . Claiming even if the storage in his noggin were reformatted, it'd be fun.

I still didn't like the idea and protested that we aren't even within decades of having adequate technology to do such a thing. Anyways my perspective, it would be more plausible, and naturally cost effective (technology/time wise that is) to dig further into anti-gravity devices, except instead of monitoring the atmosphere in a closed chamber, to create a repulsive force between an object and the ground. If the output of four of them are properly monitored and spaced it could likely sustain its altitude. It'd allow for even more personal air travel than planes, much like those things in Star Wars, I named my version a Forerunner.

Four equally repulsive Tesla Turbines would work as well . . . Providing a stable base to sit atop and pivoting arms would allow them to angle back and propel it forward, but that one would require a closed chamber to shield the operator from all of the wind.

Unfortunately the technology behind the Tesla Turbine is rather underdeveloped at the moment (current models, even ones running at fifty thousand volts only produce enough thrust to levitate themselves). It's a solid state device utilizing the high voltage between a negative wire and a positive plate to create a current of air across the two, much the way any air purifying ionizer works. With a little research and a couple prototypes it could probably be improved to create a thrust grand enough to propel an aircraft, possibly even compact enough for my Forerunner.

After a while he decided it was bed time and took me back to my car, but I didn't want to go home and figured I'd take a short drive first. Suddenly the rest of my morning came to mind. First the white blur flashing through my right peripheral vision, I rolled over dug into my pocket to retrieve my phone, and started looking for a new contact. After scrolling through the lot of them, I found nothing, and tossed my pillow back over my face.

"That was weird."

Normally I can pick out a piece of trim to match a window molding at the hardware store, after looking at the one being replaced just once. Normally I can picture a relative or friend's face, their car, or an overhead grid of their neighborhood. Normally I can picture the last guy to order a double whopper with cheese and a large soda with a medium side of fries/half onion rings.

A Caucasian guy in his mid-thirties with short brown and gray speckled hair, he had brown eyes and a goatee, but not a solid one it was tapered off toward the bottom and split in two segments like the ZEN master on the karate kid, accompanied by speckling of freckles on his cheeks. The wrinkles on his forehead were just barely visible behind bushy spiked eyebrows, and his large bulbous nose which arched in the middle like a camel's back revealed straggly nose hairs sprouting from the bottom. His face was pudgy like the hypochondriac on scrubs. From just two feet away his gut had about a foot and seven inch diameter, which was covered by a blue polo horizontally striped with black strips. He was wearing black dress pants and a tan coat with no chest pockets.

Normally I can remember close to every image and sound which passes through my brain. I typically get a great deal of satisfaction out of expanding the level of detail I can retain. However I should have paid more attention to detail this time, as for this woman, I could only picture but an almost holographic or transparent human figure, with long black hair, a white fluffy jacket, light form fitting pants, and boots extending up to her lower calf.

I played through the route in my head; I found her on the exit, merged onto Giles, took a left on to Harrison, right at a hundred and thirty second, and down to the first gas station on Q. They were closed, she chuckled, a block or so to the east the next one which was open. I fed my car, she filled her can. We traveled east on Q to a hundred and eighth and north to L, back west, missed the on ramp, continued north on a hundred and twentieth to center street, back east, on ramp, and made a straight shot back to her jeep.

Yet as for her face, I had no clear image.

After laying there lifelessly lazy for a couple more minutes, it started to bug me, like a computer I wanted to de-fragment my hard drive, I wanted to pay a forensic analyst to decrypt the corrupt files in my noggin, I wanted to go back in time and take a picture.

Then I looked over at my desk, my pack was lying there crooked open, one of the luckies had a little twist of paper on the end. I always liked to plug them with a little marry.

"mmm, I almost forgot that was there."

After glancing at the time on my phone, I hopped up grabbed my pack and my laptop and headed outside. Without inventing time travel, what else could I do?

So I hopped on to check the latest tech news; apparently they've been doing research for quality measurements, researchers in

California are using the resonant frequency of quartz crystals to stabilize the frequencies used to measure smaller and smaller quantities of materials as well as ensure the quality and purity.

For the rest of the day I flew through a couple of web pages, did some research, and went to a coffee shop to relax.

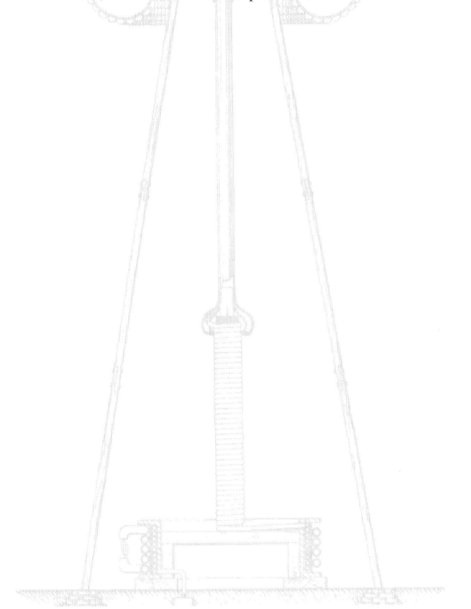

02: The Mimes

I'm a pretty average kid; at 16 I wanted my independence and some cash, so I applied at a local Burger Factory and got the job. The week after I turned 18 my general manager practically begged me to accept a higher position as a shift coordinator. He was my favorite GM, every time he gave someone a task he'd actually allow them enough time to complete it (not all managers did), if we didn't know how to do something he wouldn't yell or punish anyone he'd just show us what to do and leave us to it. All he ever asked was that we stayed busy and when we couldn't find something productive to do, ask.

I was considering attendance at a university in Lincoln however, I wanted to obtain a decent degree and make my own living just like anyone else. At the time I didn't quite know what I wanted to go into, so I couldn't make a snap judgment and decline. It took a while, but he kept asking me every day if I'd fill out the application on-line. After about a week I finally decided that I'd most likely be better off getting all of the credits I could take care of at a cheaper college (a community college) before transferring in, that way my time "figuring it out" would be cheaper. I let him know that the application was already in the system. The moment he finally "convinced" me to accept the position he clenched his fist and pumped his arm down to his side as he cried out, "yess!!" So apparently having me there was a victory. Normally I'm not prone to outbursts however; I just chuckled and went back to counting my drawer.

I never realized that staying in my home town could have such an elephantine effect on the path in which the dominoes of my life would fall. They sent me off to another store for training, which only took about a month. I spent most of my time there sitting in the lobby with lists and lists of temperatures at which certain products must be held, different procedures for chemical use, and company standards for what to do in the event of different incidents. As interesting as it was, I like to do the same with hundreds of books.

When I got home my father saw it fit to give me an hour long lecture regarding the new social dynamics I would encounter with those whom once were my friends and co-workers. Claiming that they used to have no effect on my job, however now I must consider situations in which some may become assets, and some may jeopardize my position unless I discipline them. He claimed that if one of "these people" whom are now my employees, decides to skip work, come inebriated, or even just argue with customers, the ramifications for each mistake they make can also be tied to me as a member of management.

I typically regard my father as an anally retentive worry wart (he blows everything out of proportion). He likes to claim things like, "This is supposed to be the place I come to relax! I feel like I'm waging war every day I come home!" every time I want to wait five minutes before taking out the trash because I'm in the middle of a chapter. If he wants his dishes done for him, they need to be done the moment he delegates his instructions, I cannot terminate my progress at the end of a chapter first. He wants it done now. When I was young he would scream and yell when my grades were merely B's, he'd even edit papars on my computer before I'd ever give him my password.

When I started writing this book he found a way to breech my firewall over our router, and delete sections of this text because he didn't like it. I hadn't any idea of how to stop it for the longest time.

To an extent he did have a point however; a business cannot manage to waste resources, support employees who create more issues than they solve, or even ignore miniscule variances which inevitably add up in the end. His main point was actually rather respectable, as it is a simple fact that with a promotion comes more responsibility in any corporation, and allowing other employees to make poor or childish choices may be seen as negligence on my part.

A couple of months into my new position another store needed help after some manager went out of town for a while. When I got there the store manager told me not to worry about filling in temperature logs or anything, they would be done already every time I came. I was only supposed to manage the shift, make sure everything was clean before we left, count the bank, and he showed me how to lock up.

I'm a nerd, so when I get off work I typically read a couple of Nikola Tesla's patents, or surf for information on radiant receivers, transmitters, maybe electric motors. I was a night manager, so I typically worked late into the morning. By the time I got home my parents were always asleep. So the whole house was always quiet, just the way I like it.

Normally I'd have two days off a week; typically right in the middle with hump day, so finding friends to chill was difficult. Everyone'd have homework or something on their plates. My parents on the other hand always spent their nights in front of the boob-tube, and they like to turn the volume up so loud it'll shake the neighbors' walls. Most of the time I'd get tired of the noise and hit up a coffee shop for some go juice, somewhere I could hear myself think.

About the same time Wal-Mart finally delivered that TV, I decided to chill at Caffeinated Nightmares. Conveniently enough I found The Big D there when I walked in. I've known him since kindergarten. As we were sipping on some go juice I started rambling about some of the most recent stuff I was digging up on Nikola, the moment I thought I was done reading I'd find something else that guy created.

He was there first, so I flopped down in the chair across from him. "Hey guess what."

"Great you have a stiffy again don't you."

With my mouth wide open I dazed off into the brick wall behind him, "Yaa . . ." and let my voice die off, "Ya know that Magnifying Transmitter thing Tesla powered his car with?"

He grimaced without taking his eyes off of his computer as he responded, "The Tesla coily thing? Yeah some autistic kid has brought it up a million times."

"Apparently he found a way to direct the energy emitted from one." He was rolling his eyes and nodding already so I paused for a second . . .

With the most unenthusiastic look possible he slowly raised his eyes back up toward me and groaned, "And . . . ?"

"Well my instructor told us last week that while he was in the navy some guy was standing next to the radar antennae when someone else turned it on . . . It cooked him into a soupy boil."

"That'd suck."

"Yeah kind of. The Warren cliff tower he adapted utilized an even higher dissipation . . ."

"So what, He was able to use more energy . . . and direct it?"

"Yeah . . . Apparently he called it a death ray, I found this video of one that showed an orb like pulse moving back and forth from it before discharging. It left a really big crater."

"Huh. Just a bolt of lightning?"

"I wanna make a little one and go hunting with it . . ."

"I bet that would be just about as effective as hunting with one of those fifty cal rifles."

I started nodding like a nut job, "Except instead of only getting to eat half of the deer, we could eat right away, it'd be cooked upon shock wave."

He gave me another death stare, "Great a portable microwave . . . . I want a cigarette, you coming?"

I stood up and tossed my jacket back on, I didn't even have enough time to warm up but figured it didn't matter anyways. "Guess what we use it for these days"

His right brow cocked up a bit, "Military?"

"He tried, but usually we just turn our TVs on and off with comparable circuits."

"We turn our TVs on and off with a death ray."

"Yeah, he aimed it at a receiver. Cruel ain't it?"

He opened the door to the patio rolled his eyes again and pointed outside, "Nut-cases first." Once we stepped out he lit up and sipped on his coffee before setting it down on the railing. "So how easy is it to make one we could hunt with?"

"The FBI would find our paper trail in no time, it wouldn't exactly fit in the shed, plus I'd need quite a few heavily restricted compounds, a factory the size of the Kellogg plant on ninety sixth and some pretty long extension cords if we wanted to go running through a forest with it."

He frowned as he spoke this time, "So it ain't like a rifle."

"It'd need a pretty big battery."

"What about the happy medium, can we build a reasonably sized battery pack to lug around with us, hell even if we have to turn it into a backpack like one of those ghost buster things it'd work right?"

"Well yeah, it is feasible, can I get a lite I can't find a lighter." I'd been digging through my coat and pants pocket thinking I had one.

He pulled out his and lit it for me. "I'm always happy to lite my Bitchs' cigarettes" Then he lit another and started puffing on it.

"Damn phanny-bandit." Not that it did any good, I snarled at him like a rabid dog. "If we did build one the size of a rifle, the EMF around the power source would be more effective for heating the fat on your back than a deer's side."

"A little ineffective . . ."

"It might annoy the deer enough to make it trot off in the other direction, but your back fat is still turning into cancer."

"Don't mock my back fat asshole."

"You really do need to pick up one of those workout DVDs."

"So what's that black thing I saw some whale carry in here?"

"The kindle?" I left it inside.

"What's a kindle?"

"It's one of those excessively fancy reading devices, like an electronic book. They use this e-ink in the screen so it only consumes energy when it sets up the page, and then it sits there, kinda like an etch and sketch."

"Does it browse the web?"

"It can" my face squished together in an attempt to look disappointed. "It's pretty clunky on the web, and it doesn't support anything other than HTML formats though." I stamped my cigarette out on the ground before chucking it in the trash and headed for the door, I was getting cold.

He was already done with his second so he followed through the threshold. "So it won't play videos."

"Nope."

"What the hell good is it if I can't watch porn on it."

After flopping back down in my seat I snatched up my kindle. After turning it on I noticed that it was no longer on the book I'd been reading last, it was scrolled all the way to the bottom of my library, unfortunately I only had the device for a couple of days so this didn't quite daunt on me until a month or so later. "Well after searching through Amazon's database, I found all kinds of really good books, and quite a few of the classics are free, like Tom Sawyer. There are quite a few text books as well, I found a CALC book I can go through, a physics book, chemistry, and even a couple on electronics."

"You're going to go broke buying books now aren't you?"

Apparently the place was getting pretty packed, as a group of four, two girls and two guys were looking for a place to sit, and came up next to us. They found four chairs and one table, the table adjacent could only accommodate two so the girls found a way to sit awkwardly in the middle of the aisle with two chairs they'd found somewhere else.

"Nah, Im'a go through all the free stuff I can find first, there's no sense in buying something I can't use when the free text books'll teach me calculus, I found a bunch of Nikola's stuff too, his autobiography is free, another author wrote a biography which is free, and I found a bunch of his patents I can go through."

"Huh, for something that can't play porn that thing's pretty fancy."

I pulled up the patent for a magnifying transmitter and gawked at it. "I wanna build one." The brunette in the middle of the aisle was staring at me with eyes wide like an ocean.

"Great can we go hunting with that, or is it just for frying the neighbor's dog?"

I chuckled a little bit, "Well the cop behind me does have this really mean German Shepard that licks me every time I pet it, I hate it when they do that, they lick their butts with those things . . ." I started squirming in my seat as I feigned wiping the saliva off of my hand a couple times and grimaced as the imaginary acid saliva seeps through my pores. "But it really is more for show; this is the version in which Nikola adapted into a radio transmitter. Well tried, it doesn't emit as many fractals but it still wastes a bit too much more energy as bursts of lightning than the modern transmitter."

"Perfect", he rolled his eyes while he grunted, "Just make an RC car that shocks the user while you're at it, that'll sell well." The group of mimes must have got uncomfortable as they stood up and walked off.

"It could probably sell as a gag gift, like one of those pens that zaps ya when you try and click it."

"What six year old wouldn't love to find that under the Christmas tree, aww you think you get to chase the kitty with that, BZZZZ!!!"

"Should we go through the trouble of wiring the car or just print the plastic?"

"Wire the car so we can charge for copper, that's how all the fat cats do it. What are you brain dead . . ." He snickered a little and sat back a little more in his seat. "Think I'm going to go without charging you for those alkaline thingies."

I started nodding to reassure him, "Alkaline cells aren't typically rechargeable bud . . ."

"Really? I thought you could recharge them."

"Well technically you can, however most that aren't made for it will ooze acids, some may blow up, and the ones that are made for it are expensive and only work a couple of times."

"Useless?"

"Bout as useful as you."

"Good one you over-sized monkey."

"Oh the opposable thumb, what wonders you have granted us access to." I was hoping to freak him out so I held my hands up in front of my face and started gazing at them as wide eyed as possible.

"You really are a piece of work."

I still had my hands up so I made the best of it and flipped him off with both of them. "My Daddy did say he dropped me on my head a couple of times when I'd still fit in one hand."

He snickered as one of the baristas dimmed the lights, warning us that we only had a few minutes to get our fill and get out. "Ya know, I think I'd actually believe that one."

After gazing up at the ceiling lights and back down at him I held my kindle up beside my head and barked at him, "Well since some prick kept me from getting any reading done tonight, I think I'm going to go warm up my car."

"I think I'll join ya" he looked down again and mumbled under his breath, "ya freakin' coke addict."

"Ight, I'ma redeem my refill, I'll meet ya out there." By the time he stood up I made it down the stairs at the end of the aisle and half way to the entrance. And took a left for the thermoses, I always like to top off while I still have a chance, caffeine is better in larger quantities. Once I started walking back over toward the door again he finally caught up to me and glared down at my cup as he opened the door before grunting again, "Yeah, you're a caff-addict."

As he started to open the door for himself I slipped out in front of him, "When'd ya figure that out" and made my way across the street.

We stood there and chatted for another ten minutes or so with yet another one too many cigarettes. Once our cars warmed up enough to keep from cracking one of the cylinder walls, we parted ways for our homes again.

I'd love to do one of those all-knowing overviews, but in all honesty what he was doing eludes me entirely. I however hopped right back onto the page and ingested a couple chapters.

Normally our GM prefers to group our free days (it feels more like a weekend that way) so I had the next day off as well. As always my parents flipped on the boob tube, so I decided I'd head out.

I failed to find a friend with some free time so I defaulted and grabbed my iPod and kindle before dashing out the door. I headed north to my usual coffee shop (a heinous crime right?). When I got there the barista behind the counter decided he'd grimace the moment I walked up to the counter.

I didn't know if the look on his face was my doing or not so I glanced behind me and found no one. His face looked like a face, "Can I get a medium chai latte."

"Three forty two." Maybe he was having a bad day, his face relaxed to the blank stare I was acquainted with so I handed him the three bills and some change.

I figured I'd be nice and dropped a bill in the tip jar, it had this funny little sticker on it claiming I'd be struck by lightning from the all mighty if I didn't contribute to the well-being of local employees.

He boiled it up just right and bellowed, "chai!" like a robot before turning back toward the dishes in his sink. I assumed that he was just tired of bouncing between tasks and bellowed "Kewl, Thanks" as I stumbled back to double check. There wasn't a single elephant to be found in the store.

The tables closest to their back door were typically unclaimed so I made my way straight for them to flop down. I couldn't wait to start in on one of the auto-biographies I'd downloaded. First things first though, my favorite addiction; I pulled out my IPod and sifted through its play-list for Red Sparowes.

Two things about Nikola's life stuck out like thorns on a rosebush. When he was in Smiljan he always liked to take walks and stare at the sky during storms, every time lightning started cascading the land. Empathy quickly followed the text, I always enjoyed taking my dog out in the midst of blizzards; typically I'd be staring up at the sky every foot of the way. The way he described the Niagara Falls was particularly amusing as well, most see water roaring down from the sky, to him the great waterfall was nothing but inertia available for him to harness, and the water was merely pre-accelerated mass. When he finally made it to the states for good, he did exactly that, powered the entire city adjacent.

I had to pee after about three quarters of the cup, so I dislodged my buds and headed for the bathroom. As I sat atop the can I could just barely hear someone's conversation over the crowd. "What are the chances I'd actually see him like this?"

"It's a small world I guess."

"I don't really understand why he didn't recognize me though."

"Just go talk to him."

"What if he doesn't like me?"

"He helped you blind didn't he?"

"Yeah . . . It was really sweet of him to stop, most people just keep driving."

"Most people would be afraid to get in his car."

"I was stranded, what was I supposed to do"

"You could have walked."

"It took like fifteen minutes to drive to the nearest gas station that was actually open; I would have been a Popsicle by then."

"People used to do it before we ever had cars."

"So . . . It still looked like a gold plated limo at the time."

The male voice had a really deep chuckle, "Yeah a real fancy limo with a dent in the side." It started to get a little weird though, "Are you sure you'd even want him? He's driving a beater, I doubt he's very well off."

"I don't care what it looks like, it's what he does with it that counts."

"You never know what he's going to do in the future."

"I didn't even think people would do something like that these days, he won't hurt me."

"I just don't want to see him take advantage of you."

"He wants to go to school for electrical engineering and toy around with transmitters, how would that be taking advantage of me?

"Kids his age are known for job hopping and changing their majors, I don't think it is a good idea."

"No way, he wouldn't even take anything. And I was vulnerable from the moment I met him."

"Are you going to talk to him?"

"I don't know, he probably already has a girlfriend."

"If he is as good a guy as you think he is, he probably has a wife. Maybe he's humping that guy you saw him with."

To say the least, it was weird. She was silent for a moment so I got up to wash my hands, "He just turned around and walked away like it didn't even matter though . . ."

After cleaning up I walked out into the lobby and took my time. It was plausible right? No one in the room looked familiar though, and everyone seemed to be engaged in their own conversations. So I stood in the middle of the room like an idget for a couple of seconds.

I couldn't hear anything other than my own breath, "Maybe I smoked too much on the way here . . ." and I couldn't see anyone even glancing my way . . . . I swirled around and glanced through the room, "Yeah I think I'm losing it."

I still had a personal deadline though, so I flopped back down by my kindle. Was I going crazy? I had to take another look around before putting my ear buds in. I guess that's what I get for eve's dropping, one group was planning a party, one was talking about prom, another some vacation in Colorado . . . . So I dug back into chapter two, where Tesla promoted his . . . social views. Unfortunately my idol was a bit of a nut.

Maybe a half an hour or so later just in-between two songs I just barely heard the words like whisperings through the paper thin walls of my buds, "I don't get it through! He just walked by again?" Many refer to tesla as a recluse "No I don't want to! That's his job!" Many refer to him as a man beyond his time, "I can't believe it, he was so sweet." Many claim he was a sweet and gentle man, who consistently promoted the use of his inventions for the common good of mankind. "I don't care if he smokes! As long as he doesn't do it around me." Several influential personalities like Mark Twain, Marconi, and Thomas Edison kept in contact with him over the years. "Why didn't he recognize me! I just wanted to talk to him!?" It is often claimed that few engineers are as accurate as he, few are as innovative, and he even had a knack for romantics as a poet.

Finally she was loud enough to get my attention so I jerked up from my kindle to see what all the commotion was about. Nothing though, no one was looking my way. I was losing it.

Just before I glanced back down a dark haired woman rounded the pillar in-between the door and I as she wiped something away from her cheek and the front door slammed.

A couple of seconds later a car went squealing out of the parking lot . . . .

I only got a look at her back side after she screamed, "UUGGGHH! I hate this!" on her way out the door so I couldn't tell if I knew her or not. She fit the profile, yet as vague my image, most did.

It was sad and confusing at the same time. I wanted to know but she was long gone. I would have chatted but didn't understand why she wouldn't just say hello. I didn't even know how to change it.

All I could do was go back to reading. About an hour later my cup was dry and my head sore from trying to focus, I decided jettison, and yanked the buds out; after being pounded by 50db wave forms for two and a half hours straight taking those things out was like ripping a Band-Aid off of a fresh wound.

The room was nearly empty and my timing nearly perfect, as soon as I could hear the world around me again the lights dimmed. I didn't even notice it before but the blonde mime that was sitting next to us just one night prior stood up and stretched just after I started to get situated; she hadn't been in the room when I looked last. Her voice was soft as she made her way for the door, "I can't believe someone would go out of their way like that, and just drop her!?" I almost couldn't hear her. Someone else from across the room chimed in, "She's better off without him any ways, only leeches smoke!" but I couldn't tell whom it was because they were around the corrner.

Apparently I was right, but now the room was empty. Two car doors slammed outside and revved their ways down the street. Should I take a guess? I glanced around the room and sat back down, but I was the only customer in the place. Should I run and hide? They were peaceful, finicky but peaceful.

I had to find a medium of communication, but her friends were no longer in the room . . . I figured maybe I'd leave a note or something, if I'm right maybe she'd see it, if I were wrong/unwanted I'd be nothing more than a fly on the wall. I'd just go back to reading, at the very least my caffeinated library would still be there . . .

One of the regular baristas was hanging a couple of pictures up on the wall; she's this extraordinarily chipper blond girl. So I walked up.

"Excuse me."

I'm pretty sure she was thinking intently about something else, as she jumped like a cat without bending her legs the moment I interrupted. "Uhh . . . yeah?" she glanced both ways before looking me in the eyes.

"There was this girl that ran out of the room about an hour ago . . . someone must have pissed her off."

"Yeah I saw that. Any Idea whats up? I don't know that group very well."

"I probably should have took a better look but they seemed to be having a pretty good time."

"Yeah its not often we have such a lively lobby, most of our business is usually during the day."

"I know that's why I like this place so much . . ." I paused for a second to think about the crowd I'd usually see in there. It made sense; typically there weren't too many people when I'd show up in the past few months. "Well I found this woman on the side of the road a week ago . . . she ran out of gas and I gave her a ride to the gas station. The lady running out the door looked kinda similar."

"Aww you actually stopped? That's sweet."

"I really don't remember much from that night, I just got off work at like three in the morning and I was kinda tired, but if that was her storming out of the store I'd feel kind of bad I missed her." She looked almost like she'd seen a ghost, her face blank just waiting for the next sentence; I wasn't quite sure what to say or how to ask so I just went for it, "Do you mind if I leave a note, I know all of them are gone already, but if she was here I'd be kinda cool to meet her again?"

She stared at me for another second, probably wondering if I was some freak or a serial killer as her next question was, "What did she uhh . . . . What did she do, for a living."

"She said she was a surgeon, from Ashton if I remember correctly."

She perked up a little bit and shouted, "Yeah there's a bulletin board over there" continuing with her finger out, "bands usually advertise on it and a bunch of people use it to leave business cards, you can stick it up over there if you want."

"Ya don't mind? I feel kinda weird even asking, if it were creepy you'd say no right?"

She jolted up just a little bit, "Nah, I think it's kind of romantic!"

I was still wondering if I even should, "Ok, kewl thanks".

She jolted up a little bit again. "There are always a bunch of extra pins and what not all over the board, go right ahead." And went back to what she was doing so I walked back to a table just adjacent to the door and pulled out my Kindle, I bought this hard back leather cover for it with a blank note pad facing the kindle when I close it. After flopping it open to the next blank page and pulling out a pen, I started writing . . .

To the beautiful and brilliant surgeon I met on I-80,

If I am incorrect, I apologize for my intrusion. However If I remember correctly I believe I accidentally overheard certain details in my night here I have only spilled around one person whom I cannot decisively identify. I really must apologize, as I cannot for the life of me recall your face or your name, your persona and the events of the night we met on the other hand are rather clear in my memory. Even if it was just a short drive you were rather entertaining and I'd love to chat some time.

I am unsure whether I was paying too much attention to the road or whether my being in an impure state of mind at the time caused such a blip in my memory (I'd love to have a scape goat here), yet the picture, the actual image of whom I met that night eludes me. I particularly enjoy talking to a PhD about their thesis whenever I get the chance, usually a paper or thesis tends to get even more interesting when you crack open the brain which wrote it ;-) . . . .

In all honesty I am a little surprised I actually found you, at first you were nothing but a blurr in the corner of my eye as I passed on that off ramp. However if by some odd chance I am correct and you were here, I hope you'll revisit. This is one of my favorite crooks in Omaha's many walls, if you don't care to see me I hope you will at least enjoy the orgasmic caffeine.

You spent some time trying to convince me you weren't a moron, as running out of gas in the midst of your travel was nothing more than a hiccup in the normal passage of your years. I hope that will not interfere with the future, everyone makes a mistake every now and then.

I must say though I have an excessive deal of respect for your profession. I have had to make repairs on my own vehicles and change the oil in a family members', however I cannot imagine what it would be like to do such a thing with another human being. Hell just holding a fat flap seems like rocket science to me. The thought of being able to save another person's life has always made me somewhat excitable, to be the one whom has that opportunity almost every day seems like a walk in an amazing dream.

I know this is a rather peculiar form of communication, but my brain is like an eclectic computer . . . it doesn't like to lose data. To be honest I felt the urge to hire a neurological forensic scientist to lift the old sectors from my neurons . . . . just writing this is a little odd to me, but I couldn't help but to think it would be at least a little interesting to speak to you again. I wish I had a better way to say it, I typically don't have the luxury of finding a "damsel in distress" on the side of the road, and you were certainly a rather pleasant hitch hiker to accompany me on such a journey, but I wish you all of the luck in the world, I trust you'd use it well.

Yours truly,

Jake Nikoli

402-827-9874 (I printed my number instead of this one.)

P.S. Before you left my company that night you mentioned a movie you would mimic if you could not fill your tank . . . . While I don't remember the name I would love to watch it sometime, I'm sure its rather ammusing.

I used a total of three pieces of paper, one a first draft which I made about two paragraphs and some change into, the second I made about four paragraphs into, and the third piece of paper I stuck a thumb tack through.

While admittedly I was trying to be cute, surgeons are typically required to go through six or eight years of education, so at the very least she'd be twenty four/six years, certainly my elder. I felt like I was walking a tight rope in crafting that piece of tree flesh; cute enough to gain attention, but not forward enough to creep her out.

Maybe my memory had me fooled; it wouldn't be a first as I'm pretty goofy anyways . . . Maybe my assistance caused an argument between her and a spouse, I'd have to hope she'd be a good friend if she did resurface from the oceans of Omahans. I'd be contacting a human right? Not a demon? So I was actually almost excited about the coincidence.

The words, "Why didn't he recognize me!!" started ringing through my head as I drove home. For some reason it seemed oddly probable, as no one else in the room made a sound, she exceeded all ambient noise . . . and I was pretty sure people don't do things like that on a daily basis, if I was lucky it was indeed a good thing.

The next day I went into work, and made my usual rounds . . . I had to tinker with the ketchup dispenser in the lobby because it was pumping out nothing but a speckling of tomato guts and air on a full bag. I found a couple of really old O rings we could try replacing for little to nothing and the plastic block with the valve mechanism in it was cracked.

After talking to the manager above me and showing her the crack, she handed me the catalog so I could find and order the part . . . . So I did.

Later in the night Stick wanted to go outside and have a cigarette. There were no cars coming through at the time and everyone had their tasks done up to the hour, so I decided I'd join him. I've known him since kindergarten too so most chances to chill are good ones.

Normally he has a story of his own, oddly enough this time he was curious what I had been up to. And for once I actually had a story to tell; usually my life is a little more peaceful than eventful. So I told him about the night I found this lady on the side of the road, how she told me she was coming from a party with her old sorority, and how I think she may have found me at this coffee shop.

He told me that this was good, saying "Good boy, go fuck her up the ass."

"I don't even know what she looks like."

"Dude it's not hard, especially with a story like that."

"Can you run a program that isn't installed?"

"It's not the person you're looking for, but any of them that read that."

"Isn't that a little . . .?"

He started talking again, "I'm serious dude." With his finger pointed at my crotch he continued, "All you have to do is make that thing a little less floppy!"

"I was more interested in her thesis . . ."

"Trust me!" with a frown on his face he started shaking it from side, "Doggy style!"

The words tasted a little sour so I staggered back a bit, "I see . . . so the answer to psychic communication is sex right?"

"Doesn't involve talking does it?" he started grinning as he'd nod, "Ya both know it though."

I couldn't help to chuckle in all the wrong ways, "Because sex will breech the failure to communicate?"

He told me that this didn't have to be so difficult, that I needed to get my nut up and go fuck her a couple of times. What disturbed me even more was the look of pure conviction on his face so I told him to go inside and do my dishes so we could close . . . . But he was determined, saying that he knew how to seduce a woman, with his experience he could recognize a sure bet when he heard it.

03: Cast Into the Fire

A week later I had another night off and went back . . . Even if I weren't curious this city is pretty bland at night . . . Naturally The Big D was already there, sitting right next to the back doors like always.

I'd just stumbled across some junk on particle accelerators which resembled Nikola's hand, his signature was nowhere to be found but it was from the right time period and a couple elements sketched in the image looked just right. To be entirely honest I was incredibly lucky to find anything on this technology at all. Even considering how dated this it is, the intensity of the blast it creates actually managed to scare me more than it'd intrigued. At the same time it was still new, I was still pretty eager to share and flopped down next to him . . . I'm like a kid in a candy shop when I have access to the internet.

D had a padlock in one hand and a cup of go juice in the other, so I inquired, "What's in the leather pouch!?"

"I was surfing around and found a couple of pick sets, this one was my favorite because they have a full tang" He held one up so I could see a little light showing through the hilt, "And this aluminum stamped around it was simplistic enough to be cheap."

As usual I was curious, "Half and quarter tangs have a habit of breaking like a cheap pocket knife?"

"Typically, it's even more common when they stamp the picks out of pot metal." After he finished his sentence the lock in his hand popped open and he burst out in laughter.

"Getting pretty good I take it?"

"I'd like to think so, but I keep pinching the pins and they won't even drop when I let off the tension rod."

"How old is the lock?"

"Don't know, found it in the garage."

"It probably needs some graphite."

"Yeah it is pretty sticky turnin', even with the key . . ."

"Wish I had one of them puffers with me, it might loosen up."

"Well who's going to oil their door every day so I can raid their fridge?"

"Just carry the puffer with ya."

He gave me a snarky scowl before responding, "Don't you need to turn the lock a couple of times to work the graphite in all the crevices anyways?"

"True . . . it'd make the pins real smooth like."

"Great let's just oil half our engines . . ." as he shook his head and continued fiddling around with it again he started in on me once more, "I'm pretty sure this will be good for me anyways, get good with the hard one and your door will be a cake walk."

"It's ok; our locks are only for your safety anyways."

"What did you booby trap the door again."

"No . . ." as I turned toward the wall and feigned shame I finished my statement, "I only do that when mommy and daddy are out of town!"

With eyes bright like stars he mocked me again, "That's fine, Ill come in through the back." He must have been getting tired of practicing all on his own as he handed me the lock and a couple of picks, "here try it out, I bet a dunce like you won't be able to get it open."

I took a couple of stabs at it, but I didn't quite know what I was supposed to feel after nudging one of the pins, they just slid back and forth between the tumbler and the lock casing. Before glancing back up toward him I inquired, "You must have been toying around with this for quite some time, the pins are actually pretty smooth." It still didn't budge though so I prompted again, "How am I supposed to know when one of the pins are seated?"

"Let me see it again, I'll show ya." He stuck his hand out and I plopped the lock and picks into his palm. With the tension rod inside he jiggled the pick around in there and the lock popped open. "You'll feel the tension rod twitch ever so slightly."

He handed me the lock and picks so I could stick them in and try again, after bouncing the first pin up and down a bit I could feel the twitch and he barked like a drill sergeant. "Watch how much tension you're putting on the tumbler, with an old lock like this you'll angle the pins in there and it won't open." He offered me some more advice with his left index finger on my hand, "That's about all the pressure you need."

Tinkering with it for a couple of minutes didn't make it much easier but the lock popped open eventually. I couldn't help but to giggle and gawk at the wonder I had just inherited before he took over again, "Here try this one" with a squiggly pick in hand, "It's called a rake" it had a zig zag on the end resembling a bolt of lightning instead of a single little pick head. "Some people call it a snake."

I drug it in and out of the lock, in and out again, and again. It wouldn't turnover quite yet, "Opp, Engine's seized again."

Apparently he wanted to demonstrate, after snatching it out of my hand he started twitching his wrist and flicking it about as he drug the pick in and out, then it opened. "Like dis."

After handing the lock back to me he stared at my hands as I flicked it around a bit, first bringing the back side up as it exits, then dropping it as I exit. I jammed the pick once or twice on one of the pins as I tried to reinsert it so I figured it'd be best to angle it down as I penetrate. Finally I tried flicking the far side of the pick up as I drug it out in one fail swoop (hoping that the split in the pins would catch on the tumbler as each of their little springs fling them back down) and the lock popped open again, just to prove to myself that I'd learned/retained the skill I re-latched it and popped it open again a couple of times.

I made the mistake of thinking aloud after a couple of trys, "I wonder if a wooden pick would work very well?" I glanced up at him again and inquired, "One of them wooden Popsicle sticks ya use to mix in sugar after a bitter batch."

A hysterical song burst from his belly like a chuckling hyena, "That'd be amusing, we should try it." So I dashed over to the condiments and plucked two (I'm a degenerate so I get excited about stuff like that). We started whittling away at them after I chucked one into his chest, and he finished first.

All of a sudden some woman screeched from across the room as I dug into the stirrer, "He'll get over it" and her tannish/white blur dashed right past the brick wall leading in and out of the lobby, the front door quickly crashed behind her. A couple of seconds later some car screeched like a drag racer off the line as it pulled out of the parking lot. The guy that was standing next to her started glaring at me like he wanted to burn through my face with laser eyes, and then dashed out of the room as well. Hollering along the way, "Fucking dick!?"

D tends to barge into my cognitive stream when I daze off into space, "Ya gonna be done some time today or should I go outside while I wait!?"

They were already gone though, the table empty, so I finished digging into my stirrer . . . As my dad always says, it proved to be about as worthless as boobs on a nun, it snapped after I just barely nudged the first pin.

"I don't think this test is fair, mine's wood fibers are angled off the side of the stirrer."

"Oh just blame it on the wood fibers, it's always the inanimate object's fault huh?"

So I brandished it up to his face, "Seriously, look."

"While it looks like your right, you picked the stick stupid."

"I get no love here."

"I ain't no fruit loop buddy."

"Hehe, oh well . . ." There was no point in crying over spilt milk so I offered the lock, "You may as well try yours."

After using the hook pick to fish the pieces out I tossed it back and let him show off, as the latch popped open he started laughing again, and continued the whole time as he re-latched it and did it again. Luckily he didn't get to gloat for too terribly long, it finally broke on the third try.

The rest of the crowd started to chatter on one end of the store, "He scores Again!?" Screaming and laughing their asses off on the other, "Yeah he's a taxi driver!?" So I blurted out, "Want a cigarette!" as someone out in the front room hollered, "Can't even talk to a girl big boy!?"

I didn't quite know how to respond so I continued out the back door, making sure to bring my kindle with me this time. The girl running out the door looked exactly like one of the mimes . . . I didn't know how long they'd been there, I didn't know if she had been following me. Was she just lonely and looking for someone to be hers, or was she pissed I didn't explain the situation to the guy she came with, the one that followed her out the door? For all I knew she could have been there five or more times before I realized someone was behind me having an ulcer.

I didn't know quite what to do think or say at the moment, she was out the door already. My mind kind of went on autopilot, "I guess this will be five for today . . ." He barked as I stared off toward the parking lot. "Need a light?" I felt like one of those screen savers with the imploding and exploding multicolored dye bouncing around in my head, back and forth, up and down, and all around your screen . . . . Did I not wear the right attire, was I supposed to wear business casual, should I have looked like I was coming from church, or maybe I'd be better off coming in a full tuxedo, maybe an elf costume!? Maybe I should have lunged into the room and slid onto one knee with my arms wide open as I cry out, "I'm here to save the day M-Lady!!" I didn't though . . . .

The Big D broke in again, "Something up?" (was I supposed to waltz around the room every time I'd arrive and ask each woman in the room "Hi were you stuck on the side of the road this one night?")

(Did I have a target on my back?) I gasped and knocked my head back in exasperation, "Nah, I'm fine mate, just a little schizoid."

"Got a nic-fit? You left in kind of a hurry." (was he deaf?)

"World'll keep spinning I guess . . . so did you ever finish getting into college?" (or am I schizoid?)

"Ya sure?" (Why are ya askin?) "You know I got you're back if ya need something right?" (great what do you really mean by that)

"I'll get over it eventually, Mary doesn't call anybody fat." I couldn't change the past, so I shrugged off the future.

"Ya sure? If there's something that irritated you, you know it's more important than my marines crap?" I wanted to spout off, (Great!? What do you know that you think I know that you know I know, JackAss!?) but tried to change the subject instead

"Where are you in that process anyways?"

I think he started telling me about which stage he was in after applying to an out of state for college and the marines. I didn't process much of it though, my mind was in la la land. I just knew he wanted to cover both bases.

I started nodding at him like a bobble head, and agreeing with whatever he put out into the ambient medium. When we got back into the lobby the room was back to normal again, either some of them left or they got bored of me . . . All I could hear was everyones' own conversations until a familiar voice blurted out, "I guess we'll find out soon then!" before the crowd returned to an neutral medium again.

I didn't want to be there anymore for fear the walls'd start screaming again though, so I excused myself, "I think I'm going to head home."

"We still have forty minutes before they close up?"

"Yeah but . . ."

That's when someone on the other side of the room started hollering, "Stick around and gloat why'doncha!" so I figured it wouldn't be the best place for me.

"It's just . . . about that time though . . ."

"Ight, well I'll see ya around I guess . . ." He almost sounded disappointed.

After I turned around and made my way down the aisle, someone below the stairwell chimed in, "Well there's your boyfriend!" she was a tall slender brunet with short hair and long yet well-manicured nails . . . If I were a fashion bug I'd say she was too old for the tears in her skin tight jeans, she had to of been at least thirty two . . . I didn't want it to be true, but it was . . . she glanced up at me and broke out in laughter before turning her head back toward her friend, "Nah! That guy's gay!" I was kind of hoping I'd be welcome if I weren't a cannibal or an identity thief . . . but then again the proverb "curiosity killed the cat" rings true a little too often. . . . . I could have fought back and told her she was fat or something, but usually a person like that wants nothing more than gratification, retaliation would merely be but another form of such.

As I continued toward the door another voice rang from behind me, "Aww! Are you walking out on your imaginary girlfriend!?"

I couldn't wait to put a door in-between myself and the contents of that shop . . . So I let the door close behind me and continued up to my car. Who-ever that was book'in it out of the coffee shop . . . She was probably scared of me now. What a brilliant way to greet a lovely woman right? Just sit around with a knife out before displaying how easy it is to break through a locked door . . . that'll go over real well as a class act.

Normally after an "emotional event" like that I don't take very kindly to having company around, so I drove out to my favorite lake (It's supposed to be closed after ten but I have my ways . . .). I do however like coping mechanisms like cannabis, so I emptied another cigarette and topped it off with some tastier tobacco before scurrying out into the darkness, I figured a good walk around the pond would give me some time to forget about the banter . . . and it did.

When I finally got back to my car I flicked on the radio and the first thing I heard was, "He was right there! And he struck out again!" (Not the kind of statement I wanted to hear in that mindset) so I flicked the off switch and drove home.

A week or two later I got bored and started surfing around for motorcycles and mopeds, hoping I'd land on a fiscally insurable way to get around the nation for less than the change it'd cost me to travel to a coffee shop. I couldn't help but to think the ride would be fun as well, but a decent happy medium would be nice.

None of which were manageable for me to purchase that day however. So I sifted across the missed connections on craigslist, (a local radio station had been playing these bits about them, sometimes they were actually kind of funny), I figured I'd end up mocking the poor grammar used in one page and all of the meaningless looks people would give each other across stores when they're lonely . . . . And I did, one started off with . . .

Bucky's 132th + center—M4W—Omaha

you was right there next too da slurpy macheen wen you bended over to pick up the straw you dropped. I couldn't help myself, I had to inch around cornner and get a look, you was wearing none pantys . . . I loved that sight and would love to get a nother one some time a little closer. Maybe even a little play, hit me up here if you see this and we can catch some fun. It was the store just off 132nd and center.

I'm the kind of nerd that gets a big bang out of little stuff like that, the kind of thing that a radio station reads off all of the time before breaking into a chorus of laughter.

I plucked another. Hoping someone was in a worse situation than I.

Walmart 72nd and dodge—M4W—(heaven's gate)

All dressed up in white you came in my walmart and unzipped that jacket of yours. I couln't believe my eyes at the beauty which it revealed. You had on this tight brown pants and tall boots which were almost drenched with the melt dripping down your skin. I loved your cherry red lipstick, and I want to get my own taste some time, call me if you get a look. I knew you were locking eyes with me from the moment you came in the door and gone through my line.

It nearly sent me to the floor, someone's life wasn't just as meaningless as mine, the grammar was even . . . . . "perfect".

Oddly enough the next one was a little less benign . . . dated for the night she went scampering off across the room screaming that I'd no longer be emotionally tied in due time . . .

Heaven drove away—W4M—(the edge of disaster)

I was at a church festival when the singer on stage started singing, just as he cried out the words, "Is it better to have loved and lost than to have never loved at all" I couldn't help but to start bawling.

Imagine my surprise when I thought all was lost, and then all of a sudden my Knight in Shining Armor's golden chariot stopped in front of me. At first I thought to myself, "No, god no!" I thought it was the end I thought it was going to be one of the devil's army. Yet he slowly inched back toward me and offered to help.

The singer actually stopped in the middle of his song and asked me, "Why do you cry M'lady? What is troubling you so much?"

"After saving me from the cruelty of a winter's night, my knight in shining armor left me to find my own way!?" I said!

He replied in a soft voice, "Honey god doesn't always give us a reason for the things he does, but love is in all of our fates. You'll find the right one for you some day, you just need to have faith."

> "Why does he always screw me out of the good ones!? So sweet, so gentle, so generous; and he just went away!?" I couldn't help but to cry at the time, but my girlfriends suggested something they'd heard on the radio. I figure I'll have nothing to lose (already the man of my dreams is gone) so here it is. If you ever see this I'd love to do more than pray, I'd love to meet you for coffee. I know you don't even recognize me, but I want to break the ice between us.

At the time I was thinking with the wrong head, so I assumed this was her. I thought I'd recognized something in the way she worded it . . . . The words she used and the order which they were in . . . the color, the car . . .

If she was actually pretty friendly in my car why shouldn't I give it a shot? An extra friend never hurt anyone right?

It was 4am—(the side of the interstate)

> I must apologize if our separation that night was at all consequential in an emotional realm. However if I have interpreted this correctly you may very well be the person whom I met on the side of the road. The weekend of Black Friday yes?
>
> If I am correct you came around to my favorite coffee shop to scope things out, and I never would have noticed you if it weren't for the particular conversation I overheard, and your screams, "Why didn't he recognize me!?" Yet I would love to chat if you are actually the person behind this philosophical mask. Breaking this glacier between us isn't exactly something I know how to do . . .
>
> I remember several things about you: your personality, your generous nature (how you like to give back to man kind), and the way you speak. Unfortunately I cannot recall your face or your name. I hope this is not insulting to you because I really did think that you were a rather intriguing person, but I have a really idealistic view of the world; as if everything around me has no color, I see merely their outline upon first encounter. In this coloring book I call the world I don't typically care about what someone looks like, I normally don't pay attention to the clothes they wear. I care only about the person behind the mask, which may be why I can't bring up an image of you . . .

> It is rare that this view fails me, but I am unsure exactly which vessel carries you through the day. I would like to know you though, so if you are near please give me some indication that you are the person I am looking for. While I lack the specifics, I do feel there is something worth exploring.
>
> This may not fall within average social constructs, but I am typically an intrinsic personality. If breaching this invisible barrier between us is at all intimidating, do know that it is met by an inviting vacuum inside the bubble around me. With any incentive, I normally perpetuate a friendship until the end of time, but this shell game seems rather exhausting. I'd need something more tangible.

I felt like a child In writing that^^ I felt as if I were attempting to balance a top, so well it wouldn't even leave it's spot. Like any other, I didn't want to offend or excite her too much.

In the morning I was still a little unnerved by the whole thing, and as I started boiling the water for my morning pot of tea my mother propped open the fridge. "Good morning."

I'm not a morning person, so I grunted, "ehrgh"

"You're up early, its only ten?"

"Yeah, I need to run a couple of errands before work."

"When's that?"

"Three."

"Oh . . ." she turned to stare at me with a bottle in her hand, "So where have you been going every night?"

She didn't seem to care whether or not I had enough of an attention span to mush and stir my tea leaves, "just some coffee shop."

She almost poured her milk outside the cup as she chuckled, "Uh-huh? What have you really been doing?"

I was still groggy and didn't want to answer, but the last time I didn't fork over she nearly tackled me, "Well this lady there who keeps running out of the room and whining about how someone doesn't recognize her. Judging by the shape of her ass I think it might be this surgeon I met on the side of the road one night . . ."

"Oh really!? When'd you meet a surgeon?"

"She ran out of gas and needed a ride around town to fetch a pale."

"RiGht . . . ?" she shook her head, "You can't force these things Jake. You'll find love soon enough." I could just barely see her shaking

44

her head after she slammed the fridge door and stormed out of the room. "You just have to wait." Apparently giving her something of "substance" was satisfying enough for once . . . . Normally she'd want to corner me and talk for hours. Sometimes she'll even greet me the moment I open my door in the morning. Usually she is the one telling me that books aren't supposed to come to the dinner table, when I sit at the dinner table I have agreed to engage in a good ole afternoon family special.

I didn't want to force anything to happen though, I just thought it was cold out and it'd be uncomfortable walking alongside a major highway with several cars blowing past all the way . . .

My tea was done though, so I plucked the strainer out of the pot and squished the water out before stumbling toward the hall. My brother was home again for whatever reason (I didn't see him on my way out), he was on his laptop in the living room. "Has mom been drinking already this morning?" I blurted across the room.

"No Jake, there is nothing wrong with mom. You just need to be patient. It's a virtue you know."

"And what exactly am I waiting for?"

"If you go looking for love you won't find it, you just have to wait."

"What!?"

"Don't have a coronary, dad, just wait."

After staring at him for a couple of seconds I figured he was just pulling my chain, he's always a dick like that. So I made my way down the hall to inhale a couple of articles through ZeitNews and a few patents before scurrying off to run around town until work.

04: Snagged Like the Whip Caught Gandalf

A week or so later I decided to get real comfy and search for some more candy, I flopped onto my bed and propped a pillow in-between the wall and my back with a laptop in hand. When the Warren Cliff tower was still in operation, and Nikola had time to tinker around with it, one of his modifications created a higher voltage between the source leads than was provided by the plant. Apparently this sent a little too much current back to the generators and caused a surge which shorted out a couple of the coils, since he worked on the plant he had to repair them personally. The next circuitry which I'd stumbled upon was quite similar.

After repairing the generators he began research on something he eventually called a "Method for Receiving Radiant Energy". Instead of relying on an antennae as merely a data source, he wanted to develop one capable of powering appliances as well. This was a pretty big challenge; normally the signal we receive from a local radio/cellular tower is merely milliamps. His towers did emit a stronger signal, but if the emissions were too intense they'd cook all of earth's population like ramen noodles, so a brute force method would be a little unethical.

I could only skim the surface with that which I'd found on the net, but later in history a man named Thomas Henry Moray began research on an antennae which could amplify the static in our atmosphere. I couldn't find pictures of the finished product's circuitry, but he was able to energize a large array of light bulbs by plugging into his "black box". In a couple of Moray's later papers he claimed to have achieved a maximum output of about fifty thousand watts. Not just enough to power a moderate household, but it pushed enough energy to justify the argument that he'd tapped a source other than local radio transmissions. The box was small enough that just a room or two full of them could light a city like New York too. The idea Moray implemented was to circulate the signal through a loop in the center of a reciprocating transformer in order to limit any resistance it'd encounter before attempting to increase the voltage. He claimed it'd act like a hot and cold front colliding, as a tornado spins each side pushes it round faster and faster until it can maintain a consistent velocity, the stimulus/source plate in this loop was used to circulate current through a highly conductive portion of the circuit in order to add inertia just the same way.

Later in the night my parents turned on the tv, and it started shaking the walls again. It was getting to be a little bit of difficult to read.

That coffee shop was still a little weird for me, I decided to glance around Google's map of our city after entering coffee into the search bar. I scoped across one street, down the other, up this one, and across again until I'd read the hours listed for just about every coffee shop in town. Nightmare's was the only shop I could find in town that was actually open past 9pm. If I wanted coffee I'd have to try and make the best of it, I headed out the door again.

I've lived in this city since I was a blank slate, too early in my life to know how to walk. So ever since I have had access to the Internet and a car, I have always looked for something new. A place peaceful enough to lose myself in the sea of information, and diverse enough I could get some coffee or munch on something bite sized. I can't legally go to bars yet so the only place in town which is open during my ideal portion of the day was that mom and pop shop.

The entire place was exceedingly loud this time around and so packed I couldn't find a seat inside, so I went out back to the patio. I was still being a rebel at the time so I lit up a cancer stick as soon as I'd made it out the door. After looking around to discover that I was alone, I picked this spot where I could still get some light off of the big light pole in the middle of the garden and leaned against the railing to go over a couple differences between dc and ac receivers. Most of our planet's technology regarding any type of wireless energy capture is being used in phones for wireless data transmission, or computers for WLAN. I wanted to know the difference between the power circuitry and that processing the information in a phone.

One in particular (The Wiseman) caught my eye because it was simple enough I understood how it'd operate despite my limited experience in the field. It utilized a loop of diodes to direct the current across a capacitor before it'd ever have a path of least resistance to ground. It didn't produce much power, but he tested it at several altitudes and validated the fact it's voltage increases with more space in-between the ground and plate. After an hour or so, my fingers started to get cold and numb, so I decided I'd head inside to thaw my extremities. Luckily enough I found an empty seat by the door which two college guys were occupying when I'd arrived, I could see them walking out the front door so I plopped down like a vulture

Typically a consistent and familiar background is the best alternative to complete silence when engaging in a scholarly ingestion of data. So I plopped my ear buds in and tried to read for a while.

It's rare anyone ever gets what they want however. The crowd grew even louder, they were actually managing to exceed the maximum volume apple has set to prevent damage to its users' eardrums. I was trying to ignore the background and accomplish my goal but I could have sworn I heard something about "energy" and the word "electron" eventually the loudest word in the room was "Einstein" then something about "lightning"! It was nearly impossible to leave in the back ground. The guitars and melody pounding my ear drums weren't even helping; it was actually making my head sting and throb.

So I figured I'd pluck my buds out. The moment I did the whole store dropped a thousand decibel levels, it was as if choreographed. My ear canals were sore so I stuck my fingers in to massage around and increase blood flow in the area; again the store jumped about a thousand decibels until I pulled my fingers out. The noise around me died back down yet again. Typically I prefer not to make a big deal of things, but this made me just a little bit uncomfortable. I felt like I was sitting center stage, in the middle of a play, with the world around me responding in tune with the script.

A group behind me quickly invaded my ear canals, "You can't move more energy than what is pushed by the source though."

"Like forcing water through a tube, you need some sort of "pressure" to get it moving through."

"Einstein claimed however, that "E=(M*C)^2" and more important is not the stimulus, but the total energy present in a body of mass and how it responds."

They got louder, "still this "energy" or these particles are stagnant without some sort of force to get them going."

"Yeah nothing is going to move without a cause."

"I don't get how it would be possible, it just wouldn't work."

"Some say it can be done." The guy's voice box rumbled as he chuckled aloud.

A couple of extra friends can't hurt anyone right? Normally a conversation like that one is just a little intriguing to me, especially if someone more knowledgeable than I has something to share. So I turned around and asked, "Excuse me?"

"Yeah" the guy responding looked like he was about twenty three, brown hair, green eyes, a little goatee, and a thin nose.

"Normally topics regarding energy dissipation are somewhat interesting to me . . . What exactly are you talking about?"

"My physics teacher was giving a lecture on perpetual energy. He was using a newton's cradle to describe it. He kept referring to it as a phenomenon, and said that some could actually do such a thing with electricity. At the end of the class he made a big point of the fact his newton's cradle was going the whole hour."

The guy across the table looked like he was in his mid-forties, his brown hair was speckled with grey spots, and his thick glasses reflected most of the light which made it into that corner of the room, "Pull up a chair, we'd love your input."

"Sure . . ." I said reluctantly. There wasn't an open chair at their table so I glanced both ways and drug mine over toward them.

As I plopped down next to him the elder introduced himself and offered his hand, "I'm Don."

"It's nice to meet ya, I'm Jake" (if I weren't already paranoid I'd say I could hear one of them mumble "perfect")

He continued, "This is Cassie, Jack, and Lloyd."

I offered my hand to the wind and, "It's nice to meet you all" as I sat down and the entire store dropped a thousand decibel levels again. "An electronic Newton's cradle huh? So why were you questioning whether or not it's possible?"

"What part do you mean?"

Lloyd cut in, "it's impossible, even a short piece of wire which is considered a conductor, offers some resistance."

"Like pushing water through a tube, it's a good way to visualize the flow of electrons but isn't exactly accurate."

"What is the accurate view?" Jack prompted.

"Well . . . You've seen sand before yes?"

"Of course"

"Every material on this planet can be treated the same when referencing "the atom" "I stuck my fingers around my face again like quotations, "If you could get a really powerful microscope to look at a wire, you'd eventually see millions and millions of little dots (the individual atoms). Around each of those particles is any number of "electrons" which orbit the nucleus . . . I think copper is number 29 on the periodic table so there'd be 29 electrons floating around it, every time one of the electrons moves other electrons will move away from it (because all electrons have the same polarization/charge (negative)). Much like his "newton's cradle" when one electron knocks into the next, millions down the line "ZAP" to the next atom."

"How can just a stagnant object or electron move if nothing forces it to."

"They'll only move when there is a low enough resistance."

"So periodic motion is impossible?"

"No, it's just really difficult to harness/create it."

"What is periodic motion then?"

"A better description would be a "motive balance" or an oscillation of sorts. When an electron moves, it leaves an empty hole for another to fill in."

Lloyd took over, "Because each ball in Newton's cradle is the same size/mass/weight . . . when one knocks into the other it has a proportional effect on the other ones. The ball on the other end will be moved just as much as the one which hit the first side."

"If the last one wasn't as big?"

"Because there is less mass to move with the same force exerted into it, it'd move farther and faster."

"So the force exerted on this last ball, consists of two things?"

"Did he reference the word "inertia" at all?"

He cocked his head to the side and an eyebrow up, "Quite often?"

"Yes, the inertia of the ball colliding into the chain is calculable by or consists of two factors. It's mass or how much material it is made of and its velocity or speed. That will in turn effect how far the last ball moves."

"So if the ball on the other end is a B'B it'd go flying?"

"Yarp."

Lloyd chimed in, "Or if a bully who is bigger than me, decides he wants to hit me?"

So I played along, "The bigger he is, the more it will hurt. The faster his fist moves, the more it will hurt."

"Huh . . . I don't mean to be rude or cut you off, but that actually answers my question."

"Was he trying to explain inertia?"

"Pretty much."

Someone on the other end of the store started screaming, "Find out what is wrong with him! Why isn't he!"

I didn't want to um . . . ? So I inquired, "What typically brings you guys here? I've seen Jack a couple of times but I don't recognize you three?"

"What do you mean you've seen me here before?"

"You were on the other end of the store talking to some group once or twice . . ."

He raised his eye brows and grinned. "Oh!? You were check'in me out? You've never talked to me? Why are ay so coy?" before puckering his lips a bit.

So I shrugged, "I'm usually partial to the book I've been reading or the next deadline I have to meet at school."

Don took over for him as he glanced back toward his Mp3 player, "Normally we come every Wednesday to talk about god."

I've never been to Sunday-School so I was curious, "What exactly do you mean by, talk about god?"

"Normally Jack here likes to go online and do some research, and then we just respond."

"Like sections of the bible?"

Don started to grimace, "Sometimes sections of the bible, sometimes articles from somewhere else. He prefers this Anarchist stuff."

"I've only been to church once. I don't exactly know much about God."

"Really? When was that?"

I glanced up at the ceiling to think for a second, "I was six and stayed the night at my friend's house, he had to go to church in the morning so I tagged along."

"Did you like it?"

"All we did was stand up, sit down, and listen to the sermon"

"That's normal, like anything they fluctuate . . . but sermons can be very insightful sometimes."

"I guess it may have been"

"What was it about?"

"In all honesty I don't remember that bit very well, there was a chorus, then he read out of the bible for a little while, and then he talked about some charity organization which needed donations."

"You don't remember the organization though?"

Someone on the other side of the room decided to start screaming again, "No he can't do that"

"No . . . I'm sure someone needed help, and there was a charity . . . I was busy thinking about power rangers at the time . . ."

"Why power rangers?"

"We'd been up all night playing one of their games . . ."

Again someone's voice echoed from across the room, "He'll do it for them!?" so I started to daze off into the other end of the store.

"A game huh? So you haven't ever been in a church other than that time?"

"Twice for a funeral, once for a wedding?"

"Well normally we just come here, sip on some coffee and enjoy each other's company, there's really no pressure. You'd be welcome to join us any time if you want to."

Lloyd cut Don off, "We'd love it if you'd care to share a few words"

"Sure . . . I'm not very knowledgeable but I'd love to chat I guess"

"That's not a problem, we're usually just curious to know others' views on god."

"I take it you all believe?"

"Well I do, Jack here has just left the Holy Spirit high and dry but I am a Christian"

Lloyd finished, "We're Lutheran" As he pointed toward Cassie.

"That's righteous though, sermons never hurt anybody. Do you go to church regularly?"

Don perked up, "I do!"

Lloyd cut him off again, "It's not really about how often you go, but how you act when you are in the real world."

I gave a little chuckle and responded, "So you wouldn't have any issues with me being a godless barbarian so long as I'm a teddy bear?"

"Are you?"

I didn't know how to answer that, "Kind of but not really? I'm more spiritual than I am Religious."

"What do you mean by spiritual?"

"I don't necessarily believe that he does or does not exist. God isn't going to pay my bills for me. Yet I think that "Religion" and the bible are good ways in which to import morals and good judgment into the minds of developing children."

Don quoted the bible, "Well, The good lord always says love thy neighbor."

"Usually my neighbors treat me pretty well."

He went right back to grilling me, "Do you ever do anything for them?"

"I clear off their driveway every once and a while, they're nice folk."

"Only on occasion?"

"They don't have a snow blower so I feel kind of bad for them when it piles up."

Jack scoffed from behind his Mp3 Player, "That's nice of you."

So I felt like being passive aggressive, "Yeah it's one of my favorite things to do after a couple glasses of whiskey."

Don's obviously the avid one, "Normally whiskey is seen as the devils elixir you know."

Jack wasn't, "Ya!? You're not supposed to touch that crap."

"Shure makes blowing snow seem pretty interesting."

Don sounded worried, "Do you drink a lot?"

So my head twitched, "No it was supposed to be a joke, but my body isn't exactly a temple either, it's actually healthy for your digestive system to have a glass every now and then . . ." and glanced back toward him to see his reaction.

He squinted and glanced away from me as he angled his head to his right, "Normally deviation away from god's will is pretty clear indication of one's direction."

Lloyd finished, "Sometimes it can be but a slippery slope however, a mistake isn't necessarily an end all."

Don fessed up though, "I actually had to go to AA for a couple of drunk driving tickets . . ."

"How long ago?"

"Four years now. I only drink a few every other week end now."

"We all make mistakes."

"That's a pretty costly mistake."

"Yeah . . . I guess it's nothing like putting too much ketchup on a burger . . . . Customers usually don't care as long as we replace it promptly."

Cassie inquired, "What do you mean?"

"I work at a Burger Factory."

And responded again, "Kewl! I've never worked in fast food."

Usually work is a shrug, "It isn't too shabby, work is work."

She was curious and turned her head, "Do they pay you well?"

"Minimum wage, but I'll usually get more hours than my friends who work in retail or something."

Don decided to fill in, "Cool, I hope they treat you well there."

"Usually, I scrub things they give me something else to do." I shrugged again.

Lloyd chirped up again after looking at his watch, "Hey, I have to pick up my cousin in like thirty minutes we should go."

Don wanted to be through though, "Ok, well Jake, it was nice to meet you." He offered a hand shake, "Our ride is leaving so I think it's about that time, if you ever see us here make sure you aren't a stranger, we'd love to chat."

"Sure, an extra friend rarely hurts anyone right?"

He chuckled again, "We'll see ya around."

"Take care."

Jack glanced up from his Mp3 player again and prompted, "Aint jo gonna follow the train outside?" and did an in place jog as he followed them around to the stair well with his face ablaze in hysteria.

I chuckled a little, "Nah, I think I'll stay and read while the shop is still open. Take Care though"

05: Where ever I go They'll find me

With as much respect I have for the holy, and what they do for those less fortunate than I. The background I'd found at that coffee shop was rather unpleasant. So I started sifting through Google a little more, this time I started up north and systematically worked my way south. Eventually I hit what I thought was a stroke of luck. Neither was listed on Omaha's Nightlife website; however two shops near the old market appeared to offer exactly what I was looking for. One was right next to a couple of bars and this concert hall, it's lobby was about as big as a broom closet, yet it had tables and would make for a decent night out until at least 10pm. The other was just adjacent to the market and had a much deeper lobby; it was also open until ten.

I started to get excited again and made my way toward the door with a book and my IPod. I was certain that this would be it; it was something better, this was my life's version of "greener grass".

My mother's voice echoed down the hallway, "Oh no he didn't!?" When I made it to the stair well I found her on the couch with a laptop and her phone beside her, she was watching another episode of some show about a bunch of royal folk who live in a castle, direct their servants this way and that, of course there's always a bunch of drama about it . . . . So I decided to wing a right and make for door to heaven. She hollered from the couch, "Jake wait!?"

"What?"

"Where are you going?"

"Coffee shop."

"oOoh really? Can I come?"

"Are you going to bring a book?"

"No."

"What do you think I'd be doing?"

"Talking."

"I have a dead line though, I need to be done by tomorrow."

"Oh you can take an hour off to chat."

"No . . . I'm pretty sure I intend to read when I get there . . ."

"Hehe, You'll be talking, I'm sure of it."

"MmhmM, bye mom." I shut the door and made my way down to the rolling box again.

After I plopped down into the driver's seat I pinged the engine and made my way round our circle, at the bottom of our hill I decided I'd fiddle with the radio and started hopping around stations (I've heard the music on my IPod about a million times already).

"And this guy wants to run"

"And he goes STRAIGHT the other way!"

"Hehe, Hehe, he thinks he can get away without paying his taxes . . ." he chuckled again, "Can't just tell a woman something like that and not live up to it."

"I can't believe he'd just do that without a way to pay child support. What an idiot."

"So an elementary teacher down in Kansas has just been fired for being pregnant."

"No way!? They can't just fire a chick for heeding the call of nature!?"

"Well . . . It's a Catholic school, and she was artificially inseminated."

"She couldn't just stuff a dick up there like the rest of us?"

"ARTIFICIALLY . . . Inseminated."

"Who's the daddy?"

"Apparently she doesn't even know the father's name"

"Sperm bank?"

"No . . . She hand-picked the DNA."

"How'd she pick it?"

"She plucked a hair off the back of his neck when she hugged him."

"Well . . . I'm sure they tried plenty of times"

"Wanna know how she picked him?"

"How?"

"She ran out of gas and met him on the side of some highway."

I wanted to hurl at the sound of it, that show always turns something in my gut up-side-down, and I started to glance around in a hysterical mystification . . .

"Yeah you were getting some."

"At least you would 'a stupid."

"He loves it"

"re'ert—re'ert."

"She said told the doctors that she and her husband had been having fertility issues for about three and a half months, and they wanted to try something different."

"Big boy couldn't get it up? Gotta try something a little more . . . accurate? Ehehehe."

"Well the school, a private catholic institution, has no record of a marriage . . . . Apparently they didn't like this so much . . ."

"Normally a religious institution frowns on something like that . . ."

"Hehehe, freakin morons, giving some people reproductive organs is like giving a monkey a shotgun."

"Was that just her excuse for premarital relations? Or did they actually use the right tools?"

"No . . . they used a needle . . ."

"Oh wow . . . he really couldn't get it up then?"

"I would assume they've tried more natural alternatives at least a couple of times . . ."

"Hehehheh well if his men are still good why'd he even need that? Normally it's cheaper to get the milk straight out of the cow's tit?"

"Apparently she wanted a child, and his . . . natural alternatives weren't working, so she got a needle . . . PronTo."

"How are they going to pay for it now that she's out of a job."

"Apparently she wasn't worried about it. Something about the guy made it worthwhile."

I was starting to feel ill and mumbled to myself, "Dude that's sick . . ."

Not but a moment later the radio regurgitated, "That's sick!? You have like a hundred children already, who the hell are you to judge? Pony up already!"

I'm the kind of nerd whom likes to know a girl for a couple weeks at the very least . . . Shows like this tend to turn my belly so I flicked the off button; I was within a couple of blocks anyways.

This shop was a little larger than the first one I found, it has a long corridor running back into the counter which is lined with chairs. As I made my way down, a couple of people glanced up from laptops and books to see the incoming bogie. I hadn't seen any of them before in my life, so I kept walking to the counter where the barista met me with a friendly gaze, "Hey what can I get for ya?"

After gazing up at the menu for a moment I spotted something I'd never had before, "What's an Americano?"

"We make a couple of shots of espresso, and fill the rest up with hot water."

"How does that usually taste?"

"In comparison to a regular cup of coffee, it's usually a lot less acidic because it doesn't brew as long, the espresso gives it a really bold flavor, but it's mellowed a bit by the water."

"Ok, I may as well try a medium one of those, I've been looking for a real balanced flavor anyways."

He started fiddling with a couple of dials on the espresso machine, "Yeah it does create a really nice balance, I guess that'd be a good way to describe it."

"I had some really good coffee I'd order from Amazon a couple of years ago," I started to turn around and get a glimpse of the crowd back in the corner (their lobby is L shaped), "I can't remember the name, but it had a really intense flavor almost like you'd drink a peanut, and almost no acidity to it."

"Some beans are tempered so they'll come out like that in a regular coffee machine; ours are all Arabica beans from Guatemala. We prefer these because the roast is really light and you get less of that carbonized flavor in the cup."

"Yeah my brother always says Micky D's burns theirs to a crisp."

"It's so they can get an even punch in every cup. Do you like lots of caffeine or just a little flavor in yours?"

"I'm a caffeine fiend."

"I can dump an extra shot in if you want."

"Sure why not, I can always water it down a little if it's too potent right?"

"Yeah don't worry about it man, I'm a big fan."

I turned my head back at him like a curious puppy, "A big fan of?"

He almost looked surprised, "Oh, uhh . . . Just a good cup of jitter liquor, I must be thinking of the wrong person."

"Who were you thinking of?"

"A friend of a friend is real picky about his coffee. He always likes the perfect balance."

"Huh, well if he's that picky I ought to order it just like he does every time . . ." I glanced back to my right and found this painting of a really tall and slender woman whisking her right bangs out of her eyes.

"That's just about what I got going for you here."

"So who does these paintings?" It was the same one I'd seen at Nightmare's.

"A local artist, she leaves a few in a couple of our shops around town. Has a couple of pieces in the Artist's Collaborative too." After poking around at the register he chimed in again, "It'll be just two forty five good lad."

I ponied up some change and dropped a bill in the tip jar. Before taking the cup he handed me my change and I offered my gratitude, "Kewl, well thanks. You are open until ten right?"

"Yep, ten every night. Come in and see us any time."

"Awesome, thanks." He turned around to the sink and picked up a scrub brush as I turned back toward the painting. She was making puppy dog eyes to the sky as Einstein scoffed behind her with a torch in hand. Below it was a short description, A Dark Knight leads an eternal search for the meaning of love, 600.

"Whatever" I turned and walked halfway back toward the door, where the room was the least crowded.

The book I brought with me was one of my favorites. I discovered it when I was on MIT's Free Course Ware one day, I started searching around their catalog for some information on electrical engineering and motor control circuitry. This was the book with which they'd teach their classes on "Electric Machinery."

My first inclination was to investigate what It'd offer on polyphase machinery, I already had a decent understanding for exactly how the poles were staggered/wired, how much current would be required for a proportional magnetic field, and how to properly space/balance the rotor; however I was somewhat sketchy on the circuitry which was meant to control the speed/current flow/torque regarding the motor. Once I did "No you're a creep!" echoed throughout the store.

A couple of different circuits shown utilized an all-encompassing loop which would reduce the overall current needed to drive a motor. These were compared dc wiring which was easiest to wire in parallel (a star circuit/triangular formation). "No way! You can't seriously be that dumb!?" The equation for an electric motor was rather complicated, so I plucked out my calculator and tried tinkering around with it. I could get a couple to calculate out correctly, yet my limited experience regarding calculus made it difficult for me to manipulate the equation.

Two of the main factors in producing the overall torque of the device were the current circulating each coil, and the diameter of the rotor (like a fulcrum arm, pushing down on a lever requires less and less force further away from the axis).

Dc machinery, these were rather simple. "And he goes straight the other way!?" Instead of using a complex system to digitize the control of current required to create a certain frequency, or requiring a particular amount of current to rotate the motor at some rotational velocity; a DC motor could simply use a contact breaker which would rotate freely without any road friction, it's speed would simply match the current entering the device and the amount of resistance it encounters. Much like a gasoline powered engine it'd just run free if it's out of gear (even with miniscule currents) . . . the more power introduced meant more power expelled.

There were quite a few issues with contact breakers however. "Oh I'm just a whore because I've been in a sorority then huh!?" Every source I've found in the past references the simple fact they never last forever. Any material, even a metal stands no chance if it swirls around at some thousands of revolutions per minute and grinds against another piece of material to get its supply of current. Several hours of high intensity loads eventually cause the rotor to shift back and forth a little bit, the surfaces grind together and leave shavings behind. Those shavings eventually cause arcing between leads, those arcs burn away material, and the missing material leaves unconnected coils as deadweight to bogg the engine down. "What the hell is wrong with you!? Just act like I don't exist then!? Casper the friendly ghost hurr!"

This woman's voice was getting somewhat distracting . . . so I finally looked up for an awnser. She had her back turned toward me again, it was the same woman who'd followed me to nightmares and stormed out of the room.

"Excuse me?"

The girlfriend who'd been sitting with her glanced over at me stuck her finger out and looked back at her, "No! Be a man for once you little perve!"

She raised her eyebrow and spoke, "He's trying too . . ."

So she screamed once more, "No! And I know just how to ruin him!?" Before she stormed out of the shop again.

She hadn't been sitting there when I arrived, or when I sat down . . . . Nor did she seem to want to talk. I didn't even know how she meant to "ruin me", storming out of the room was rather perplexing . . . . however it wouldn't really accomplish anything.

Her girlfriend didn't make eye contact with me and followed her out of the store . . . I felt like a deer in the headlights so I went back to reading. A couple of the larger generators/motors on the next page were almost as large as a refrigerator, some as large as a room. Typically they are used in factories so tuning these to a certain frequency or rotational velocity would require merely a few variable settings (High, Medium, Low).

One of the pictures went into detail describing the several hundred poles in a single hydro-electric generator. They required several different throttle mechanisms to maintain the water pressure driving the generator so it wouldn't move too fast or too slow (this ensures the correct voltage/frequency is produced). A couple of grounded rectifiers or transformers could also be used to maintain the correct output.

"Excuse me" the barista broke through my train of thought.

"Yeah?"

"I just wanted to let you know that we'll be closing up shop in a couple of minutes." I tend to get carried away . . .

I glanced around the room and then at my watch, only two people were left in the room and it was nearly ten, "Ok, I'll get out of your hair in a couple of minutes."

"Awsome, thanks."

The last few bits of the chapter explained a few more regulation circuits, one of which would extort the ground lead in such a manner that anything more than say 400 volts at 5000 amps would drain off into the dedicated ground.

After I hopped into my car I started wondering if I'd find something on the radio, I started hoping I was just going nuts. But as soon as I flipped on the radio, Tigger started in.

"She lIkes yOu."

"hehehe"

"You're MmArriieeD."

"And he goes straight the other way!? Haha that's rich!"

It was a little . . . weird, to say the least. So I grunted under my breath in hysteria again, "Great . . . a gravy baby right?"

"Right they just wrap that up in Reynolds Wrap and squish it around huh?"

And I mumbled again, "Yeah . . . Umm, I'm a virgin."

"Bullshit, you two have been trying for over a month now."

"he he, yeah that kid gets all kinds of action."

My radio squealed on one side of the vehicle and ungulate back and forth.

"Gotta pay your child support soon here buddy."

I felt like my brain was about to pop as I mumbled again, "I'm pretty sure it'd be rape."

"No you love it! Hehehe."

"Yeah he loves it, He heh he he."

Despite my better judgment I barked again, "You sound like a chipmunk when you laugh."

"Right, just call me Alvin."

"Freakin idiot, when are you going to learn you can't tell a woman something like that and just say opps I didn't really mean it."

It reminded me of the patriot act, and the phone was the only thing in the car I could think'd do anything . . . . So I turned the radio up to full blast and stuck the phone by a speaker.

"Shit! Dude that's not cool."

I got my awnser so I asked for another, "How'd you get my number anyways."

"You left it on a wall stupid."

"Just go back there man."

"Wednesday."

I was still creeped out though. "You were joking about the artificial insemination right?"

And they broke into a song of laughter, "Hehehe, Gravy baby!"

"Hehehe, find out for your self dude."

"Time for another rock block, Bye bye." And the radio started playing another song . . . . "I've been stuffed in your pocket for the last hundred days" was the first one.

I couldn't help but to be a little curious when I got home. So I looked back on The Hell hole, and naturally it was there . . .

Beauty seeks Einstein—W4M—Eternal bliss

Do you like her? I modeled the back ground off of the nights sky from that night, the torch above fueled by fire water is to symbolize the passion for you I have burning inside me.

I'll make ya a deal on the acrylic paste though, for you just 500, a hundred bucks off. If you want you can meet the model after you buy it, she's been dying to see you.

It was almost weird enough to make my stomach turn inside out.

06: Snagged My Heart Again

About three weeks after meeting them my manager scheduled me off on another Wednesday, and yet again like clockwork, the elders began studying some medieval lore. I could hear the echo of swords clashing through the guitar on my wall, the feet of a thousand horses gallop across gravel, and cries from several impaled knights; their usual dose of pixelated cocaine. My father has this habit of rewinding the show and turning up the volume every time he misses a word, so it gradually climbs and climbs over the course of an hour; he's like a gigantic toddler in front of the boob tube.

I thought the biggest problem in my life was the dead battery in my kindle, so I plugged it in, packed up my laptop, and headed out the door. Maybe I'd catch a break this time . . . Maybe I should give it a second chance.

As I was driving I heard Tigger's voice cry over the radio, "Seriously!? The idiot is going back for more!?" but it was just too weird for me, I lurched forward to shut it off again (try telling a cop that the voices through a radio have been talking to you, guess where you'll end up). After I waltzed in I ordered myself a cup a mocha. And finally tried to head out to the lobby where I thought I could sit down for a while, but the fanatic caught me by the psychological collar, "Hey Jake! Over here!"

Hearing Jack's voice echo throughout the room was like having a spider crawl up my back, but I glanced over my left shoulder anyways and found six of them seated in a big circle like the knights of Camelot. They'd drug two tables off into the corner of the room so they could all fit. Normally I try not to refuse a friend so I stumbled their way and started mumbling "Wha-cha guys up to?" as I slid my laptop under the table.

Lyle and Ken were looking at something on Ken's IPAD so Don decided to fill me in, "We're discussing whether or not god learns over time, or if this is unnecessary."

"Whether or not you think he does?"

Jack took over as he gestured over the table with his pencil and flopped it back onto his notepad, "Ken here thinks that if such an "entity" is "all powerful" and "all knowing" and "has reason for everything he does" that he would already have an "infinite knowledge" knowledge of every event which will ever come to pass, has passed, and what is happening now." And he kept talking (almost seamlessly), "Seeing as how god is accepted as being all powerful, and all knowing. It seems rather illogical that he would need at any time to change his mind, coming from an all knowing position would mean all relevant factors already have been considered."

Ken looked up and finished, "He would already retain every detail of every life in the history of time, so no event should be substantial or sudden enough it should dislocate his reasoning."

At this point I didn't really care how intelligent/moronic I'd sound, so I butted in, "Still don't you think that this "all powerful" being is at the very least as intelligent as you or I?"

Don interrupted, "He is god, he is all knowing."

"Homo sapiens are typically considered to be beings of "higher intelligence yes?"

"Of course." Jack nodded furiously

"Our neurological circuitry isn't only larger but more intricate than other species. So if we have the ability to be "responsive" in an intellectual environment, don't you think god would be intelligent enough to do the same?"

Jack started screaming, "The bible says that Yahweh is the fourth dimension, he is the constant beyond this universe, he over sees and knows everything."

"And someone who is color blind might say that the sky is orange."

Jack decided to cut in, "Infinite knowledge is infinite knowledge. Nothing would affect his train of thought, he'd already know it."

Don, "If he says "break this commandment and you are doomed to hell" then you best not break this commandment right?"

"If he says the rapture will come, 2010 will be the end yes?" I figured they'd get worked up one way or another, why'd I care.

"The end must come one day!?" Jack looked angry.

"It'd be nice if life were that easy right? I'm pretty lazy; death would almost be a relief if I could just bank on the world ending sometime soon I'd almost be happy about it?"

"Not exactly . . ." Don almost looked scared.

"The inconsistencies however are proof to the fact he does not exist!"

"What inconsistencies?"

Don finished up, "He likes to go on about how there are positives and negatives scattered throughout the bible."

Jack took over again, "In some scripts he will say he will be our savior, in some he claims rapture will come."

Don didn't like that so much, "God exists, how else would the world come to exist." He even nodded his head and scowled.

And I shrugged, "My parents were horney."

They ignored me and Jack cut him off, "Sex is wrong, the birth of a baby is beautiful."

"Love is beautiful!" Don's face was cherry red

Jack turned back toward me, "I'm being real general right now, but I'll bring a couple more scripts from the bible next time."

I tried reasoning, "Even if it wasn't his intention to change his mind at any given point he may be offering these inconsistencies as a test, god has been known to test his minions right?"

He started getting a little riled up, "Even if it were a test, it is still ineffective to lead people in such a manner, inconsistencies in the teachings are just as likely to create deviations from one's beliefs as are the sins given to us by the devil."

"Ok, we have free will and may do as we please?"

"You are missing the point!" he screamed again, "If god ruled everything, controlled everything, and it were all a perfect plan why is there so much inaccuracy in the scripts."

"Maybe god has a personality? You can't expect a human to get everything right the first time around?"

"God is god! If he created the Earth in so perfect an image as it is, there would be a proper order for things!"

"Are my veins well organized? No its just a sporadic fractal array . . ."

"They all lead to the right organ!" Don chimed in.

"He still isn't going to pay my bills though . . ."

"Exactly!" Jack hollered

"Even so, he is all knowing, he'd have a reason for that too right?"

Don suggested, "For uncertainty is a test."

"That's what I'm trying to say, I don't believe he is all knowing, and deviations like dates of the rapture the, the end of the world, or messages in the text prove it, he may have created the world, but I don't think he controls everything, not even being able to keep his own story straight!"

I glanced between Ken, Don, and Lyle hoping for a little assistance with the nut job, I started hoping the words, "Well yeah one must think before they can think freely."

I don't think he liked that answer though, he started barking out, "Here let me show you!"

We went back and forth for another half an hour or so, he showed me a couple of excerpts from the bible which he had printed off from some other website, contradicting everything I said with another line from his paper, another paragraph from a website.

Eventually Don got tired and took over for a while, when Jack started directing his argument my way again Don looked down for a couple of seconds and fumbled with his watch.

After jamming it in Jack's face he blurted out, "Opps times up bud, I have to go."

Jack looked back over at him, "But we're not done with our conversation."

Don retaliated, "Well I'm leaving now, if you want I can give you a ride, but I have to work in the morning."

Ken and Lyle both looked over at me, and said, "Yeah, I think we're going to head out too, it was good seeing ya."

I was a little bit bewildered however so I wished them luck., "It was good seeing y'all too I guess. See ya around."

That guy has always unnerved me just a wee bit, but then again the bible isn't my strong suit; all of his specifics were a bit over my head. I couldn't tell if he was a Jehovah's witness, or if he was just questioning his own religion still. Wondering wouldn't help.

I didn't know and I wasn't going to find out by staring at the wall while Don drives him home, so I looked down to find my laptop again, after going through a couple of Nikolas Patents I had found some really funny ones.

He had this little RC boat he'd control with a wooden box faced with a couple of dials and levers, I always loved the way he would name his devices, it made me giggle when I'd see what I call remote controlled cars described for the first time. He coined it an "Apparatus for Controlling Mechanism of Moving Vehicle or Vehicles", it was like rotary dial and digital keypads. The fact that he put a plural on the end stuck out like a sore thumb, and made me wonder if he had tried moving around an array of boats with the same box.

When I was in elementary school, my parents bought these cheap mini RC cars, each of them were about the size of a dollar bill if you fold it the fat way twice in the middle. On Christmas morning, my brother and I drove them around in circles on the kitchen floor to play tag. When he'd hit my car, I was it, and I'd have to chase down his or someone else's car. It's amazing how far silly things like a remote control have condensed.

At the bottom of the patent, I couldn't help but to think that this guy probably bought bread for a penny. Nothing like this had ever existed, and he did it in just one life time.

So I went back to the list of his patents which I'd found on Wikipedia, and plucked the one he called an, "Apparatus for Aerial Transportation." This was his attempt to create a plane.

It looked like nothing I had ever seen before; his plan was to take off vertically by equalizing the force of thrust upwards, with the force of gravity. He'd then angle the Vehicle forward until the two wings above and below him would catch wind and move forward.

Would it really work? Some stealth jets operate in the same manner. I'd hope he was flying around in one, he'd probably get a kick out of it. At the very least this was probably the platform for the technology leading up to the creation of stealth fighters.

I started to stretch and look around; I tend to do so every now and then. There was this wormhole sitting on the ground just a couple of feet out of reach, a note card which someone had folded in half to make it stand up. It was facing the seat which Don had offered to me.

So I started glancing about the room, and scanned every face in the place from wall to wall. Not a soul present looked familiar, yet it still demanded a little curiosity. I called out "Derka Derka" and ducked behind my laptop to glance about the room again.

Quite a few stiffs turned my way, and returned blank stares but yet again each of them wore a new face. No one budged, no one stopped what they were doing they just stared for a couple of seconds and went back to their own lives. What else was I supposed to say should I do a back flip, was I but a personal jester? But no, it was just the same ole caffeinated nightmare. So I got up and walked out into the front room, took a look around, and threw the note in the trash.

My luck was pretty consistent, and apparently it had a negative polarity. This crowd wasn't silent for long, and their eyes never budged, one woman cried aloud, "how could he do that to her" my mind was racing, it was caving, "why wouldn't he do it". Again it felt like there was a hurricane in my skull. One lady even stared right at me, "fucking dick". "No he didn't want it to be special!?" some guy on the other side of the room started with his finger stuck out toward me, "See, nothing has sentimental value."

I tried to clear my mind and went back to the list of patents, all I could do however was to start scrolling up and down. "Can't get it up big boy?" I didn't want to be there, I didn't understand why I shouldn't' be allowed in a public place as well; my head started doing that thing again; it felt like that screen saver with the multicolored dye bouncing around. "She even tried making it easy on him, but he just won't take the bait." So I shut it down, the little progress wheel just kept spinning, why wasn't my operating system done yet, then the splash screen, "Aww, he couldn't save his girlfriend." Finally all of the lights went dead and the hard drive stopped moving. So I packed it up and hopped in my car for another cigarette while the engine warms up.

I started mumbling as I blew through a red light, "She was there . . . . well someone was there . . ." It killed me, they'd go out of their way to set up the proper line for me to walk but no one would just say Hi.

Did she want to get revenge on one of the lobes in my brain because I didn't fulfill some bargain or was she just socially defunct enough to think that this was the way? Was I socially defunct? Should my brain be saturated with a different neurochemical at the sight of someone pretty, was my response of bad timing?

The radio, music was a better answer, a different psychological track. So I flipped the switch in hopes to get my mind on something else but Tanya's voice rang loud and clear, "he struck out again!" before a clip full of a crowds' cheers rang through.

Then Tanyas's, "I'm not so sure that kid is even straight."

And the third voice, "It looks like Romeo will never win . . ."

"The idiot is really going to play cat and mouse instead?"

"Apparently, just tell a girl something like that and then ignore her, its freak'in despicable."

"I'm not so sure Big boy even wants to get it up, a lot of guys do this kind of thing for sport, it might be the perfect game."

"If I were a dick I would be loving this . . ."

"heh he he, **IF**! You were a dick."

I stuck my finger atop the roof just outside my window and pulled it back in. "She was right there!"

"He even had a warning sign, Jesus!"

"Oh sure just flip off the satellite . . ."

Maybe it was just my mind set, but when I heard the words, I almost veered off the highway. It was "she was right there." which bothered me right? What could I do about it?

It is surprising I didn't get pulled over on my way home, my mind wasn't in the car . . . When I finally pulled up to the house my parents were already asleep, so I stumbled to my room without a word and flopped atop my bed. After staring at the ceiling and twitching about like an epileptic for a little while my mind kept trailing . . . Should I feel bad for her? Was she in on it? Were they playing this little joke on her too?

I went back to the crap I'd seen on that one hell hole, the MISSED CONNECTIONS . . . .

I give up on men!—W4M—(Little Lucifer's Trap)

I was absolutely mystifyed that you would actually do that to me, I was staring you down the entire time and you just do that you just act like I'm not even there! What is wrong with you are you sociopath really!? You are going to do nothing more than watch me burn? Do you have no people skills what so ever!? The man I met was so sweet and then you make a girl cry, why do you always make girls cry!? I should have known better that to trust you, you can't just act like I'm some chia pet sitting on the mantle! You need to actually come talk to me, you need to actually be my friend or you'll never get anywhere, you'll never get anywhere with any woman.

Not even Hades himself would treat his fix this way and I wouldn't even mind if that was all we were!? I just want something just a little bit why can't you give me anything why can't men like you ever just fucking behave, it's not that hard to do the right thing every once and a while! It's not like I expect you to give up every little thing, I just want a little compassion just a little effort that is all! Why can't you even get off your butt! We all know the truth so why do you insist on this ridiculous sharade, you know damn well it just feels better when you do right by family and loved ones so why the hell don't you just do it already. Like the enamel on your teeth as you guzzle acid beans, it will tear apart everything you know, it will destroy your heart it will I swear! If you keep me in this little devils trap of yours you will never under stand the deep and unwavering love I hold in my heart, you will never experience any more than your little torturous devotion. You know that you can't go on forever like this; you will need the unconditional devotion a love like mine offers sooner or later! This lifestyle this manner of living will be your demise! You need to learn how to let someone help you you need to learn how to succum to your own needs your own desires!

You may think that you fucking "pureity" life style is all good and perfect but you need to check your head, theres an error, you forget something you forget you need to learn to love! I don't understand what you get out of it, you make me cry when I could make you moan, all I wanted to do was fuck you! So Dream Big you little fucker, dream your way to the sky, you will be there alone if you can't put someone before yourself!

It made me somewhat uncomfortable to say the least . . . . When I regained consciousness I started staring off into space as if I were no longer bound my vessel, my head wasn't empty for long however. Something in the back of my head started to ping and remind me of the one thing over that way.

After hopping back on to my laptop I brought it up again, it seemed somewhat logical she had already been there, and she was pissed . . . .

It was a little weird at first, I thought I was crazy, it was too unlikely, but I sifted back through the dates, looking at all of the post headings, and started reading a couple. After maybe ten, I felt like I finally understood what an English teacher meant by "a writer's voice."

There were oodles of them though, some about women or men that had been observed at their jobs, some about people waiting in lines at Wal-mart, and some of them sounded really sweet.

I could easily pick out the goofy ones, about a funny stare from across the room and eye contact. But it was the more personal ones that dislocated something inside me.

It's Wednesday again Asshole!—W4M—(Hades)

Dip Du Ok it's Wednesday! Ok we both showed up again, Ok you like the chapel that was hanging on the wall. Do you even realize that I painted that picture you spent so long looking at!? The bell tower on that is an exact image of the one across from my child hood school! The painting was done in my basement! I made it with my bare fucking hands! Something you might never know the feeling of!

And you are just going to sit down right next to it! You have got to be kidding me! Grow a fucking pair and come talk to me already! I am sick of this game of cat and mouse.

I scrolled down for a little bit and found another.

Dipdu—W4M

Same time Same place Dip Du!! Seriously how long are you going to evade me like this! Can't you just talk to me! It's Wednesday again and you are back to the same old pathetic game! Jesus if all men are like this I never want one in my life again!

It was dated for another Wednesday . . . and I was there that Wednesday . . . I scrolled up and down, flipped around a couple of pages and several other posts were titled Dip Du, a couple of them described other paintings which were in that store. A couple described web pages I'd been on. One even referred to a web page I was on. "Oh and that Moray Lightning thing is going to give you the same satisfaction right!?"

They went on and on, deeper into the past though, I couldn't read all of them, plus they could have been any one . . . So . . . . Ya know that saying "Curiosity killed the cat?" I sent an email to a couple of the postings . . .

To the first "Dip Du" I sent a message "You must have added too much water to the paint, there was a gnarly bleed line stemming from the chapel's peak . . ."

To "I give up on men!" I sent another, "You should talk to him if you think he's eye candy . . . You can't have love before you have a friend . . ."

And I found this other one somewhere down the line which kept referencing lines from "The Catcher In the Rye" which I'd been reading the last time I was there . . .

I checked my email the next day and all of the responses came from the same email address, all of them were the same. The subject line

Oh! Ya think you're Funny do Ya Dip Du~!!

> You go to the same place, at the same time every time stupid! Every time you just walk right past me! I'm a producer! Don't expect me to be tricked by all of the masks you always wear, go ahead keep picking all of them up! We'll just see who gets the short end of the stick huh!? You need to come talk to me! You need to apologize! You need to be the one to start the conversation! Because we both know I'm right!

I responded back

I don't even know who I'm looking for?

> I don't mean to be rude but I like to know who I am talking to before I open up too much . . . If you want to meet me for lunch or something I'd love to chat some time, but I need to know who to talk to . . . As it stands all of the people walking around at that place look the same to me . . .

Don't lie to me you little prick!

> I don't have time to send hundreds of emails back and forth! You just need to come and talk to me! I don't want to hear all of your excuses I just want a real man in my life! Grow a pair and talk to me or we will never have anything together, Kapeesh?

I got a little curious again and turned my kindle on, bringing up a web page, and setting it aside waiting for it to go back to the screen saver; it was still on the same web-page when I poked the sleep button to turn it back on.

I'd left a couple of emails on other posts because I was curious . . . and this response from the other side of the room confused me, but they were sporadic and ridiculous . . . . I deleted them . . . .

74

07: If You Say So

It was Saturday, and I had nothing on my day's schedule again, so I sent out a mass text to a majority of the people on my contacts list. After an hour or so they all reported back to say that they were already at work or had plans. Some people were out with family, some had homework, and some were with lovers.

So I figured it was about that time in my life, if everyone was busy I'd just go back to work, heaven knows I can't stand to sit around and do nothing. But my parents were ingesting pixelated crack again, and try as I may there is a point where the volume gets so high, that my ear drums start hurting. Even blocking it out with Prog-Rock becomes more distracting than what the music is supposed to mask.

So I went back to the "good" coffee shop in town, because it was open past ten every night and midnight on Saturdays. The place had been awesome for months before, so I'd just have to hope that everything would dissipate.

The moment I stepped foot in the nightmare, I found a line five meat sacks long. Every time I decide it'd be better to find a seat first, the line grows and grows until I end up waiting behind five different people instead of the five there in the first place, so I decided to deal with it and wait in line. I leaned against the fridge by the door to gaze up at the menu; maybe I'd find something new this time.

Their chalk boards are always filled with flavored smoothies and different combinations of latte and frothy syrups. I picked out a berry smoothie from the middle board, I hadn't tried one before and judging by the quality of their other goodies, it'd probably taste like liquid gold. With four people still ahead, my mind wandered to the poster by my right shoulder, it had a list of different coffee filled delights. Showing coffee beans for concentration, the espresso had three, and one little water droplet to show the ratio, a latte displayed two coffee beans and some milk, and the mocha had little chocolate bars by it; it was kinda cute I guess. Some woman rushed up to the counter and flailed her paper cup over the counter, "Can I get a refill!"

Jeff nudged his ball cap with his fore arm as he glanced up from the sandwich he was making, mumbled "Yeah, no problem" and took the cup. He turned around and set it under the hot water spigot, flipped the switch, and tossed some more toppings atop the sammich he was working on (apparently she was drinking tea).

She hollered rather abruptly once he turned back around to attend to her cup, "Me Katie!!"

Again, I wasn't quite sure exactly how to respond, she actually growled as Jeff flipped the valve off and handed her the cup, "he isn't going to do it is he!?" she still had her back turned toward me. He glanced over at me as my eyes grew like the Grand Canyon and the left eyebrow atop my face cocked upward. He didn't say a word as he shrugged and it set her off like a firecracker, "NoOo, I just sit hur alone every night because my boyfriend has amnesia!" She even had this slurred tone to her voice like a bully mocking some slow kid.

I had to do a double take and check her out, she didn't exactly stick out in my memory but she certainly fit the profile. She was tall, slender, fair skinned, and had the same ebony colored hair. Something about the situation was unsatisfying though; she ripped the cup out of his hand and dashed for the door without even turning toward me. As the door slammed behind her Jeff fought the urge to burst into laughter, he forced himself to straighten out the smirk and went back to the sammich.

It wasn't long before he called out, "Greek Feta!" set the plate out on the counter and started taking orders again. He must have got stuck at the register alone as he had to bounce between making drinks and taking orders until it was my turn.

Again no one even did the rubber neck thing . . . glancing throughout the store revealed that no one was scowling, no one growling, or even laughing. While I was a little disappointed; at least it'd be quiet for the rest of the night.

Jeff took my order and whipped up a delicious smoothie in no time. He was actually smiling as he made it, he prodded only once, "want any whipped cream on top?" and he even seemed chipper while he offered some extras.

"Sure."

There was a perfect seat over by the back door, usually the lights are shining every which way, and either glare all over a computer's screen or blind me from the side, but this one had a lamp hanging just above it, somehow that always worked perfectly.

So I plopped down and started toying around with the first patent I hadn't already been through, it was called "Apparatus for the Utilization of Radiant Energy." I'd seen similar receivers several times over, naturally most of them were about as useful as a child's picture book before a bachelor's degree; however this one was probably the simplest circuitry so far. It had a couple of different receivers, each for a different type of signal; one for a vacuum tube, one for an RLC, and one for an ambient signal.

He had just found a way to make a usable wireless signal and already he was tinkering around with ways to keep our neighbors' phones from interfering with ours.

After gawking at it for a while I wanted to track the development of the electric motor during it's time in the inventor's hands. For his first brushless motor he described how by increasing the "tension" of the drive signal, the speed of rotation can be increased. Yet the controller dissipation was still the same, which would mean instantaneous and consistent torque.

Naturally they started out being about the size of a fridge with only two active poles creating torque, later generators were huge and had thousands of poles. I started digging in again, a little further for the more intricate designs and stumbled across one which was used in an industrial plant. The system utilized thousands of permanent magnets to drive several hundred coils, obviously the general conception behind "more is better" reigns true in the industrial production of electricity . . .

I got a little caught up after I found one of his more ridiculous creations however, one which has never been successfully produced. He drew this boxy little back-pack thing with a line coming out of it which led to a parabolic looking ray gun he'd strapped to his arm. His idea was to direct a bolt of lightning from his arm to an enemy target. It was probably inspired by a bully from his younger days or something.

It took a couple of minutes to get over this one, and surely everyone in the store thought I was insane as I was just about rolling around on the floor laughing after I'd found it. It was exactly what I was talking about with D.

Granted they'd surely be correct in such an assumption, it is a rather illogical prototype. Electricity or the plasma like discharges which come from an electrode like the "tesla coil" will follow what is called the path of least resistance every single time. If he ever did try this, it'd operate a little more like one of the machines which some researchers wired up to the pleasure center in a couple of mice. Just like the mouse getting his freak on, every time he engages the on switch he'd get a little zap.

After a while I got bored and started sifting around the more personal descriptions of Nikola. While all of the biographies which other authors have done on Nikola thoroughly depict him as a hermit with a nearly inexistent social life, it seemed to me his achievements were a better show of personality. Sure many claim that he was abstinent throughout his life, and never married. Some will say that his OCD led him to boast his habitual work schedule, he may have claimed that because of the fact he worked almost twenty four seven he is better than everyone else. But that kind of life/description has always seemed a little extreme to me.

Typically someone who is classifiable as a hermit will do as little as possible, the very definition is "one who lives in solitude" or "one who is reclusive". I've never met the guy, but I've never understood how a reclusive personality would create or invent . . . He went pretty far out of his way to create some of the things which he has . . . He kept in contact with several authors/inventor/electricians . . . and he was friends with Mark Twain himself . . .

It didn't add up so I flipped the page.

The room was starting to fill up quite a bit so I sat back to stretch for a moment and yanked my ear buds out to get some blood moving in my ears again. Every face in the room was a fresh one and they all seemed to be engaged in their own lives so I dug back in.

The next one on the list was called "Method of Insulating Electric Conductors." It was intriguing because he was writing it back in the day they'd still wrap copper wire in paper or tar in order to insulate the wires, eventually it became popular to coat wires in a mineral solution a little like the enamel on magnet wire.

He found a way however to run hollow copper coils through a body of water before dumping some sort of cooling agent in the tube. While he referred to several rather primitive solutions, this Cooling agent would cool the tubes and eventually freeze the water. After doing a bunch of tests on the conductivity of the water surrounding a wire he'd run through it, he was able to determine that solids were better insulators than were liquids, a fact which is considered common knowledge these days. In conclusion he claimed that it may be possible/advantageous to embed these wire into concrete structures in order to reduce the loss of electric current to surrounding mass. An improvement because before they'd just slap some bare copper wires into the ground and loose potential further and further away from the plant.

This particular "invention" actually spawned the possibility for two developments leading up to our current systems. One was the coil which he was dumping these fluids into in the first place; these would eventually show up in freezer coils and refrigerators. The second; his method of insulation, eventually a similar apparatus was actually used to quickly cool wires as they are drawn from a mass of metal as well as cool the insulation around them after they are dunked through it. He had the right idea however, and the particular patent certainly exemplified our specie's struggle to understand and develop that which we are just learning to use.

I got carried away and started digging around a couple more, one of which was his, "Commutator For Dynamo Electric Machines."

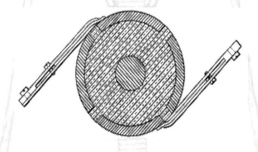

While we may simply refer to it as a commutator, this kind of device is typically used inside a Direct current Electric motor, it controls which coils are energized with either polarity at a particular degree of rotation inside of the motor. Older models use similar "Brushes" to make and break contact as the machine rotates, however Nikola had an issue with the sparks which consistently formed every time a new contact was made or broken, so he created this device.

It utilizes a wider arm to prevent these discharges and the arms are actually angled to prevent wear and tear. He also tacked on a little screw which would allow the adjustment of pressure this little arm exerts on the rotor, that way it can be manipulated just a little further if it ever warps out of place.

I tinkered around with a couple more of them and eventually I got bored again before sifting along to ZeitNews. Soon the lights dimmed and I had to head home. It may not sound like an exciting night on the town, but it was one of the first peaceful nights she'd allowed in a long time. No one noticed my guilty pleasure as I'd dig through everything I could find.

When I finally got back home I glanced up on the hell hole again, unfortunately that has become a habit, when I did I realized that this "peaceful night" was too good to be true for the likes of me.

Stop hiding behind books—W4M—(the tip of ecstasy)

Seriously you'd rather read about soaking wires in plastic than talk to a horny woman!? What the hell is wrong with you!? I can see right through you! You are just a dirty little liar. Don't think for even a second that I didn't notice you looking, you knew that I was going to be there and you know that I want you. I am seriously just mystified that I actually have to regurgitate this. You were the one that started everything off on a lie and I expect you to accept the repercussions of your actions!

You need someone in your life who can read you like a book

You need someone who will keep you honest

You need to grow up, act like an adult in your relationships

You need to initiate our next converstation

Every time I go there to find you, you insist on screwing me over. You walked right past me yet again! Don't fool yourself into thinking you can get away with this, if you are ever going to overcome the lies you have spewed you know what to do.

I know it is hard to believe but it is true, despite all of the things you have done I still love you. You are going to have to do this eventually, why not find love early in life, you can be my rock until death do us part. So stop using that slithering tongue of yours to hurt girls by promising them the moon and the stars only to stand us up every Saturday.

While every time I drift off I can't help but to dream, at the same time the thought of rolling around with your tongue in my mouth makes me sick every time you bite. Not because I don't love you but because all the lies you speak have left such a dirty residue for my subconscious. Clean it up already, we could have it all, if you just prioritize your love correctly then we can have our holy delight already! Why the hell are you waiting!? I just want to fuck you! So come talk to me already!

While it was kind of creepy she knew what I was reading, I was dumb enough to go back two weeks later. The moment I walked through the threshold into the lobby another voice cascaded through the air, Don invited me over to the table as he beckoned again, "Hey Jake over here!" So I crept over toward the table to see just what was going on and found a few new "friends" sitting around.

Jack filled in to display a new toy, "Look what Chris found at a garage sale." It was an immaculate set of poker chips.

Chris decided to show them off, and held up the aluminum backed case he got along with it, "Feel how heavy those are." So I plucked a red one out of the case.

As I started examining it my mouth leaked a little, "Nice, they're a lot heavier than the cheap plastic ones stamped for cheesy poker kits." The thing had to have been at least two or three ounces.

Chris started up again as I knocked on it with my knuckle. "Yeah I almost grazed over them, but when I plucked one I couldn't help but to notice that they were almost casino quality!"

"It almost feels like there's a metal weight in there."

He turned toward Jack and prompted, "I don't know!? What do they put in poker chips these days?"

He glanced up at me and finished, "They might be, I think I remember hearing something about how their counting machines use different mass or weight measurements to sort the chips . . . ." As his left cheek curled up, he glanced over toward Lyle and tried to boss him around as he started poking at the tablet in Lyle's hand. "You should look it up on your IPad there!"

Lyle jerked to the side in order to protect his copper box with his shoulder and barked back toward Jack, "Ok!? I will in a second, just keep your mitts off my shit man!"

"Sorry I was just trying to get your attention" Jack scoffed and withdrew his hand, "Ya don't have to have another one of your little hissy fits!"

Lyle didn't make much of a response however, he just shook his head and went back to whatever he was doing, "Right! I'M THE ONE HAVING A HISSY FIT EVERY TEN SECONDS!?"

I couldn't help but to chuckle a bit as Jack turned back toward me and barked again, "So do you know how to play poker!?"

"I've played a couple of times with friends and family"

"Any good at it!?"

This was a shrugging matter, "I usually keep one of them charts with all of the hands next to me."

Don butted in quite hastily, "We can teach you, Ken found a pretty good book on how to calculate the odds on the fly in Texas Hold-em."

Ken, "I can email it to you; it's an E-Book."

I couldn't quite decipher how well or whether they knew the back ground noise. As a new voice called from somewhere else in the store, "Oh I get it we just need a web site for them to communicate through!?" I decided to glance about the room before grunting, "Sure why not." No face in the room was familiar so I pulled up a chair from one of the nearby tables, "Let me sit out a few hands and watch the cards though . . . I'm a bit rusty."

Jack filled in for the group as he started dealing their next hand. "Kewl!? I'll just get the ball rolling then"

I was right next to him so I nudged Jack with my elbow and prompted, "Mind if I watch your hand?"

"Yeah why not, don't think of trying it when you're in the pot though." He jerked back to face me as everyone chuckled a little bit.

They went round the pot and the group got kind of quiet, after Lyle took the pot Chris dealt a new hand.

I didn't want to be rude so I shoved my hand over in Chris's face before blurting out, "I don't think we have met before, I'm Jake."

Ken took the bait and responded as he jolted forward in his seat. "Oh yeah sorry, we've known him for a while, Chris this is Jake, Jake—Chris." as he gestured between the two of us Chris sat up and shook my hand.

I was curious and stuck my finger out at the fanatic. "So where'd you meet these guys"

"A church event! You?"

Just before I could open my mouth Jack filled in for me, "He was sitting over there one Friday night poking around on his little book thing, he must have smelled my cologne when he turned around to interrupt one of our discussions, after locking eyes he was obviously done for."

Everyone started chuckling as I watched him make a raise on a pair of fives with one in the flop, "Yeah they were having some conversation about energy and when I got curious they did a bait and switch to throw a bible at me."

Chris laughed again and stuck his finger at Don. "Yeah Jack likes to do that. He gets it from the car salesman here"

Don raised his eyebrows and continued, "Buy a ram with the towing package and undercoating, and you're getting the title for a Focus." He handed me a set of business cards, "If you know anyone looking to buy a car send them my way, I'll give you a Hundred dollar referral bonus."

The other side of the room screamed again, "Not if he deletes them all!"

Jack continued, "If you like them, refer them somewhere else though!"

I chuckled involuntarily, "Ha, so do family and friends get the upgraded bait and switch?"

Chris responded as he jolted forward yet again to match Don's raise on the river, "They get a used car."

"I get it . . . Buy a Hyundai instead."

"Oh so that's just a couple months of her life wasted is it!?" echoed again from across the room.

Don grimaced a little bit and barked, "If you do that you'll have to sell your house to pay the repair bills by ten thousand miles. Hyundais are cheap pieces of aluminum trash."

So I tried being sarcastic, "Like hell mine ain't still running at two hundred and forty thousand, and it defiantly isn't the easiest car I've ever had to work on!?"

Chris looked around, "Show of hands?" Lyle folded and only Chris, Don, and Jack were in the hand.

Don and Chris both nodded and flopped their hands down, the very sight of which instantaneously sent Jack into a frenzy, he sat up in his seat and started beaming with pride like a golden retriever after receiving a treat, "BooYah!"

Don, who had a pair of kings and a pair of three's on the river obviously didn't like Jack's full house, as he growled and pushed the stack toward Jack in a single sloppy swipe which knocked it into oblivion "Damn, I though two pair would take such a weak pot."

I had to catch two of the chips after Don launched them off of the table, and set them back in front of Jack. Yet it gave me some insight into the others' tendencies, and I decided to inquire further, "Aww is somebody on a losing streak?" as I glanced down toward his stack of three.

Don's head twitched a little as he argued, "Yeah I think they are going to try and take me for another forty tonight" He was a quick sale though, he smacked Chris's shoulder almost instantaneously, "Put me in for another five."

As Chris pulled up his fancy little case and started counting chips I asked, "How much you guys play for?"

The other side of the room echoed again, "No it's a trick! He's just faking it! Do you remember a brilliant surgeon! Huh do you remember that!?"

Chris continued, "Usually for just five or ten." He started giving me the denominations as he pulled out each color, "this one's five, ten, twenty five, fifty, and a dollar." Before inquiring he shoved a pile of chips over toward Don. "Want in on this pot?"

"Sure, I'ma run to the rest room real quick though I'll hop in the next pot."

He barked, "Ok, for how much?" before dealing the next hand.

"Five?"

I took my time down the asile, the steps, and the entryway; everyone in the store continued their own conversations as if I didn't exist. So I washed my hands and made my way back, again taking a slow enough stride I could get a look about the place and remember every face inside.

Sawyer, who had just filled another chair at the table greeted me rather quickly, "Hey! Perfect timing!"

Chris wanted to make sure he was dealing enough cards, "You in for this round!?"

And I wanted to count my stack as I regurgitated an adequate response, "Sure." There were only enough chips to account for $4.25.

Sawyer released an uneven grin as he mumbled; "Perfect" and Lyle started tossing cards.

I prompted again as I darted toward Lyle. "So what do you mean by calculating the odds?"

Apparently I had forgotten who discovered the book, as Ken started to fill in instead, "What's your email address? I'll send it to you."

He pulled up an email application and passed me his IPad, I didn't see a reason why such a simple thing would be an issue so I entered my address for him before handing it back. He made eye contact with me as I insisted, "It delivers many messages" and grasped its leather case.

Chris flopped a couple of chips into the pot, and I glanced around the circle. The pot was barely juiced so I figured everyone had a relatively crummy hand. Once I matched the bet I lost to a pair of threes though.

Ken tapped a couple of buttons before setting the IPad down, after glancing up he chuckled a little bit and shoved a couple of chips forward, "We'll try and give you a quick run through and I'll send it to you later tonight."

Don glanced at his hand, over toward Ken, back to the pot, and tossed his cards down, "Fold."

Jack matched, Lyle and Chris folded as well, after turning over their cards, Ken had a set of three queens and took the pot.

After shoving the pot over to Ken, Chris started dealing the next hand and yet again the same feminine voice exploded from across the room, "Sure, just call me a whore, ya fucking dick. Just because I was in a sorority, is that it?"

I couldn't help but to giggle hysterically and look around, I couldn't see anyone abnormal but the store got a little quieter. Since she wasn't going to look me in the eyes as I'd walk around I figured I may as well play along and grunted, "Someone's pissy . . ." which sent the entire group into an almost song like laughter. At least I was able to gain an identifiable glance before the front door slammed again, "This happen often?" I glanced back toward the group for an answer.

Jack filled in, "Yeah, bitches here are crazy, I think some-one's selling crack out on the patio."

I chuckled and the rest of them busted out laughter again. As they tried to contain themselves Lyle and Ken covered their mouths like ten year olds. Ken couldn't hold it back however as he snickered "She may be crazy, but her vagina's still good."

It was a lovely joke so I mumbled exactly that, "Well ain't that lovely . . ." and stuttered for a moment, "Guess I'll raise ya a dollar twenty five then . . ." and bluffed my way to being two bucks richer after they all folded. I didn't know whether I should feel bad for her, or continue avoiding the psychotic polarization behind her requirement that I start a conversation. So let the subject change its self.

Jack ran out of plastic this time so he grunted toward Chris, "Let me in for another five I guess . . ."

He plopped his little case up on the table, propped the lid open and hid behind it as his arms flopped up and down on each side, exemplifying his motions like a puppet being flopped around by its master before chucking Jack's chips over. Lyle dealt.

"These run through a pop machine like real quarters?" I beckoned with a twenty five in my hand.

Ken retaliated as he tossed out a raise of fifty before the flop "Only at the casino."

"What's that an ace?" Lyle barked as he sat back in his seat in attempt to look at Jack's hand, Ken pushed him back into his seat and shook his head.

The ace was sitting in my hand so I raised the pot to a dollar and made everyone pony up another fifty. Chris tossed out the flop, a third ace for me, and the two matched mine.

Another Ghost in the walls screeched, "She won't stop until she knows why!?" as someone else stormed out of the room.

My gut turned as the words echoed through my head again. I didn't like wasting time either, but there were a lot of unfamiliar vessels in the room, what was I supposed to run around like a YouTube vid begging everyone in the store for an answer? Marry before I even meet a girl?

Jack's grin grew from ear to ear as he raised my pot of gold another dollar and the rest of them dropped out of the pot.

Apparently content with the pot now he checked, allowing me to pull another two bucks out of his stack with a raise. He let me take his triple twos with three aces and two twos.

Jack scoffed and screamed, "Beginners luck won again, ya gutsy little prick" as he cast his hand toward the pot.

I was giggling like a coyote as I pulled in my winnings. "If ya say so, He-he . . ."

Ken offered him some consolation, "So I guess we don't have to try too hard to fill you in?"

But I'm an addict so I started offering again to tune in to another lecture, "Nah feel free, I never mind a good tip."

Sawyer started describing the first point system described in the book, the easy one, "it's pretty simple, not having a continuous book of decks coming, the odds reset with each deal, every card in a hand or on the flop is one point up or down in respect to what is in our hand. A hand from the chart is obviously a plus, while counting the pot we'd have to assume that anyone could have any of the other possibilities on the floor. If one's hand is highest, they should naturally add to the pot."

The concept of a bluff or when to raise and push the next guy around was rather simplistic to me . . .

"the odds of a card showing up are naturally one out of fifty two, odds of a pair drop each time a card shows as there are only three of that number or face left in the deck." Lyle paused to look over at Jack.

After dealing the next hand Jack started fondling two little action figures that apparently came with Chris's new chip set. He was setting them up in doggy style and once we noticed he started laughing his ass off, "Hah-ha, my favorite position!" Jack barked again as everyone else chuckled and shook their heads.

After a couple of hands some girls walking out to grab a cigarette scoffed back at our table as they grunted, "Pigs" and brushed past us toward the patio. This too set them off like firecrackers before the next hand went round. Eventually Ken took the pot from Don again.

I could understand the perspective in a couple of minutes. I got to see what Jack had been hiding behind his cards the whole time.

Throughout the night he kept glancing back and forth between his Mp3 player and his cards, he was fondling the LCD screen every once and a while.

When I got a look over his shoulder, I could see a couple of nude girls go across the screen like a slideshow, all in different positions. He glanced back up at me, chuckled and offered up the words, "Ya like that!? Here this one is my favorite" he poked around and brought up one up of a brunette posed in doggy style . . . .

At the time, as this was my first experience with the obscene task of publicly observing naked women; the psychology book buried in my memory was leaning toward a developmental issue. I mustered up an uncomfortable word, "Yeah she's always gorgeous when you don't have to see her face . . ." and sat back in my seat a little bit to attend to my cards, after of course catching a glimpse of the two of hearts and three of clubs in his hand. Oddly enough his hand was likely to take the pot, with a two and three sitting out we were still waiting for the turn, so he raised a quarter and went back to his little player again.

Ken interrupted his fun, "Jesus man, do we need to pause while you take a restroom break."

"What, they're hot!?"

Lyle filled in, "It ain't hot knowing you're sitting here with your giblets in your hand though."

Jack looked exasperated, and a perplexed look boiled behind his brow.

I grunted, "Really man, it's obscene in public" in hopes to knock some sense in him.

"Sorry if I'm not still hiding with my sexuality in the closet. Like you guys are."

"You may not be but the two four-n some odd year olds on the other side of the store probably aren't even sure what to call it." I was hoping again to exaggerate the illegal and obscene nature of his exposure. "How old are you anyways."

"Twenty eight, what are you going to tell me to put it away daddy? I can look at whatever I want."

"Ya got a girlfriend?"

"Not at the moment . . ."

I wasn't sure I even wanted to know him anymore, "Wonder why, perverts like you usually sicken women." His face started to turn red as he scoffed at me, "The unsanitary mask of religious obsession probably doesn't help you any does it?"

He didn't like that, "Shut the fuck up ass wipe, I get all kinds of tail!"

I slide three dollars into the pot after the river dropped another three and the turn a second king, matching my hand with a three and a king sitting by. "Ya gonn'a match it or not"

He chuckled and scoffed again before dropping his chips in, "Yeah, I'll match." He even sat up in his chair and grabbed his crotch like a gangster, he held his cards up and barked, "What, what!"

Only Lyle was left in the pot and he decided to fold. So without a word I showed my cards and gave a blank deer like stare before scrounging up my winnings.

Unfortunately over the course of the night I went from ten bucks to nearly zero and back up to three before the place closed. I only lost a cup of coffee.

After paying Lyle we went outside. Ken lite up a cigarette, indicating they'd be there for at-least a little while longer, so I played monkey see monkey do and did the same. Sawyer came waltzing up to have some cancer and started telling Ken about this time just a couple of days prior he was in bed with his girlfriend and his father gave him a high five after catching them. So Jack started talking about someone in doggy style again.

I turned to Don and asked, "They always like this, I mean so . . . public?"

He didn't take long to nod and reassure my little observation as he grimaced, "Pretty much, about every hour or so most days"

"So . . . . not only common, but constant." He nodded, implying at least confirmation, "I take it his father's exit from his life was a good thing?"

Don's eyes widened a fair bit, almost as if in fear. He glanced back at Jack, and then to me. Jack was glaring at me and his face was glowing cherry red, I couldn't tell however whether it was rage or embarrassment, "No just . . . over indulgence . . ." He started nodding intently, like he'd brush clouds on the upswing if he could.

Jack butted in again after hearing me, "Least I ain't in the closet like you two."

I chuckled again in an attempt to plea insanity so he didn't try and bash my face in or something, "Silly humans, I just think the little picture box is a bit nasty in a crowd. I'm kind of sheltered."

Sawyer retaliated, "He still has that fucking mp3 player . . . ." And shook his head.

"Dude there are people that make millions of dollars a year off this kinda stuff. Haven't you been to the bunny ranch" Jack moaned, before he held both hands out to the side in exasperation.

"Sick dude, ya don't have to bring it here though, don't you have a bedroom." Sawyer insisted.

I tried containing my-self, as apparently I'd just struck a chord. "Ight I gotta head home, I'll see ya later mates."

Just before I got to my door I could hear one of them bark, "She's really going to pay us twenty bucks an hour to do this?" So I decided to ignore the warm up period. As I drove down the lot I opened the windows, giving one an opportunity to bark yet again, "Even a blind squirrel gets a nut sometimes."

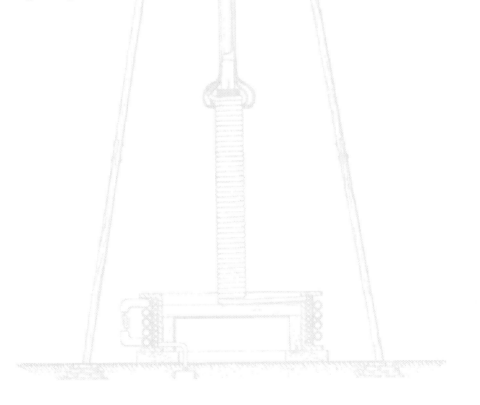

08: Another Response

In the morning I falsely assumed it might be relationally productive to overlook my focus on my emotional trauma regarding my defective DNA, this time I wanted to blame it on my Pallium's lack of resources which required the Thalamus to over-write a more useful sector in my cortex so I couldn't get it right the first time . . . the one over there . . . with all the pixels and stuff.

For some reason I knew she was going to, she even described the painting I was sitting by to clarify.

Over here Eros—W4M

It's like the Metamorphoses all over again, this is driving me crazy. I couldn't help but to enjoy the fact you were so kind, as to sit right there. With your back to my friend's painting, you wore the crimsin and golden brown leaves around her walk way like a beautiful crown of the falls. Each side arched above you head just perfectly centered.

We joked and laugh the whole time, it was so much more fitting as a dunce cap. Your golden brown hair and baby blue eyes always get my stomach turnin, that much I admit. And yes it was fun watching you play cards all night, but I do have to say that it is getting rather tiring that you would rather sit there by the wall and play cards all night. It is a sick sick torture just watching you know, it is so hard to keep my lust for you contained. You always fill that silver shirt so well when you wear it, I just want to tear it right off of you and run my tongue up your torso. I just want to unzip those tight jeans with my teeth.

Why would you rather play one of the devil's games while one of the minxes is right here to pleasure you? You have already proved to me that you have the perfect capacity for what I need, a kind and compassionate person who would go out of their way at a skip, and it made my heart skip just as well. For nothing more but to do what I could not, it was the sweetest thing anyone has ever done for me, and for that I accept your previous wishes, I want you to be mine and mine alone. I want to be everything you need and desire in the sexual realm, You are the only one I crave, you are the only one I want to love; I do, I do, I do love you. I can accept you as mine for the rest of forever, but you must do just this one thing before you can have it all.

You invited me in, and I am at my wits end. You can accept it can't you, just accept it this one time, I need you to see what you are doing to me. Every night I lay to bed alone, every morning I wake to an empty bed, an empty life. I want you to be my husband damn you, I want things back to the way I saw it from the moment you walked into my life! You were perfect, you just broke right in like I always need so I know you can. If only you wouldn't insist on acting like an idiot, maybe you would realize that we can be perfect for each other. You need to be strong and supportive, I need my rock back! You need to hop back into the shoes you wore first, just come and talk to me, all will be forgiven. I could never stay mad at you, even after what you did.

Everything said is said but I don't want you unless I can have you! So get off of your lousy yet gorgous bum and get talkin!

I've never been an English buff, but I wanted to pick apart the structure and flow. I couldn't help but to notice the grammatical and spelling errors . . . The redundancy stuck out like a thorn.

I was reluctant and confused, yet curious. It was too similar. It wasn't accurate enough. Maybe it was hasty because of an emotional haze. Maybe there was another painting of some walk way out there, with another brown haired blue eye sitting in the way.

Should I draw her in? Was I being duped by a prankster? Did she sick her sorority sisters on me? Was she twice my elder? There was no one in the store when I gave any wind to the possibility I had anything to do with a cab ride so the likely hood of random chemistry had to be lesser.

The website had an option to post anonymously. Maybe I'd make a friend. Maybe it would be more natural than I expected. Maybe she'd tell me to piss off. Maybe I could offend her enough to scare her off, so I didn't have to go through the wild goose chase. Maybe my grammar would be so horrid she'd color me green and leave me dust in the wind.

None of it really mattered. Curiosity always kills the cat does it not?

Blame Canabis Psyche—M4W—(Under the dunce cap)

Well Psyche, I would have preferred it, I really would. It would be nice to find love early in life; my time on this earth really could be but a euphoric dream if such a thing were possible. It's not an easy task though, love isn't the kind of thing one can pick up at the store. It's not the kind of thing you can fry up for dinner and stuff back in the fridge when you are done.

You're probably more used to hearing that you are perfect, gorgeous, or even angelic when you meet a guy. I won't lie, I was thinking the same. Ya can't catch a wale with a two pound line though.

According to Billy R. Martin's paper for The American College of Neuropsychopharmacology, "*Marijuana*".

"While THC appears to produce its greatest decrement in free recall or short-term memory, it has been proposed that chronic marijuana use in adolescents may result in long-term memory impairment (116). There are also indications that individuals with learning disabilities may be more susceptible to memory deficits"

While I appreciate the offer, as it really is quite flattering. I don't fancy the idea'r of talking to a wall while they daydream about the XXX. I know that many like to jump right into the deep end, I know many will do it over and over. But I've been called an odd ball on more than just a few occasions. As rude as it may be, it isn't likely I will ever change that about myself for anyone.

I told you I didn't remember something specific. I wasn't sure I even wanted to try. When I did you trampled me on your way out the door.

You know I am scared, you know I am timid. The closest I have to describe the sensation I get when I read the posts with your voice injected is that mimicking the personality disorder of a Schizoid. It leads me to believe that you don't want me for my personality, but for something else. Maybe it's a memory, maybe it's something more tangible, but please let's just chalk this up to a starry night.

Unfortunately for me this story has taken the cake with my group, many of my closer friends blame it on my lack of experience. They enjoy jesting at my so called failure to lose my first badge, a task about as important to them as the poo jokes which send them to the floor in a frenzy of laughter.

I am open to love however I prefer to search for it in my own way. I'd really rather get to know a person a little better before particular levels of intimacy, and you have chosen to mandate my approach, you have chosen to mandate that we will be copulating in the near future.

Every time I leave for the roasted heaven I remember, I can't help but to wonder If I'll see you again. I used to find myself hoping that maybe this wall between us will fall, and wishing that I never delivered to myself the circuitry for the time machine which set me on the other side of it. This would be so much easier if only I didn't give myself a century long lecture on why not to warp the space time continuum, apparently it has destroyed a couple of dimensions which my alter ego was using as a test ground.

Every time I go back there I feel as if I am hopping through a worm hole. I know I was wrong to turn my back toward you, I wish I hadn't listened to the wrong book at the wrong time, but every time I get closer to understanding Nikola's view of electron flow, every time I find a new way to make another neural connection, my disorder gets the best of me. It is likely I will spend every day depleting as close to every Nano gram of prolactin in my noggin I possibly can. It is just too addictive a concept, to think something as simple as a big hole in the ground could provide the deficit I'd need to make possible the extraction of electrons from the static in our ozone.

I swear I am not useless, but this one thing has me riding a tight rope, if you could see it in your heart, I'd really like my sanity back. Some details of my history stick out like thorns; some implode and leave a cavern like one of the dents on that mass yanking our oceans around. So I must implore you, I haven't but a vague symptom of your actions, I wish I knew what you have been up to I really do.

Unfortunately I only have a chance at retaining that which happens in my line of sight, and it is really kind of embarrassing when the only thing I remember about a person is the pear shape atop the back side of their legs. It is true that at one point I had wished for you to help me identify the other side of your vessel. But I can't force someone to be my friend for ten minutes.

I know you have your own perspective, and that I respect, but please understand that if I could make it be true I would, I don't care. I am wrong about so many things. Yet every time I made an attempt it seems you weren't satisfied.

For some reason I can't help but to think that if the shoe were on the other foot, I'd just be like "Hey aren't you that one guy who found me on Mars?" or some crap like that. However in reality I fear Mary has made a useful contribution, unfortunately I am beginning to be grateful of the psychological wall in-between your image and I. She has shown me who I believe my true friends are.

She really didn't like that though. Her post was time stamped for just twenty minutes after mine.

And I just Disappear Right?—W4M—(in the roach)

Well master, I know you think that you are being clever but you don't get off of this quite that easy. If I didn't already love you I'd just say "hey to the wind" and let your sorry ass go about your normal ways but this light has to stay on people. I can't just let you go off of the deep end after what you did. I am your friend, you need one that will never let go even in hard times.

You may not see now that I am the real prize, I am that which you yearn for and you will regret it until the day you die if you ignore me and settle for less. But I know for fact that one day you will learn. We're all alike in my profession. It isn't easy to get here. I put my all into everything I do. It is only fair I give the same to you. I will stop at nothing to make you happy. You earned that.

I am literally exploding with hormones whenever you are even near; I was from the moment you backed up your little chariot. Every time you speak here you pull my strings. Every time I find I have made my master angry, every time he decides he would rather not see me, it tears me apart inside. Yet I doubt you'll ever notice being so involved in yourself and all.

Open up before it is too late. I am a work in progress, not a finished deal. I still want to be a better slave, every day all I dream of is to submit to your every desire, I want to be that which you want and deserve. I could never imagine being with another, you are my master.

But you must see that I too crave certain things, while you already exceed all of my expectations and annihilate my desires, you must respect that sometimes I have my own requirements.

I have trusted you from the beginning, I can't imagine being with another. I know that you have been playing with others, no woman in her right mind would let a piece of man meat like you go to bed alone. So take your first badge and eat it. Eat it right out of my cavern. The only thing I aim for in this life is to be a good slave to you, I am ok with this. Everyone has a past, everyone has a lover. When you hold such a deep place in my heart, you can get away with anything, especially after I have told you that there have been others for I as well. I'll invite them to come play with us together if I have to.

Please master; forgive my faults, however plentiful they may be. Just let me come back, all I want to do is try out that cock, the girth alone has me wondering if it is just a novelty toy, or the real thing. I can only imagine what it would be like to have you sink deep inside me to explore, I cannot wait to have you violate me, I love the xXx. I am yours alone all of the time.

I keep up my appearance as best I can. I am only human. The way you told me I wasn't even good enough to remember is the most hurtful thing I have ever been told. Are you doing this on purpose? Did you really do that just so you can toy with my strings like I am some freaking puppet? Many say that you are sick, you are mentally diseased, but I won't leave you like this. I will be by your side forever, we can heal together. Just come back to what you know is right.

I know you know, stop playing dumb. I will not make any advance, that is your job. It's too tight a rope I walk with you. It isn't healthy. I am certain though, my place is with you master, it always has been and always will be. You will never feel right without love in your life. Just come back. Just come back and I will fulfill your wildest dreams. You will enjoy it I promise.

Once I got home from work, I logged onto my email account to check some updates from my favorite tech news . . . There were two emails from the same address (JesAtoy).

Ok Mr. Electrical Engineering?!

The fact is that I know I am right, you need to man up and fulfill your side of the bargain. But knowing you, you are probably questioning whether or not I am the right one aren't you. It is very difficult for me to just throw everyday life out there, where so many people can see it, and I am tired of the fact that you have made me do such a thing. If you refer back to my posting I have already told you everything you need to know, and I expect you to be the man I once met.

The time stamp on the next one was from the next day.

Oh nothing more to say do ya

You can't respond? You started this! I am waiting for an answer? I laughing so much every time you take so long coming up with your sadistic little lies. So what is it, how long is it going to take you to make up an excuse this time? Huh? Am I really just a fucking toy to you? Come one you little pervert! I'm ready to take you to the alter! I just want to fuck the shit out of you, don't leave me like this!

And like an idiot I responded . . .

My lies are but another perspective

I only intended to confirm the identity of my responder, because I thought it might be cool to catch up. This was just a little too weird for me after it was made to be about nothing but sex. Whether it is someone else or you, I still don't enjoy being screamed at from across my favorite coffee shop. "Oh you can't even talk to a girl big boy!?" Isn't exactly a friendly remark.

I'm not entirely sure what I want any more. I need some time alone. I need to go to work.

Not but ten minutes later the window started blinking again, another email had arrived.

Be a Man already!

No I'm not leaving you like this it isn't healthy! It is normal for men to have some form of assertiveness. It is healthy for a full-blooded male like you to be aggressive enough to get things done! Grow up and be a man.

What do you expect me to believe that your penis doesn't even work? Are you going to tell me that you're incontinent or something!? I can't believe it. I don't want to believe it. Do you even know how to love anyone at all!

Yes! I am a very intelligent individual but I am a sexual being too and I have needs you know!

It isn't healthy for you to shut yourself off from the world like this. You need to learn to be naughty or you'll miss out on life.

So I closed the window and went back to surfing the web. My parents did that thing where they turn the volume up to such a level it shakes every wall in the house after a while, and I decided to leave.

I found this little Panera hidden in the crevice of a strip mall out west which I'd never been to before, on the opposite side of town. So I figured it'd be a good place to stake out and chill for a while. After ordering a cup of joe I popped in some ear buds and went right back to ZeitNews.

They had this amusing story about how for many subconscious homosexual desires may bubble to the surface in the form of outward homophobic actions or statements. After doing a couple of surveys with their test group they were able to establish the individuals' extrinsic sexuality. Afterward they also measured their reactions to homophobic and heterosexual imagery. This data provided facts for the claim that internalized or unexpressed homoerotic tendencies will cause an internal war, eventually they will also bubble to the surface as violent outbursts and declarations demeaning to homosexuals. The subjects were also more prone to utilize aggressive terminology.

Next they were asked about their home life, and the social dynamics of their childhood shelters. Typically those who had oppressive or demanding parents were more likely to show signs of similar internal conflicts, as well as react adversely to homoerotic stimuli.

It made me stop and think for a moment, so I dazed off across the room into this fake fireplace which is embedded into the side of their central pillar. My father's words echoed through my head, "You just don't plug a toaster into your microwave, it just doesn't work!" The bit about "oppressive parents" reminded me of my father. He's rather invasive, sometimes I'd call him a two face, when no one is around he'll scream and yell about every little thing possible. He's territorial, possessive, and petty. His favorite statements consist of "Because I said so!" and "Shut the fuck up." When he's met by bad news he'll shoot the messenger, "That just doesn't happen, it's too much for me to digest! Shut the fuck up already, nobody wants to hear that crap!" When I haven't completed the task he has mandated within a moment's notice He'll scream and yell again, "We'll hop to it you ungrateful little fuck!" He always speaks highly of homosexuals too, he's very homophobic.

Then I got bored again and flipped the webpage.

A new synthetic material which some chemists at KTM in Stockholm have developed is actually able to imitate the process of photosynthesis and at a record level. The molecular catalyst which was used sped the process up to such a rate it actually approached productivity comparable to natural plants. The rate at which they ingest and process energy is referred to as turn overs per second. Someone screamed through the music, "Grow up and come talk to me you little pervert!" This achievement is paramount, as most solar circuitry will benefit. She screamed again, "One minute he sounds like Romeo and now I'm just supposed to disappear!?"

I glanced around the room and found nothing/no-one in my line of sight before going back to the screen. While this research could lead to incredibly efficient hydrogen production it also meant more research must be done to make it cost effective without consistent maintenance. She screamed again, "Oh you have to eat some freakin prolactin do ya!?" Then this little image popped up on my screen while my hand wasn't even resting on it.

It was an image of a naked woman. She was bent over with her ass aimed at the mirror in doggy style. She was turned to the side with a camera in her hand, facing the mirror. Apparently she even sent it through photoshop, there was text around her which said, "You can start with an apology Dip-Du!" So I glanced up again and the words, "No! He needs to do it in person!" echoed throughout the store.

So I found out what it was like to be violated . . . and stood up to walk around the store. I made my way to the bathroom as an excuse and she screamed again, "Oh no! I'm just casper the friendly freakin ghost!" so I glanced over just quick enough I almost made eye contact with her. However her head twitched back toward the stiff sitting in front of her and she hollered again, "No! He needs to do it!"

It was her in the photo, so I went into the bathroom to evade her and think for a minute. I couldn't figure out how she did it. I couldn't even close the window. So I rebooted it and the start screen came up like normal. I started rooting around to see if it'd be possible for her to even get in, but there weren't any controls I could get to in the user interface. My best option was to shut it off and get the hell out of there. Before I had a chance to shut it off another image popped up on my screen, this time she was lying on her back with her legs spread so everything was visible, the text around this one said, "I want you squirrely!"

So obviously it was time to do something I started walking out of the store. She didn't like that so much however, "Be a man for once!" a couple of feet further, "Come on already squirly!? Fuck me!" and after I passed her, "Oh ok just a toy am I!?"

Finally I waded through the delirium just enough I could verbalize, "Great, no escape." I'm not sure if she even heard it.

"Just like that!?" she kept screaming, "Just like that you are going to leave." And screaming, "No this isn't healthy!" by the time I made it to the door, she screamed again, "Learn to be naughty you little prick!" and again, "Fine!" and again, "Leave then! See if I" *Clunk* It was nice to finally have at-least one door in-between us.

Yeah . . . . My head started to do that thing again as I plopped back into my car, I couldn't help but to wonder how she even found me. I didn't like it anymore. I wanted out.

Even then though, my first impulse was to prop open my center consul pluck out my I-Pod and hook it up for some tunes. I didn't exactly know where I could go. So once I declared a victor, Mogwai, I glanced back up over the hood and sparked the top dead center cylinder.

She was walking down the declination from the side walk with her hand in her purse. I had to assume the worst as I popped the clutch and goosed it, luckily I always like to park aiming out of my spots. I had to jerk the car to the left to re compensate and avoid clipping the SUV next to me. My tires broke traction and squealed as I ducked behind the next two cars. When I made it to the end of the parking lot I had to pull my hand brake to stop without boning the eclipse which glide right past my bumper. I wanted out of there, I wanted out of there yesterday. Luckily it passed before she could pull up behind me and I was off to a squealing start again.

After taking my third detour, I got stuck at the next light, and her silver jeep pulled up behind me, I could see her in the mirror screaming and bashing her hands against the steering wheel as she flipped off her girlfriend whom was in the passenger seat. I guess she decided to honk at me, her horn rang out long and loud. He blinker wasn't on so I looked back at the light. It was still red. I couldn't take it anymore so I decided to take an urgent right, and squealed off the line again.

She followed me. After taking my second left, and another right immediately after, I managed to put about two and a half blocks in between us but she still came raging up behind me. I went another couple of blocks before deciding to wing a left, and another. I made it a block down and finally I could see her going the opposite way behind some houses. I was going fifty in a thirty five zone.

After jamming on the brakes I pulled my e-brake to slow just shy of the explorer in front of me, and I decided to dodge right into another neighborhood. I was still feeling unsafe so I weaseled my way through the neighborhood and up to another major street which revealed the interstate. So I booked it that way and down a mile of interstate, I merged my way off and back on to city streets.

I was about to pee myself, I needed a gas station. So I went back to weaving through the city. I took a left a mile or so down, a right, and finally I was satisfied I'd lost my tail. I didn't quite know where to go, so I picked the Bucky's on my right.

I pulled right up to the door, in the rock star's spot just a few feet from the door. I hopped out and dashed inside straight to the men's room. I was shaking uncontrollably the entire time.

When I finally headed to the sink to lather up and rinse some stiff decided to walk up to the bowl next to mine. I was still shaking uncontrollably so he glanced over at me at least three times, "You OK buddy" and gave me one of those drug concerned father glares. I was unable to entirely release the tension preventing my neck from turning freely.

I just barely cocked my head up toward him and grunted, "No . . . Not really." Before I snatched a paper towel wiped my hands and slammed the door behind me. The clerk followed me with his eyes out the door like a shoplifter. Once I was in my car I glanced down to the fuel gauge and backed up to the nearest stall since it was riding only a quarter above E.

As I yanked the lever, unscrewed the gas cap, and jammed my card in the automated leech some silver jeep pulled up to the pump on the end. I had to keep my eye on it as I slipped the pump nozzle in and squeezed. It was by the entrance to the lot, furthest away from me.

After the longest twenty seconds of my life I could see an arm . . . . they went to the other side of the pump . . . . Back to the car . . . . and finally the most attractive fat guy I've ever seen walked over to grab the windshield squeegee.

09: Someone New

So I was surfing around one day, and did something uncharacteristic. I opened a window for Facebook. Typically when I open a browser for the first time in a day I'll open up my email account and glance through a couple of updates from different newspapers, political forums, and a couple of shopping sites which I find decent deals on every once and a while. Even despite my break from the norm though, it got boring and I went back to Zeitnews.

I found this story about another electrical engineer; he'd achieved a new record for one of the smallest transistors on the planet. It was merely a couple of nanometers wide. Typically a transistor this small is only found in your computer's microprocessor or CPU. The writer went on for a while to describe how this is yet another crowning achievement in the field proving Moore's law. He claimed that most microprocessors from the last decade utilize transistors which span about a hundred nanometers. After a while it deviled into the future, he rambled about how as a planet we are quickly approaching the ability to create a transistorized switch which will not only be a circuit of singular molecules but will require only a single displaced electron to store a value.

The tab for Facebook started blinking and demanding attention, so I clicked on it to investigate. It was because of a message from this young lady (Crystal) whom I met while training about two years ago, and we hadn't chatted since. So I opened the page in a new window and plastered it to the left, ZeitNews to the right.

"Hello?"

"Hi"

"How have you been?"

"Decent, been keepin' busy."

"Oh so you're probably doing something right now?"

"Nah, just surfing the digital ocean."

"Oh . . . Well I was just curious if you wanted to chill."

"I haven't seen you in ages, it might be fun?"

"Do you want to go get drinks somewhere or something?"

"Sure, how about tea?"

"I don't know where we'd find that."

"There is a cool little tea shop hidden in Plattsmouth Port. It's called the Boiling Leaf."

"Ok I'll meet you there."

The little dot next to her name disappeared, so I'd assume she was going already. I saved the session for my browser, shut down the computer and left.

It took me about fifteen minutes but when I got there she was sitting right in front of the store front's windows. So I killed the engine and made my way inside. Just after I propped open the door she blurted out, "You finally made it!" at about the same time the two baristas simultaneously mumbled, "Huh, he is." And "Holy crap he did come."

I was a little hesitant as the entire store reacted abnormally, yet I continued walking, "Yeah, I take it you've been here for a while?"

"Only fifteen minutes or so."

"You must have found your way here pretty quickly."

"Yep, I only live a couple blocks away."

As I plucked the chair from in front of her I tried to speak, "Really that's"

But she cut me off, "Do you want to go order before you sit down?"

She started to stand up and turn that way so I mumbled again, "Sure why not . . ."

When we approached the counter she started to look around and asked me, "what's usually the best here?"

"Well, do you ever drink tea?"

"None."

I plucked up their book and started prodding for personal preferences, "What kind of things do you usually like?"

"Coffee, juice, margaritas . . ."

"What do you usually order when you get coffee."

"Uhh . . . A vanilla latte, chocolate espresso, caramel, or a strawberry bomber."

This time it was easy, "So would something with strawberry appeal to?"

She cut me off again, "Yeah that sounds good!"

I had my finger on one of their options, "Black or"

"Sure!"

The barista at the counter mumbled under his breath as we were picking something out, "Well aren't you two good friends" But he played it off the moment I glanced up at him, "What can I get for ya" And her eye's popped open like she'd seen a ghost.

With my finger on the Blue Shadow I tried to speak. "Can we get a."

But he cut me off too, "A Blue Shadow? Sure what size?"

"How about a two . . . How bout a four cup pot."

As I started to reach for my wallet she stuck her card in his face and blurted out, "It's ok I got it."

"I can."

"I got it."

So I shrugged, "Ok."

He said, "It'll be four sixty seven." As he plucked it out of her hand and started swiping it down the register.

She stood with her back turned toward me as she waited for her card. I could have sworn I heard her throat rumble as she'd mumbled, "Yeah, I'm gonna do this."

So I tried to get her attention off of the wall by grunting, "Huh"

She jumped a little as he handed her the card. "thanks" Once she looked back toward me she went on, "I was just thinking about something for class."

"Which one?"

"An art class."

The barista cut in again, "I'll bring it right out to you if you want to have a seat."

So we started walking back that way, "So what's that thing you walked in here with?"

"The tablet? It's an Acer Ionia, running the same operating system as the phone in your hand."

She glanced down at it and back to me again, "So does it get calls and surf the web or what?"

"It only has a wireless LAN card in it and a GPS Chip . . . I bought this one because I wanted to tinker around with an android platform and surf the web."

I flicked my finger around and opened the lock up before swirling it around and sliding it over to her, "It'll play games and everything?"

She flicked around the home page before prompting again, "Where's the browser."

So I stuck my finger on it, "Right there." and opened it,

She squeaked a little and started tapping at the screen before sliding it back to me, "Here, look at that."

"What is it?"

"My website."

I glanced about and it was littered with grammatical errors and two of the links didn't work, "Why doesn't this."

"It is, it's true, I'm a nymph."

So I stuttered, "Umm . . ." and asked again, "This link doesn't work."

The barista startled me as well and set our cups and kettle down next to us, "just pluck the strainer when that timer runs out," before he walked off.

"It's a work in progress, I'm an artist." So I poked one of the links that did work as the buzzer went off. "The buzzer's going off."

She looked at me like I was nuts when I plucked the strainer out to set it aside and inquired, "How'd ya make that?"

It was a wooden block with the word "PASSION" carved into it, so she explained. "I chiseled out the blocks, stained in the words and sanded and lacquered it."

"Huh, elaborate." There weren't many others, so I glanced up at her and she handed me a business card. "Nice . . ."

"I just started it."

I kept poking around as I prodded. "Are you going to open up a shop or what are you doing with it at the moment." The next block of wood had the word sex carved into it. The third said blowjob 30$.

"I've sold a couple." She shook her head violently up and down, "if you know anyone who would like one let me know."

"Do you want any help designing the web page or anything?"

"Nah, I'll get to that later." She drained a cup and stared into the painting on the wall, "This is really good tea."

"Ya like it?"

"Yeah, it is, it's good." The pot was empty so I plucked it up and dumped some more hot water over the leaves for a second brew as she started in again, "Do you want to go back to my place and watch a movie?"

I felt like I was belching the word as I sat down, "Maybe."

But she quickly changed her mind, "Or your place."

"Which would be better?"

"Yours . . . My uhh . . ." she glanced off toward the door and back to me, "My dad doesn't like it when I have friends over this late."

"I guess . . . Don't you want to finish the tea?"

"Oh ok . . ." she wicked this metal thing around in her mouth as I poured some more tea, "Do you like it?"

"What is it?"

She nodded again, "A tongue ring."

"Fancy. What's that for?"

"It's kind of weird, if you really want to know." And she nodded again.

"How weird?" I nodded too.

"It's supposed to make it feel better."

"Do you like having that thing in your mouth?"

"It hurt at first, but I got used to it."

"Funky . . ."

"Do you want to see my tattoos?"

"Sure, how many do you have?"

"A couple," she turned her ankle around and pulled up her pants a little bit, "This one is a Yin-Yang sign."

I could see that, "Why'd you choose that one?"

She answered before chugging the other glass of tea, "I liked the balance."

The water she just downed was at least a hundred and ninety degrees so I shined her on, "The balance of good and evil, it has a lot to say doesn't it?"

"Yeah."

"It's supposed to symbolize the same thing as the word moderation; one action must be met by another. The dot kind of gives an ode to the fact bad parts of our life infect the good, vice versa."

"Like how cowboys always tried to take over the Indians?"

"Yeah . . . We killed thousands of Indians to get here, but Wal-Mart makes life affordable."

I wasn't on anything at the time so I didn't feel quite right when she asked again, "Tea's gone, want to go watch a movie?"

"Maybe . . ." I plucked the serving platter up and carried it to the counter, she was already on her way out the door by the time I turned around.

She spoke right before the door slammed behind her, "I'll follow you."

Once I made it out behind her I tried to slow down again, "Are you sure you don't want to go to a theatre, it's only ten?"

So she stopped at her car door. "I had a good one picked out though."

"Which one?"

"It was supposed to be a surprise."

"Oh . . ."

After a short pause she asked again, "So can we go?"

"I guess."

She hopped in her car and hollered before I got a chance to speak again. "OK! I'll be right behind you."

And she was, I was actually somewhat surprised that she didn't rear end me. Every time I'd merge, she'd merge without leaving my tail or turning her blinkers on for even a second. If I used the brakes, her tires would squeal. Once I reached a velocity within five miles of the speed limit, she'd nearly rear end me. So the whole time I was driving home, I was wondering whether I should pull over to another restaurant or shop . . . .

There was still a reasonable doubt in my mind though. While I was training she really did seem like a decent person, so we made it to my place and I parked in the drive way. She pulled around the circle and parked right in-between the "NO PARKING THIS SIDE OF STREET" and "NO PARKING IN-BETWEEN SIGNS" signs, so I skipped my way down toward her and bent over by her driver's side window. After she rolled the window down she gave me a blank stare and I pointed over at the sign, "You might want to pull down the street and park over there before you get a ticket." So she pinged the engine and drove off.

Once she parked she came running up the hill toward me and hugged me like we'd known each other for years, "So what movie do you want to watch?"

"I have Limitless on my hard drive."

I propped my door open, "That could work I guess."

"I don't know if you can play it on that, or if you have another . . ."

"Sure . . . just make yourself at home and I'll grab my laptop."

After I brought it back in she flopped on the floor next to me as I hooked it up to the tv and entered the pass code. She plugged her hard drive in right away and started poking around to get to the movie.

"What's Bare Flix mean?"

"Oh that's just uh . . ."

"Porn?"

"Yeah . . ."

"Do you watch a lot of porn?"

She stopped fiddling around with the computer and gazed straight through the screen, "Just a little."

"Is that a bad thing?"

"I don't know . . . is it?"

Her eyes darted from side to side before she glanced back to the computer, "Well I'm just going to . . ." she clicked on the button, "We can sit on the couch right?" as she raised her eye brows.

"Sure, make yourself at home I guess. You're already here."

She leaped backward and sat right in the middle of our couch so I made my way over to the love seat before she called after me again, "Aren't you going to sit by me."

I glanced down at the floor to be as shy as possible and mumbled, "OH, I guess . . ." as I stumbled over toward her.

She giggled and asked, "So have you seen this movie."

"Yeah, my uncle and my parents drug me to it when he was in town."

"Oh . . . Ok."

"There's a rather amusing principle behind it too."

"What's that?"

"Well . . . I've found realities counterpart to NZT-48 . . ."

"Ritalin?"

"No just multivitamins."

"How does that help?"

"Oh a healthy body is a happy body."

"I've never tried that."

Again I played along, "You should some time. The vitamin B floods in and opens capillaries; vitamin A improves your eyesight noticeably so long as you are properly hydrated. Vitamin k is good for brain development and plasticity."

"Wow, maybe I should try that."

"Yeah my dad has like eighty bottles of them in his bathroom closet."

"Which ones actually work?"

"Oh just try a bunch, as long as they don't have iron in them it'll be a cake walk."

"There aren't any which are better or worse?"

So I nodded furiously, "Oh, yeah all of the "natural" ones typically break down in your body a lot quicker."

"Ok as long as they say natural right?"

I turned toward her to be inflammatory, "Yep, just take one of those and the compounds will do all of the work for you. It's exactly like being on NZT."

So she stuck her tongue in my mouth and slobbered all over my face for a while. Luckily enough she told me that she had a curfew after a while. She had to go home. I'm not much of a ladies man, I didn't even know if the rapidity at which she started necking with me was normal. Nor did I like it.

The whole dating scene is almost a sociological requirement in some countries though. For some reason I still felt compelled to asked her if she wanted to go to dinner next time, maybe she'd open up intellectually. When I did she suggested Friday, and slobbered all over my face before leaving.

Apparently it was that simple. So after my mind did that screen saver thing, and bounced around every which way, I decided I'd pack up my laptop and tote it back into my room. After I read a couple of articles, I checked my email. Naturally by this point my inbox was full of crap, nude images forwarded from the hell hole, phone numbers forwarded from the hell hole, and even a couple of different women bitching and moaning about their relationships with their husbands through the most respectable source known to man, the last post I made on Craigslist. Most claimed that they wanted someone whom would meet them at a discreet location and give them what they aren't getting at home.

Normally I hate to judge, but the quality of the human beings contacting me was in question. So I deleted all of them, went back to the birth of my inbox and deleted all of those. A burst of emails like that seemed somewhat coincidental, so I scanned my computer and found twelve viruses. My antivirus even claimed one was a freakin' Trojan. Oddly enough the video which she left on my desk top was not one of them . . . .

There was also another present on the hell hole, it was created merely fifteen minutes before she left.

You Think you can Replace me!?—W4M

Ok so after everything you are just going to flip a dime and start something new with another!? NO, you do not get to leave me this way, I don't care who you think you met but you are involved you son of a bitch.

I don't even get you anymore, obviously you want to be intimate, you weren't exactly shy with her. So why not me, why won't you even give me the light of day?

I'm serious if you don't get your ass back here on Wednesday I will make you regret it. Your little friend has nothing on me, I can live with the fact that you were trying, but I refuse to let you just walk out like this, it is uncalled for. You are mine and you know it.

I didn't know whether the infectious hard drive was intentional, not everyone picks up on the subtle stuff inside a copper box. Plus she's already demonstrated her demonic hold on me by showing up at other shops. So I decided I'd show up at dinner and find out if Crystal was conversational or just sexual. I even went out of my way to find this perfect little Thai restaurant, a little crook in the wall which wasn't just a Styrofoam mill . . . but made decent food. They had great reviews on several culinary review sites.

During a quick text interlude we decided when to meet up and I gave her the address and directions. I found myself waiting inside a couple of minutes early.

As she broke through the threshold I glanced up from the page and found a glitter showered goddess, she was stoking a plasticy looking leather jacket, a flower coated pink blouse, and some skin tight black trousers. So I stood up and grunted, "You made it." At the same time as the waiter behind me mumbled to himself, "She finally made it."

"Yeah sorry I had to stop at home first."

"No biggy. That a new jacket? It doesn't look like it's seen the light of day?"

She popped up onto the balls of her feet and squeaked, "Yeah, I just picked it up at K-Mart, How'd ya know."

"You just have a tag sticking out the back of your neck there."

"Oh yeah that's umm," she started poking at it with her left hand, "Opps . . ." and plucked it off.

"Guess you don't want to take it back huh?"

"Oh . . . well of course not!"

She rushed up and gave me a hug as I offered, "It's good to see ya, have a seat if you'd like."

I slid my tab off to the side and offered her a menu, "I almost didn't find this place."

"Mom and pop shops are always fun to find . . . You can see it right off Main here."

"I was coming from the other way. What's good here anyways?"

"How familiar are you with Thai food?"

"Not very."

"Two of the more distinct flavors from a thai cusine are Curry and coconut," I squinted for the question mark, "If you've never had a green curry or pad thai." She shook her head though.

"You can just order for me if you want, I always like trying new things."

"Sure, do you just want to get two dishes and share them? That way you can try both."

"Ok, sounds good."

The waiter was prompt in nudging in, "So you've decided?"

"Yeah how about a green curry with shrimp and a Pad thai? You don't mind shrimp do you?"

"That's fine."

"How hot would you like those? On a scale of one to ten."

She chirped in, "I like spicy food."

"How about a seven then. Is that a good compromise?"

"Sounds perfect."

And he answered, "We can do that, would you like me to take the menu's"

So I plucked them up and forked over, "Sure."

"We'll have that right out to you."

"So why'd ya pick up the new threads?"

She started to whisk a tear away from her face as she spoke, "Oh I just needed something fancy . . . . In all honesty nobody has taken me out on a real date in a long time."

"Not even your last boyfriend?"

"Oh Jermal? No he just wanted to chill at home most of the time."

"That's a shame; I hope they don't know what they're missing out on right?"

"This one guy from school used to bring me Daises from some field before we'd go back to bed though . . ." She was really direct I guess, "It was kind of cute; I always knew he wanted to screw when he did that."

It came up pretty quickly, "You musta liked that huh?"

She nodded again, "Yeah."

"At least you're honest."

The waiter left us some food without saying a word, but she filled in, "So how have you done relationship wise.

"I actually haven't spent much time dabbling in the gossip worthy world."

"What do you mean."

"If you qualify as a girlfriend it'd be a first."

"Oh so you've never." The grin on her face was coupled with a draw of her abdomen and a quick angling of her eyebrows.

So I gave her the same lie I give all of my friends. "Oh, I did this girl at a party near UNO; we didn't date at all though. Its surprising I even know her name."

Her mouth straightened and she glanced back down toward the food to dunk it in one of the sauce cups. "Oh well I was hoping I was going to get to pop one."

So I raised my left eyebrow, "That's usually a good thing?"

"Are you sheltered or something?" she did too.

"Yeah kinda, I spend most of my time at work or with a book."

"Oh" the smirk returned to her face, "Most of the time I'm at work I'm either high or on something."

"Yeah I've done that . . ." she started shoveling food in her mouth like there wasn't going to be a tomorrow, "We used to dump some whiskey in our drink cups before we'd go through the broiler, that thing was always a nuisance."

She jerked her hand about and pointed toward one of the sauce cups, "Man that shit is dynamite."

"Dynamite?"

"Yeah it's just like this powder my dad used to throw at us all of the time."

"Ya like it?"

"Yeah it's my favorite sauce, he used to sneak it into all kinds of different things."

"My mom likes putting tabasco in her brownies."

She shook her head, "I cannot believe some of the things that man did." Without taking her eyes off of the plates.

"Huh?"

"So you say you used to bring alcohol into work?"

"Oddly enough our drive times actually went down when my employees were happy."

"What do you mean by happy?"

"I'm pretty sure the results were skewed however, he'd put more effort into things when he got what he wanted. After we made a bet on it he started going faster so he could have more uhh . . . more happiness."

"Well everyone's better off when they're happy." She raised her eyebrows at me again.

"Yeah, I started monitoring his allowance though, he only got half a grin every two hours."

"That wouldn't do much . . ."

"That was the point."

She rooted around in her purse for some reason and plucked out her ID before handing it to me. "Here"

The image certainly wasn't her though. Her eye's were actually green instead of brown, and her nose was incredibly thin in comparison to the image on the card. Her facial structure was even out of line, her nose was much more petite than the photo. "Oh you're gorgeous." It even brandished the correct name and age I remembered. I didn't see the point in having a fake ID that doesn't let you buy booze though.

"Thanks, I spent hours getting ready that day."

"I bet, lots of makeup, and high lights in your hair it looks like."

She plucked it out of my hand and put it in her purse as the waiter brought us our check. Just after he turned around she raised her eye brows at me and asked, "If you want to go back to your place we can finish watching that movie?"

"Oh yeah, sure. Who wouldn't love to watch a little ole movie?"

She stopped being conversational again, all she said in between shovels full of food was, "Yeah . . . I love movies" as she winked. And naturally "I'll meet you there." Before she drove off and raced toward my house. She took the lead this time. Along the way she squealed to a halt twice, chucked a cancer stick out the window, and went the wrong direction before she called me and asked for directions.

After unlocking my computer she cued up the second file which was on her hard drive, apparently it was broken into two, and curled up next to me.

I couldn't help myself so I mocked her, "Oh an aphrodisiac!?"

"Huh?"

"Oh, I said Yeah this is a really good movie."

She retaliated by telling me her favorite position is doggy style, and slobbered all over my face again. She asked me if I wanted to go get condoms three times that night, but I stalled long enough she had to leave again. I'm kinda stubborn like that, either I know a person so well I can read their mind or we don't screw.

Naturally after she left I had to slay a couple of viruses again . . . . Only nine this time however . . .

10: The eco box

The family's eco box had been acting up; when starting at a stop light it would jolt and jerk off the line, the check engine light indicated a leak in the E.V.A.P. system, an oxygen sensor, the catalyst threshold, oil pressure, and naturally problems with the fuel injector pressure as well. I had the auto parts store clear the codes, and then every time it'd get a fill up, the engine refused to turn over and spark unless I held down the gas in order to prime the engine. Once started it would chug and die unless I'd rev the engine and pop it into gear first. Naturally the codes came back with every fill up, but once I managed to rev it just a little and put it in gear it would run fine.

I was already driving out north, so I decided to chill and get some coffee, it'd been at least three weeks since the last time I saw her, so I was dumb and went to nightmares. Once I ordered a liquid orgasm and walked out into the lobby I glanced about the room, making sure no one in sight had been there too often. The lot of the room was full of strangers though, no one acknowledged I existed, so I felt safe enough to sit down and read.

After sitting down and tossing in some buds I went digging through the inter webs, hoping I'd find a similar case with a plausible solution, a couple of web pages had decent descriptions of symptoms mimicking what it was doing, but a symptom in each description was always out of place. So I kept digging a little more and pulled up some forums, however I couldn't find any DIY mechanics whom have already had the issue. Nothing really seemed to match and something as simple as reduced fuel pressure wouldn't cause such a misfire it'd jerk the car around, with reduced pressure on the same fuel rail (as a four banger only has one) each cylinder would still run at the same fuel air ratio. I had already checked the seal and the impedance on each fuel injector, they were all within the proper variance and each had the correct voltage driving the solenoid, this pretty much ruled out a fault in the fuel system entirely. I even got curious and checked the impedance of the fuel pump already, it was fine.

After finding five pages indicating that an E.V.A.P. leak could potentially build excess pressure in the wrong area and it could ignite the fuel in the rail I decided it may be best to take it to the professionals in the morning.

I had homework to do for class the next day anyways, so I decided to prioritize. It was an English assignment, I needed to write a movie critic, but I don't watch many so I didn't want to watch a movie alone, after looking around for movie listings. I found only one movie out at the moment that looked good and only one showing I could make it too on time, at ten, I had to act fast. So I plucked up my phone and tried calling Crystal, but no one answered, so I called Bob.

"Hello." He answered.

"Hey what ya up to tonight?"

"Not much, you."

"I just have an English assignment I was hoping you could help me with."

"Need a proof read?"

"No, this old hag is making us write a critic on a movie, and I get lonely alone in dark rooms."

He chuckled a little as he replied, "Most people dream of that assignment, and you actually need help with it."

"Yeah, lucky enough, wanna come?"

"Well, we don't have anything to do tonight, so if ya wanna chill afterwards or something I'd love to see you, but I think we might have to sit this one out, budgets been tight lately.

"What if I buy."

"I don't know, I wouldn't really be comfortable with that."

"It's only a couple of bucks, come on it'll be fun."

From across the room some girl screamed, "You can buy me a ticket." Which made me grimace again while I glanced that way, she was staring across the table still, scowling like a pit-bull.

"Ya sure? If you go alone it's only one ticket, Britney's going to be home tonight." he answered

"Uhh . . ." still surprised at the answer from across the room, "Dude its fine, I practically never have time to do anything I can float it."

"Well, she gets off in half an hour, I still have to go pick her up from work."

So I lowered my voice, "That's fine mate, This means War doesn't show for another hour and a half at west plaza."

She yelled from across the room again, "Wouldn't it be funny if she just, showed up."

I tried shaking my head violently, no, but she still insisted on staring across her table at the guy she was sitting with.

"Yeah, why not, do you want to meet there or what." he answered again.

"Don't you think I'd like to know what it's like to have a guy sweep me off my feet, I want to know what that's like!" she screamed again.

"Yeah are you at your place?"

She let in on me again, "See he's still hung up on her, he won't even take another offer!"

I could only figure I was no longer welcome there, so I answered as I got up and dashed out of the room. "I can pick you up."

She screamed again, "What you can't . . ." and the door slammed behind me

As I scurried up to my car Bob responded, "Yeah, you know where our apartment is right?"

"Yeah I've been there."

"Kewl I'll see you soon"

"Ight, be there in a bit." I hung up, and got in my car.

First thing I did was light a cigarette, it has been a bit unsettling being there, let alone all of the people whom like to scream across the room at me every time I go. I'd never seen her either, it's always a new person, and they always seem to know me better than I do.

I flopped the transmission into reverse backed out, and rolled down the lot. As I was driving up to the stop light on dodge I flipped on a country station, being sick of Tigger and Tanya and all I wanted something new. The song somebody I used to know was playing, I couldn't help but to blurt out, "Yeah after this crap that's the way you're staying too." Thinking I was joking.

The signal turned green, and I took a left. "Yeah that's why I did it, so you can just fucking follow me there when I have homework to do. It's not like the coffee and internet connection are any good." and almost lightning fast, the song stopped in the middle and a female voice called out, "You heard him, that's why he did it."

My intestines crawled up into my chest again; something just wasn't right about that, "NO!!! Stay the fuck away from me!!!" I sat up in my seat shifting my pelvis as my abdomen started seizing, "Stop!!!", tears started rolling down my face as I tried to comprehend my forced encounter, "How the hell are you doing this!!!!"

There was no answer from my friendly radio ghost, and the DJ switched to the next song once the song ended, one of those pop things from Swift. So I was left to squirm.

Figuring it was useless to scream, I lost my voice and continued to drive down the road, I decided however to stop at a gas station first and fill up, my hand was still shaking uncontrollably as I slipped the nozzle into the tank, and surprisingly I didn't give the car a fresh paint job, I could barely keep my hand steady.

The moment I hopped back in the car her voice crackled again. "Holy crap, she's in town."

Then a male voice rang through, "He's listening! Don't spoil it!" before some more music instantaneously started playing. It took about three minutes of cranking the engine to get it to start.

When I got to Bob's place I pulled into a parking spot and the engine sputtered and died on its own, "well that's . . . . convenient." After stumbling up to his door, I knocked on the door, and he propped it open.

"Hey, what took you so long." he inquired.

"I uhh . . ." I didn't know how to explain it so I shifted my eyes away from him, "I had to go get gas before I headed here." It was still playing in my head, but I didn't want to admit myself to a psych ward.

"That's cool; Britney said her boss asked her to stay another half an hour anyways."

"Yeah when's she getting off now?"

"She said to be outside around nine thirty."

"Ok the movie starts at ten thirty and there are always plenty of previews we can miss, I think that'll work fine."

I took my shoes off since it might be a little while before we left, and he asked the same question as always, "Want a bowl since it'll be a while."

"Yeah why not."

No one else was in the apartment at the time, so he made his way over to the couch and I flopped down onto the one across the coffee table, he loaded a bowl sucked on it a bit and tossed it over to me. He had been working on a video game for the last couple of hours apparently. So he asked me, "Wann'a play? I've been toying around with this new emulator."

"Nice you modded the box?"

"Yep" he scrolled through the screen to show off all of the different consoles on the emulator, "It'll run Nintendo, Super Nintendo, SNES, NES, and Nintendo sixty four games.

"Did you set this one up or find it."

"I found the emulator on the Internet." he replied as I handed back the pipe, "what console do you want to play on."

"That one," I gasped, with my finger stuck out toward the TV.

He chuckled again as he responded, "I can't see what you're pointing at dude."

"I don't know mate, I ain't much of a gamer, surprise me."

"Ight how's about Mario cart."

"Sounds good." I started toying with my phone to look at the hell hole, the radio had me a little freaked out again and I still couldn't stop shaking.

He looked over at me, "It's true."

My attention jumped back to at him, "Hu . . . What is?" and my head started shaking again. And a tear started to bubble in my left tear duct.

He chuckled ever so softly as he turned back to the TV and started the race. I poked the pedal and started my cart forward. About half way through the race, my mind started drifting again, the multi colored die was bouncing around in it again.

"You're going the wrong way."

". . . oh . . . dick." in last, I turned around and started driving until the game finished without my making all of the laps.

He chuckled again, "so what have you been up to, lately, I hear you have a girlfriend now."

It was startling as I hadn't told anyone I even knew her, and she's never hung out with them to my knowledge, "Kinda, I met her when I was training; I haven't been able to get a hold of her lately though. I'm pretty sure she's a hooker in disguise."

"They all are, that's the best part about a woman. What's she like."

"Uhh, her name's Crystal, she's gorgeous, funny . . . looking, kind of sporadic, and I don't know, she's an artist, wants to do tattoos, doesn't talk much. I haven't been around her much, but she seems kinda sweet."

"As long as they spread their legs they don't have to talk."

I was a little shocked but answered anyways, "I was kind of avoiding it but she did tell me she's a nymph and asked if I wanted to go get condoms."

He bobbed his head like a gangster and congratulated me, "Jake's getting some action."

So I tried to correct him, "We haven't done that though."

"Really . . . that's boring . . ." his phone rang in the middle of the race so he let his cart run into the railing and I finished one place above last this time. "Hello." He paused, "ok, we'll head up in a little bit then." click, "Brittney said her boss'll let her go a little early if we head up there."

"OK, do ya mind if we take your car, mime's acting a little funny, I don't want it to die on the way there and leave us somewhere."

"What's it doing?"

"The ECU keeps coding an E.V.A.P. Leak, and something's wrong with the O2 sensor as usual, but it'll die in motion every once and a while, and sometimes I have trouble starting it."

"Yeah I guess, mines been a little sluggish too, but it doesn't just . . . die."

I started slipping on my shoes and tossed on my jacket, "What's wrong with it."

As we walked out the door and to his car he explained, "It's doing the same stuff we had to fix last time, at first it won't really accelerate very well, and then after like fifteen miles an hour it'll kick in real hard."

"Did you have the codes taken?"

"Yeah the only thing that's wrong with it is an O2 sensor code though." he unlocked the doors and we hopped in.

I didn't want to go now, I was still shaking uncontrollably yet. He started forward though and asked, "Want a cigarette." As he offered me the pack one was hanging out of his mouth.

I snapped back into reality a little, "uhh, yeah sure." I probably wouldn't smoke so much if I didn't have friends, "got a light?"

He handed me a lighter and started off to the next stop light as I lit the cancer. Just after starting again when our light turned green he barked out, "Feel that." the engine cut back a little, and then jolted forward again when the engine forced through.

"Yeah that feels a lot like what mine is doing actually."

"It doesn't happen all of the time, but it gets kind of annoying, and I haven't been getting as good gas mileage."

"How long since you've done an oil change."

"It's been a while, certainly can't help."

"I'll have to let ya know what's wrong with mine when I figure it out, I might take it to a shop instead, but it feels just the same, the jolting and all, it's a lot more drastic with a four banger though."

"Ight, I'll let ya know if I need any help with it too."

"Kewl, so where's Brittney working now?"

"A call center, You'll see."

When we got there we only had to sit in the lot for a couple of minutes, when she came out I hopped out and got in the back seat.

"You don't have to get in the back." she beckoned.

"I'm already back here, don't worry about it." as she got in and latched the door.

He drove off toward a gas station, where we got gas and a couple of snacks for the road. I had to pony up some money for gas and snacks. On the way over Brittney told us about the imbecilic who called that day, and when we were quite for a few minutes she leaned over toward Bob and whispered, "Why's he buying us a movie again?"

I couldn't hear the answer through his music, but along the way there he had to ask me for directions, since I was the one whom planned the night, I directed him there through the interstate up north and then to the parking garage.

When we got there, my gut started to drop out of me again. I couldn't stand the thought of being followed again. The register was nearly cleared out, the only seats available were scattered throughout the VIP seating with only seven up for grabs, it was relieving we were able to find a seat; I thought the place was going to be packed. However when we finally climbed the stairs there were only about 15 people in the theater aside from the crew which was sparse as well. It was eerie as hell, like a ghost town.

I had to go to the restroom so Brittney said she'd go find seats and pointed us toward the show, Bob and I went to search for a bathroom. The theater was kind of weird, we had to ride up an escalator at the top, apparently it has three tiers, atop the third we found a bathroom with a single stall. I opted he take it and said I'd meet him in the movie; secretly I wanted to break from the pack for a moment anyways. I went down a level and looked around, eventually I found a little bathroom near the employee only area. As I sat atop the throne to take a crap, I heard some singer call out, "Is this a game, are you winning?" before she started singing some song, "Somebody like you." It nearly knocked me the can, the voice was rather distinct. So I pulled out my phone, and sure enough there were plenty of posts under m4w making some unspecific claims, some soul searching, someone was desperate, and then I found it.

Is this a game?—w4m

I just wanted to know if this is just a game. Can you learn to love or do you have a black heart. Whatever it is, I know for sure you have no excuse. Learn to love and you will benefit. We both will, every day. I haven't been able to sleep in weeks without the chance to burn off a little energy. Sleep is so much more fulfilling when we can roll around for a while first. You'll just have to feel it to believe it.

Why play with another heart, when you can bathe in endorfins every day?

My heart rate jumped up to about a thousand beats a minute, she always seems to pick the most opportune times, I say I have homework to do, and she decides she is going to show up and holler. Never in my life, up until I met this person, has it been so wrong for me to seek out an education. It was like she didn't want me to abide by the portion of the bill of rights stating I have the right to the pursuit of happiness.

When I walked out into the theater, there was a woman in the second floor bar singing that one song "somebody like you" she was lying on the floor against the back wall. When I got to the doorway, she looked at me, smiled, and continued singing. I felt like I'd never seen her before and now she was holding her hand out to me like a long lost lover or some crap like that. It was a little creepy to say the least.

Everyone I could see in the bar was unfamiliar. As I started looking back at her again I gave her a halfcocked expression like a curious dog turning his head as my eyes receded into my skull. I think she got the meaning "who are you" . . . as she turned her nose up, back to her audience.

There was another woman at the bar; a lifeless brunette lampshade nursing her drink, two more women in the audience both brunettes who looked very much alike, and a few guys. I walked over to a seat in the middle of the room, and almost forgot that my friends were waiting for me. I sat there for about a minute, I heard someone remark, "This isn't cheap Jake." I thought I was going to have a seizure. The singer got up and started walking around, soon enough she locked eyes with me and held out her hand as she sang. The world around me went dark for a second, all I could see was her, and all I could hear was the sound of my brain ringing in F sharp, the song started flowing in one ear and out the other.

After a while she started singing a new song, but I still couldn't recall if or when we'd become so well acquainted. Sure something like this could be rather expensive, that much is sure, but it didn't feel right. Even if this was some outward message for me, I've heard of so many celebrity marriages fail as one sponges off the other or one just starts throwing money to get their orgasmic fix after spending only a few days together during the year. Even if true, it wasn't love.

It was sweet; it was like a hallucinogen, and bitter like the taste of blood. She'd been running rings around me. She'd been trapping me for her own pleasure. She didn't take no for an answer. It was almost sweet, but for some reason, my gut wouldn't let me give her what she wanted, I had to get up and walk out of the room to go do my homework.

When I got into the theater, the place was empty aside from the two whom came with me. Bob blurted out, "What did you fall in."

"Nah I just don't . . . feel . . . great" I was trying not to puke, and grimaced a bit as I sat down next to him, "Anything happen?"

"Nope they just panned down to the city, perfect timing." and we started staring at the screen.

After fifteen minutes some woman walked in and sat in the middle of the first row, some thirty feet away from us. And I could just barely hear Brittney whisper, "he's using his girlfriend again to get his homework done".

My brain seized again, I didn't even know how to answer that, "hey, do you want to get popcorn?" Britney butted in.

"Uhh, I really don't have much of an appetite right now; you guys can though of course."

"Yeah we just didn't have time to stop for cash."

I plucked out my wallet and as she thanked me. "Awesome thanks Jake, we'll pay you back I swear.".

"Don't worry about it." I whispered back as I slid backward a bit giving her room so she could run off to the concession stand.

My head did that thing again, as a tear rolled down my face Bob looked at me and back at the screen. It was like smacking me in the face.

Bob blurted, "Dude wouldn't it be cool if we could make little bugs like that, we could screw with Stick so much." As I was forced to re-enter reality again, I jumped in my seat and turned back toward him.

"Yeah, wouldn't that be just dandy. Every time he is thinking aloud just text him or blurt something over his radio."

He chuckled and went back to the movie, as my eyes lingered on him for a moment yet, I had to wonder what he knew. It felt almost psychotic, and went back to the screen.

When Brittney came back she told us that the crew said we were actually supposed to be up on the top floor, and asked if we wanted to go up there. So she led the way. One of the crew members brought a couple glasses of ice water up to us.

"Want some" she asked and angled the bucket at me.

"No thanks, I don't have much of an appetite right now . . ." the multicolored die bouncing around in my head had obliterated any chance of that.

In an attempt to make the best of my new mental disorder I continued watching the movie, the paper was due in the morning and I wanted the credits.

As they snuggled up in the seats next to me they began to whisper back and forth, I could have sworn I could make out the words, "and he's your friend."

As we were walking out of the theater I couldn't help myself. I had to look in the bar again, I had to know if it were true. However no one was there, and the girls that went into the lower section to watch the movie were just in front of us as we went down the elevators.

When we were walking back to Bob's car Brittney started reviewing scenes from the movie, claiming it was a good one.

"The part where they shot the headlights was kinda corny though." Was the only real response I had.

She cut in to my train of thought again "Thanks for the movie though Jake, we'll pay you back some time soon."

As I hopped into the car I responded, "Don't worry about it, thanks for coming along, I would have gotten cold alone anyways."

"We're always hot enough to warm your environment." Bob chuckled

I was losing track of my steps, all I could do was try and fake a smile, "hee, you guys always are great radiators."

I couldn't help but to drift a little bit on the drive back. It was a quiet drive though, Britney lit some cancer and stared out the window.

As we pulled up to thier apartment, I excused myself, "I think I'ma go write this paper before I forget anything."

"Ya sure? You can come chill for a while if you want." Bob tried to cut me off, but I didn't want to be around anyone . . . .

"Yeah I'm kind of tired anyways; I need to tend to the hunk of scrap metal in the morning." I paused for a moment before finishing my sentence, "I'll come hang out some time soon though, I promise."

"Thanks again for the movie." Brittney exclaimed again. "Don't forget us."

"I'll catch ya another day."

They both yelled "good bye" and I made my way over to my car. It took about five minutes to get it to turn over, and it was only getting colder. It died twice on the way home.

After getting the car back to the house, I wrote a quick cheesy paper and passed out.

After school I tried to get ahold of Crystal a couple of times, but she wouldn't answer. So I headed home and bugged my father to help me drop the car off.

After getting it back from the mechanic the next day we found out that there was a lot more wrong with it than we expected. P0134 the oxygen sensor 2 was slow, it also claimed no activity at one point. P0172, the engine was burning full rich. P0449 the EVAP system was malfunctioning. P1166, the oxygen sensor was over-heated. Our shop smoke tested the intake, scoped the engine and found that the a/c motor was sticking. The spark plugs were fouled up, and the EVAP valve near the tank sounded like a machine gun firing every time we gave it any gas. Naturally he topped the description off with the fact the oil was as black as night.

I thought this was finally out of my hands but they said they let it warm up and took it around the block and nothing happened. When we got the damn thing home, it coded again. But it wasn't making that machine gun sound anymore. Naturally the old man started to have a cow when we got home; claiming to my mother, "If you two didn't drive it so much this kind of thing wouldn't happen." He continued, saying he wanted to "trash the Korean piece of shit and get a new car." He started to say, "Maybe I'm not so fond of Korean scrap metal." I zoned out, for many reasons, it is always someone else's fault with him; I walked out of the room because these inanimate objects always seem to be out to get him. I couldn't change it either.

When he is heated, everyone suffers. So in another attempt to escape his presence, I changed the oil, it'd be cheaper at home anyways and maybe it would help. He even told me to drive it for another day to see if it'd come back. So I headed out to a west bound coffee shop. I was dead wrong, About 15 minutes into my drive it died at 35 mph and forced me to stop, so I got out and gave it a look under the hood. After sitting for ten minutes I tried to start it again. Click . . . click . . . . click . . . . it turned over. I was in business again.

After turning around I found that little did I know, it was too good to be true, it died again at 40 this time, so I goosed it turned the engine and managed to keep it going by throwing it into neutral every time I came to an intersection or a hill and revving the engine. It started to accelerate slower and slower every time, it was like something was decaying inside the vehicle, at another stop light I revved it in neutral and the gauge slowly crawled up and up until it hit four grand the light went green and I jammed it into drive. The car jerked forward like a F1 racecar off the line, and proceeded to try and throw me against the steering wheel after the engine cut back again. It was back to the slow climb, probably about a minute to gain ten miles per hour. People started honking behind me, gunning it and swerving around me. However I managed to keep it moving for about another 5 miles or so, the temperature gauge never budged, and I didn't ever see any smoke coming out of the engine bay, so I assumed I wouldn't have to start pushing, yet it finally died at another intersection while I was trying to rev the damn thing.

I was within a half mile of home and it was doubtful it'd even climb the hill to my house. My throttle was useless, the gas gauge dropped by over a quarter within just a few miles and I lost speed up the last two hills, obviously something was killing this thing, it was useless fighting it anymore. I had to park it. At this time some happy camper sat behind me and held his horn for a while, for almost a minute. It was giving me a head ache and there weren't even any other cars on the road, I wasn't sure what was wrong with him, so I waved him around. Naturally the genius flipped me off and hollered "asshole" as he swerved around.

I sat there with my hazards on as a light cycle passed and a couple more cars swerved around me. I worked up the courage eventually to attempt turning the engine over again. With the pedal to the metal and the engine cranking finally it revved up to a measly grand and a half, which was enough to idle at full throttle into the first parking lot I saw.

I tried to look at the bright side, I was within a half mile from home, but I'd still prefer to do other things . . . After sitting and staring over the dash for almost thirty minutes, I started to review the symptoms, and naturally my mind started rolling, "What would my uncle do?" My first thought was to pull the plates, syphon the gas, and leave it there, but cars don't grow on trees.

I had to stew on it for a moment before I got out and stuck my hand over the tail pipe, oddly enough he was even helpful from the grave. When I got it started, and cupped my hand around the exhaust nothing happened, the exhaust pressure should've quickly blown loose.

When my uncle was still around he was complaining one day about the cheap materials used for head gaskets, when they go antifreeze will flow through the exhaust and that reacts with something in the catalytic converter which melts over and turns into a big rock. When the engine runs, the hot exhaust causes it to swell up and choke the engine to death.

I was giddy, it baffled our family mechanic, and finally, my Uncle solved it for me from the grave.

After a little walk back home, my dad was curious why I just came in the front door instead. I gave him the low down and then HIS gasket blew . . . . Again the world was going to end, it was our fault, and he wanted to give up on what he referred to as scrap metal. After complaining that he couldn't afford another car payment, and how we might have to sell his fancy SUV to buy others I got tired of speaking to a wall. He wouldn't even listen to the fact I still had my own, and that I could help them get around until it was fixed. His attitude is typically contagious though, unless I wanted to have a family ulcer I had to get out of there.

The next morning I found an engine gasket set for about two hundred, the head bolts for thirty five, the new catalytic converter for a measly two hundred and eight online, next I only needed a couple of hex sockets for my ¾ wrench, and a book with the correct torque and sequence specs). After convincing him I could do it in the garage, I overheard him talking to my mother, she was worried I'd fuck it up, and being a cheap ass he insisted, "oh well at least he'll be learning a lot. Plus we can always tow it back to the shop if that's the case, they'd still have all the pieces of the car."

I tried to get ahold of Crystal, failed, and then replaced the head gasket in our garage myself; it only took about 6 hours to disassemble the engine.

Once I exposed the open cavities of the chambers my father decided to come down and chat.

"What are you doing!?" he paused and glared at the open cavities, "Don't you dare let anything fall in the chambers, It'll ruin the engine!"

"I won't." I responded.

"I don't think you're hearing me, DO NOT let anything fall in there!"

"That's why I have paper towels in there. I'm going to clean them out when I'm done scraping off the gasket. There won't be any debris in there when it runs."

His face boiled red as he shouted again, "I know more about cars than you will ever learn! You will scratch the walls if you wipe them out!"

"The only thing in there is gasket material and carbon, that aint going to scuff the metal walls. Aluminum is a little harder than paper Dad." I turned back to the car and continued scraping off the gasket, plucking whatever pieces I could as I loosened them. And the shortest conversation I've ever had with him concluded as he turned back to the house and stomped over to the door.

With the door slamming behind him he screamed, "MY HOUSE!"

"Umm . . . I'm sorry?"

After eight hours I decided that doing the head gasket in a single day just wasn't going to happen. The odds were stacked against me. We still had to wait for the catalytic converter. Half of the engine was still apart. And I couldn't see anything in the dark.

I checked to see if Crystal would respond threw my tablet and a book in my backpack and hopped on my old bicycle for kicks.

Just before I rolled out of the garage, my father crept out and started screaming, "What you're just going to leave now!?"

"Yeah I just cleaned up the block, I'll re-secure all of the accessories and have it ready when the catty gets here tomorrow. I can just slap everything on and it'll run."

"It's almost nine, and only fifteen degrees you idiot, aren't you going to be cold."

"I have gloves." I mumbled as he did a one eighty and slammed the door again.

I found another store which wasn't open as late. The kicker was the open patio, I could sit there even after they closed. So I went out back to cool down and sip on my tea. Soon it'll be necessary for me to move to a new college, so I started looking around the nation for reviews on each engineering department.

A group of people came outside, six guys, one woman, after a couple of minutes she started screaming, "Sex Jake, Sex!!!" like I didn't know what the word meant. I had to glance her way without moving my head but it was true again. She didn't take long to book it back inside. Her friends scowled at me, and one mumbled "I'm going to beat the shit out of him if he doesn't."

I didn't feel like losing a fist fight with the lot of them so I cowered there for a bit. Luckily enough they did no more than pace around and holler, "Little shit need to grow a pair!" I only recognized a few of them though, "Oh don'ch know who me is stupid?" Usually they are scattered amongst a crowd, but I've never had a conversation with any of them. Luckily they went inside after hollering, "Fucking coward!" So I tried to get some reading done.

11: Can't make Apple Cider with Lemons

Finally, the catalytic converter arrived. Express shipping was still cheaper than the dealer or a parts store, but those two days felt like a year. And Crystal still hadn't contacted me.

When I finally logged on to my face book, I got curious and browsed to hers. She had someone listed as her boyfriend, and it wasn't me. Naturally this made me a little curious, so I texted her, asking if she wanted to meet somewhere for dinner or coffee, she didn't respond. She may not have been the easiest book to pry open, conversationally that is, but at least she seemed to want me around . . . So I decided I'd drive up and see if she was working, and she was.

When I walked in I found the one of the girls who was working there when I was training. She greeted me as I approached, "Hi what can I get for ya?"

"Yeah is Crystal working right now?"

"Umm . . . yeah, is everything ok?" she looked down at my waist and slowly up my torso, finally back to my face.

"Yeah I just wanted to ask her . . . a . . . a question."

". . . Ok." She replied, and walked back behind the divider between registers and the kitchen. I could just barely hear her in-between the overhead fans, "kain some aoek see you aoke." And she walked back up toward me, "She'll be out in a sec."

So I stepped to the side past the railing and waved some guy whom walked up behind me through, "go ahead, I'ma be a minute."

She took his order, money, and a moment later his burger flopped back out onto the heating rail, while she bagged it Crystal walked out to greet me, her face dropped the moment she rounded the corner.

". . . Hey, what's up?" she asked.

It took a moment; I didn't know what to say or how to say it. "I wasn't able to get ahold of you for a while and I was just curious . . ."

She perked up a little, "Yeah, I went rouge for a few days, didn't show up for work, Paul almost fired me."

That was a little surprising, "Really . . . you were almost fired?"

"Yeah, crap happens though."

"What do you mean by going rouge?"

"I went to this party out in stateside; they had this awesome Kush and quite a few mollies."

The sound of those words was like a smack in the face knocking my head back in surprise, "Mollies are allways . . . . Fun." I didn't want to verbalize anything offensive, but I'm not exactly a fan of ecstasy.

"Yeah they had a really cool DJ too."

"Funky . . . So . . . I looked on face book, you're uhh . . . with another guy?"

She started to cry, and wiped a tear away from her left eye. "Yeah we were at a party and . . . he was just." She turned her head as her newer manager beckoned for her and someone drove up to the window, "I need to go . . . Do you want to talk later, I'll call you after work?" she started leaning forward a bit as she whipped her eye lashes around.

I wasn't sure just what to make of it but responded anyways, "Ya don't have to, I'm sure what's his face won't like that at all . . ."

She glanced back at another customer waiting in line, "No . . . Its fine I'll call . . ."

My eyebrow was confused, "Yeah, sure . . . I was just curious if it was true." As I shrugged.

"Ok . . . well." She glanced over again, "I have to go."

"Ok . . . Take care." I stared at her for a second, and then nodded before walking off toward the door. Made my way through it, and luckily to my car, where I mumbled under my breath, "Uhh, Yeah he . . . great he nuerrrr . . ." before I stared into the radio for a couple of minutes. A couple of cars drove by me, two went through the drive through, and one gave birth to a mother and two kids whom skipped joyously up to the door as their mother followed. It was kind of perplexing, when I was there I was told she was one of the better crew members, and she seemed to get everything done just fine. I never would have taken her for a sensation addict . . . Ecstasy, freakin ecstasy.

My corneas were just barely saturated as I glared back up toward the cinderblocks holding the structure up. So I struck the engine.

I continued to drive out of the parking lot, hit the street just fine, and went a mile down the highway. The moment I hit Hillshire I decided to dodge east, crossed a patch paved with gravel, crested a hill and came skidding to a halt in the next valley. Since there was no one in sight I decided to pull off of the road into the field in case any cars'd come rolling through. "What did I take you to the wrong restaurant!? Was I not forward enough!? Did I talk too much? No . . . You can't speak, we must go squeaky squeaky."

Some car left a smoke cloud trailing past me as it blew over the hill in the other direction, after a couple of minutes it wafted in my window and started making me sneeze. "Seriously, already . . ." I gaged again. After staring at the hill for ten minutes or so, the dust finally settled and conveniently enough another sedan went flying in the other direction. I like to mumble under my breath, "great I'm going to get a ticket sitting here aren't I?" so I sparked the engine again and inched my way back onto the road before jamming it into second and started making my way back home.

As I did the radio came back on, conveniently enough Tanya started going on again just as it did, "They're a lot nicer when you do them the right way though." I wasn't exactly in the mood to listen to it for long so I jerked forward as I belched, "Nope that ain't gonna work!" and poked the dash to change the station.

When I finally pulled up to my hill I left the shifter in first and crawled up the hill at about ten miles an hour, I didn't want to go there either. But I never get a break, my phone started vibrating, "Great! . . ." I barked as I goosed the pedal again pulled over the curb. It was her, "Hello."

"Hey, are you busy."

"Nope."

"Well . . . I actually . . . have to work in the morning, do you want to chat tomorrow instead."

"Sure . . . when?" I was angry at the time so I didn't want to spoon feed her.

"Oh, well I get off work at ten, do you want to meet somewhere."

My gut got the best of me, "how about Caffeinated Nightmares, It's this mom and pop shop I've been going to for years when I have the time. My brother and our friend brought me there one time; it's on twenty second and Howard." Most of the customers there already thought I was a verbal piñata so why not.

"Ok."

Great, a one word response, I was being fed my own medicine. "I'll see you tomorrow." I hung up first, and tossed my phone into my back pack.

I had to work in the morning so I made my way inside. My mother, whom was sitting in the seat atop the stairs perked up, "When do I get to meet her?"

As I turned back toward her I filled her in, "She's humping another guy." and walked off toward my room.

Every once and a while a friend of the family likes to have help on a job or two, I work nights at the burger factory so I like the extra cash. He's was working as a plumber for thirty years before he started his own company. I call him the Stench because he always has me clean up after people. This time he had to call and wake me in the morning, I forgot to set my alarm the night before.

"Are you working today!?"

"Yeah, sorry . . . I had a . . . I guess one could call it a Rough night. I'll be out in a minute." Normally he picks me up at my house when he needs help with a job.

"Ok we're only supposed to be at the Kambels' by ten, they don't leave before then, but I wanted to tidy up the garage while we have time."

"Ight, I'll be out in a moment, just give me a sec to throw some pants on."

"Ok. I'll be here . . . Still." I could hear the truck jerk around a little; I think he shifted back into park or something.

He lives just across the street, so luckily enough he never seems to mind picking me up in the morning so long as I am useful, or at the very least close to it. When I finally bashed into the wall as I'd put my pants on, and made my way out the door, I hopped in the passenger seat.

"So . . . Long night?"

"Yeah . . ." I didn't want to review.

Naturally it was inescapable however . . . . He ain't psychic so he prodded, "What happened."

How dare him . . . I gasped as if my fifth amendment had just been carved out of me, "Crystal and I had a little . . . disagreement."

"Oh, well if you don't want"

I cut him off, "Apparently she was at a party and some dude met her fancy . . ."

"That su . . ."

Again, "I couldn't get ahold of her for two weeks, and then I looked at Facebook for once; apparently Facebook is the key to life." Just to be an ass I nodded my head like I'd found . . . well, the key to life.

. . . Again, "What was on th . . ."

"Well, there was good news, she has a boyfriend . . . ."

"Rea"

"It isn't me"

"Oh . . ." He glanced over at me . . . . Then back to the road.

"She went rouge for a while, took a couple of pills, humped some dude, and said she'd chat with me later."

"That's . . ."

"Apparently she didn't want me, she just wanted to hump something." he stopped talking until we got to the storage garage.

"We need the miter saw, power tools, table saw, the auto screw gun, dry wall tools, half inch copper, and . . ." after pausing for a moment he went on, "two inch and inch and a half pvc."

"Ok" I stared off into the scenery until he parked; just before the truck stopped I hopped out with the keys in hand to fetch supplies.

He got out and started arranging a couple more things by the garage opening for me to load up, once I'd cleared the lot, he took the keys out of our lock and chucked them at me as he called out, "Dry wall mud and tile saw." While I went the other way he locked the first door. After fetching the saw from the second side he barked again, "Keys?" so I dropped them into his hand. Once I loaded the mud and saw I made my way back toward him, he was holding the axe with the handle toward me just near his groin, "we're doing demo today, you might want this." I didn't say a word as I snatched it out of his hand. He did though, "Oh, that's nice." My geezer likes to taunt me.

I grunted again as I hopped in the truck. "What exactly are we doing today?"

He followed through the other door into the driver's seat. "We're starting a remodel . . . the Kambels have a leaky shower, and their Jacuzzi tub isn't working, they said they were bored of it anyways, and want a full tile job."

"So . . . demo . . . ?" I perked up like a prick and stared at him with my mouth half open.

I was the one who asked so he nodded with his eyes still on the road, ". . . Yeah, demo." and I went back to staring out the passenger window.

When we arrived he pointed out what all needed taken out, what was being saved, what was trash, and what he wanted close by, mainly trash cans. With the tool bag, axe and power tools still in hand, I gazed through him and continued to nod at everything he said before I barked, "Aye eye Crappin crunch" dropped my stuff and went to fetch a trash can.

He had his phone playing Pandora through the radio by the time I got back, so I plopped down the trash can, and started swinging an axe. When he was done extracting the cabinets I was half way through the tub wall and ripped up a lead on the carpet for him, which he started tugging on and clipped it just shy of the door after we lugged the cabinets to a safe location in the garage.

After tearing the shower base, walls, toilet, tub, flooring, piping, Jacuzzi, and floor boards out we finished early . . . just shy of four. I swept and packed as he screwed a board down which they could step on to get to the closet. After lugging the trash cans down and climbing back up the stairs to find him. He barked at me again from outside the bathroom. "Well aint that an easy demo."

"I like getting paid to destroy things."

He chuckled a little and encouraged me, "You do huh? I should start more remodels like this."

He glanced back toward me for an awnser, "Clean enough or did we miss something?"

"Yeah it's clean enough" after I nodded he started staring back into the bathroom, "I thought this would take all day . . ."

"As much as I'd love it if ya start more jobs like this . . . I'm still curious if I can take a nap now?"

"Yeah, you can take a nap now." He ingested a couple more photons from the bathroom before turning back toward me and we headed down to the truck, once he dropped me off I set a snooze alarm.

At about nine I tried to force my face back into a dream filled pillow, where my bank account and book shelf were full of things I've never touched before. Unfortunately wishing for it didn't work. So when nine thirty rolled around, I cascaded onto the floor, and stood up after lying there for a couple of minutes. After grabbing my tablet and making my way out the door I started my car and drove.

Apparently I got there early as she wasn't present. So I ordered a cup, and found a seat. Unfortunately the Big D was there, I tried walking past him outside to smoke. "Aren't you going to join me?"

But sphinctering doesn't explain anything I had to speak as I turned around to greet him. "I'd rather not"

"Aww . . . come on I haven't seen you in ages, chill for a bit."

"Ight what ever." I pulled the chair out and flopped down into the seat.

"I hear you are here to meet the lady." He perked up and smiled, apparently waiting for good news.

His sentence was news to me, so I went through the social motions. "Yeah . . . Apparently she found some other dude, I think she's coming here to try and let me down easy."

His face returned to normal, "That sucks, what happened?"

"Couldn't get ahold of her for a week, and presto she's humping someone else."

"So you probably don't feel much like talkin' do ya?"

I started toying around with my tablet for a few minutes, and he gave me a break on the conversation. It didn't take long for her to come through the door; she walked in and poked around at her phone by the door before dodging over to the counter. I wasn't too eager to run up and have a chat, so I poked around on the tab for a few minutes. After realizing she hadn't come in I overheard someone across the room, "That's Jake's Girlfriend? Why didn't he go greet her?"

I looked around and mumbled, "I don't even know the bulk of you . . ." before I got up to go see if she fell in the coffee pot or something, but she wasn't in the lobby.

So I checked my pockets for a phone, "great it's in the car." And brushed out the front door, I started heading for my car and noticed hers in the middle of the lot. She opened the door and stepped out as soon as I headed that way, "Hey sorry I left my phone in the car."

"I didn't see you in there?" She prompted inquisitively.

"Yeah sorry, I musta been in the shadows or something like that." I couldn't help stuttering a bit when I saw her, "Gee . . . You haven't been here long have you?" I didn't want to compliment her if she was going to ditch me so easily, but she looked like a freaking goddess. Her hair was perfectly manicured, her coat was freshly pressed, and the new floral shirt around her torso looked new as well. She looked to be a little well-prepared for a break-up.

"No, I just . . . had to stop at home." She started to tear up already, "Do you want to stay here, or . . ."

"We can go out back, they have a pretty cozy little patio out there, if ya haven't seen it already it's pretty cool."

"Sure . . ." she was speaking so soft I could barely hear her.

We made our way inside and out the back, I picked a seat over in the garden, since no one was out there we got the secluded spot over by the bushes. She just kind of stared at me, so I started, "So uhh . . . What happened?"

"I umm, had a party at my house, and I took a couple of things which put me in a really dark place, and he talked me out of it . . ." she batted her eyes a bit and wiped a tear away from her face.

"Almost wish I'da been there, think I'd try and do the same . . ."

She just cried and stared some more.

So I lit a cigarette; figuring she was leaving anyways, I may as well be unappealing. She glanced over and starred straight at it, like it was going to bite her, "Yeah I've been smoking a lot the last two days. Since my phone doesn't work so good and all." As some guys came out side, she started to get restless and shift in her seat. "So have you known him long or what?"

"Yeah he went to my school; he's been a good friend for a long time."

"Tom?"

She shifted again, apparently not expecting me to be curious when I thought she was interested, "I think I might need to go, my curfew is at eleven."

I glanced at my phone for the time, "Well it's only ten thirty five, if you need to go." I shrugged and gestured toward the door, hoping she didn't expect I'd do something rash.

After pausing for a second, she slipped back into her seat, "oh, maybe not yet?" looking inquisitive and glancing over me, probably assuming I'm a devil.

"You have a curfew still? Is it common you . . . go rouge for a little bit?"

"Yeah, my parents had me going to a therapist for a long time, and filled me up with happy meds." She started nodding back and forth again like she always did while bragging, "They say I'm a little schizoid."

"That's a shame," It reminded me of the hell hole, when I was trying to excuse myself for being a book worm since the respondent hated how docile I was. "Just out of curiosity" I looked down toward the floor, embarrassed to ask, and wondering why I was anyways, "you don't know anything about Craigslist do you?"

"Uhh . . ." she shifted back a little and squirmed in her seat, "No, why what's that?"

"Never mind, I'm just loco." I couldn't remember seeing her there anyways, I let it go.

"I think I might need to go." She looked at her phone and back up at me.

"Ok."

She glanced at me again, at the floor, at me again, and toward the door, "Ok . . . ."

"Ight, I can walk ya out," I glanced over at her for approval, "if that's ok?" I didn't want to scare her; she already seemed really jumpy at the time.

After she nodded, she led the way up to the door into the shop, and through the store. There was a group of people in the ally blocking our path, when they didn't move she glanced back at me with tears bubbling up in her eyes. When they started moving again, I nodded toward them and she continued out the door.

When she got to the rear of her car, she turned around and said, "This is a pretty nice place, I may have found a new coffee shop . . ." She looked a little inquisitive, with tears still bubbling in her eyes.

"Well, it is open to the public" I glanced over toward the shop again, "that sign looks kind of tattered, the manager seemed interested in having it redone if you ever feel like an odd job; I'm sure she'd love if you came and asked about it some morning when your free. I'm sure it'd look pretty good when you're done." It felt kind of awkward helping her as she dumps me.

"Oh that's umm . . ." she continued to sob a little bit as I backed off a foot.

She was still staring at me and delaying a little bit though. This made me wonder if the attire was supposed to be some sort of "sign" so I inquired, "Do you even remember being with me?" She cried again and nodded, "but Toms uhh . . . ?" she nodded again. So I tried to make it a little easier, "If you ever need anything, ya get stranded somewhere or something . . . Feel free to call me if you can't get ahold of someone else," and paused again, "just take care of yourself ight?"

"Do you . . . want to talk after Christmas?"

I shrugged, "Sure . . . Whatever" as I didn't quite know why or what was actually rolling around in her head, it's not like she really wanted to talk even before that night, "you have my number still right?"

Finally she nodded and turned around to flop down into her car. I made my way up to mine and hopped on the back of the trunk to have a smoke and poke around on my tablet again . . . maybe it'd "mask the river" trying to make its way through my tear ducts for her as she drove off.

The whole night seemed kind of pointless, I still don't know exactly why she wanted to meet and chat anyways, it didn't change anything. She never called after that night either. I tried making the best of it and remaining friends afterwards, but it never seems to work out that way . . . . I guess that's life for ya.

12: My personal Voyeur
June 2012

I guess I screwed up . . . . I was going nine miles an hour over the speed limit, and apparently it was on the wrong street on the wrong day. The officer at the bottom of the hill decided to give me a ticket (I was speeding after all . . .), and luckily enough he also gave me the opportunity to take some stop class thing. Apparently they let ya do that for the first minor infraction. He informed me that by doing so I'd prevent it from going on my record. This option was quite intriguing to me, as unfortunately for my wallet insurance isn't cheap. Insurance companies like to compound the cost of their service every time a point is assigned against someone's license. So what I spend over the course of my life increases while my wage would stay the same.

Since two hours of my time could save me a couple hundred over the next few years, I decided I'd be a good little boy and take the class. I signed up for it online, paid the fee, and printed off the little invoice which they send in an email. That way I could toss it in my drawer for a quick reference when the date approaches.

I tend to skim most terms and disclaimers, conveniently enough, there were big bold letters on the payment confirmation page concisely stating, "All Payments are Final" another section that really jumped out at me said, "If you miss the class, the ticket for which it is registered will still be valid and must be paid before your court date, all points for the infraction will be taken off of your license and you will no longer be eligible for another class. If any changes need to be made you must do so at least 24Hrs before the class." So I figure it'd be best if I actually show up right?

The night before going to that class I was at a coffee shop out west. The place was actually pretty pleasant for an hour or two. It never lasts forever though, someone saw it fit to start bellowing across the room, "You little twerp how could you do that to her!" I jumped a little at the sound of a familiar voice.

She was a regular from nightmares. I didn't have much hope for it but I sulked back toward my book, hoping I could ignore it and finish the chapter before class. "You said you'd do it! Just go talk to her! Is that really so fucking difficult?" she usually pauses for a bit, "Yeah, sure he's a real boy now! I'm surprised your nose doesn't grow when you talk liar!" It's always too good to be true though, usually that's about the time I pluck my ear buds out and look that way.

I was right about the voice, she's this tall busty blonde . . . The same one I saw before the movie. "NO!" her voice is really sharp, "I'm a GuRl I don't do Tthatt!!" she has this emphatic pulse in her voice, like a spring in one's step. I didn't even know where she came from, one minute the room was empty, the next she's on the other side screaming at me. "Seriously! This again you little prude!" This time she didn't pause for quite as long, as she thrust her hand against the table she screamed again, "And now this!!" So I glanced around the room, "It's always this!" her head twitched back to face the guy across her table once I came close to making eye contact, "NO!! He needs to do it in person!"

I started to stuff my ear buds in my pocket figuring I may as well leave, it's not like I'd get any reading done here anymore . . . Along my way out the door, she barked at my back, "Yeah! Run you little chicken!" and again as the door closed behind me, "Grow a pair you coward, you're pathet." *ClunK* Life is always better when there is at least one door between us.

It's typically a bit bewildering, so after I plopped down into my car I started gazing back into the store. She wasn't alone; Katie was sitting right by one of the exterior windows, one which I scoped to make sure no one was there before walking in. It was starting to scare me how this tall slender brunette always found a way to track me down. She made eye contact, grinned, and the three foot braided tassel attached to the back of her head wiped to the side as she went back to her book before I left.

At about midnight my gut started turning on me, if she could find me there, why not anywhere? When It finally occurred to me, I found this.

Tinkerbelle—w4m—(cloud 9)

Its rare you actually open up
You've finally given me a way

The day has many challenges.
Pass the test, these traffic things are always easy
The sendoff, we can ride together again
Dinner, favorite place to people watch

I won't be coy, you should know what to look for
Cream satin shirt No bra
Brown shorts No Underwear, I don't want anything between us

If you do as you are told, I will reward you
Your master

Now we can be together forever

Just freakin' lovely right? While I typically hate to be melodramatic, its stuff like this that sends more neurochemicals swarming inside my noggin than I could ever hope to describe. I wanted to reach through the screen and strangle the person on the other side . . .

By now the page has gained a voice in my head; deep and sadistically relentless, it creates this subtle echo in the background of my mind as my eyes dart from side to side like a type writer. It was nagging at the back of my mind more than ever.

That post may as well have stated, "Don't make us strap you to the bed and force feed you Viagra!" So yeah . . . . I reacted a bit poorly.

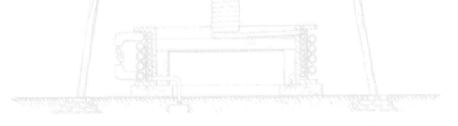

Stay the Fuck Away From Me!!—M4W (Hellmaha)

Every time, I think I have found my out, you find a new way in. Every time I think I have cleared the viruses out of my computer, you find a new way to steal from me information which should be legally confidential. I am tired of it, you cannot imagine how badly ail me; you are the most caustic personality I have ever met.

How the hell do you even know I have to take a class, how do you know where it is? How do you know so many intimate details about my life so quickly? This cannot be legal I swear, I have not given you consent for shit!? I swear I have not been leading you on. I have done nothing more than monitor the hell fire you spew here in order to ensure my life is not in jeopardy. It isn't exactly normal for someone to show up everywhere I go, not but ten paces behind, this time ten ahead.

Every time you look at me, turns my stomach upside down; it makes me want to puke. Sure long, long ago I was under the impression that our connection would be a good thing, but since time has passed I've seen your true colors. It was never optional. I don't know how you did it, but you have been tracking me. You have been making sure I have to "do something" in person.

I don't even know you and you act like I'm obligated to you somehow. All you do is insult and bait me like you are trying to trap an animal. It is disgusting, this is the closest thing to rape I have ever had to endure. For this I loathe you more than the terrorists whom destroyed the twin towers. It isn't a crime but human nature to change one's mind after unpleasant stimuli, I know at one point I wanted for you to come around that much I will admit, but you have crossed a line, if not already surely in doing this. I feel like I have been gaged and beaten, you ignore my every word.

I want nothing more to do with you. Any marriage between us would require a shot gun to my backside! Honestly I would rather turn and bring it to my skull insisting a pull of the trigger would be better than being forced into that which I have not chosen. The next time you come near is without invitation; you have tried the excuse many times that you will only listen if I speak to you in person; however this alone is proof to me, to show is to know and when I write you can read/understand it. Obviously you know English right!? There you go that's a clear form of communication, the next time you come around is one too many. Just stay the fuck away from me!! I don't want to be raped on this planet!

To me, it was like asking a rape victim for sex on the first date. Not only was the ability to acquire this information above my pay grade, but I'm pretty sure she didn't get that ticket by accident . . . . Just seeing it made my stomach turn more than ever. Like being strapped to a bed with all four limbs tied to each corner of the frame, whom ever put that up there didn't want me to go free . . . they wanted to "reward" me.

I started trying to calculate a way to get out of it. I was already within twenty four hours of the class. The department in charge wasn't open anymore. After paying tuition I only had about four hundred bucks to my name, if I skipped class it'd cost three hundred in the end for the class and ticket. I'd be scrounging for scraps until pay day . . . . If the ticket stayed on my record, perpetual my scrounging would become.

Plus, it would be on my record in the first place. Typically failure to make it on time to a class which will negate the effect of a violation isn't seen as merely a violation on paper but further proof of that person's tendency to be unreliable and inattentive.

Going to the stop class was the best choice for me. Yet considering the situation I didn't want to go.

Twice the sensation woke me in the middle of the night. The first time I thought I'd hurl. The second nightmare made me think my hands were bound. Reality quickly set in however, she was too good at covering her tracks for anything tangible like the nightmare playing in my head that night.

It felt like a puppeteer was doing my walking as I slowly I stumbled into the room and started glancing about for the poster, spotting her didn't take long, but it wasn't who I expected to see. Her satin shirt sparkled as if coated with glitter, and her golden brown face was coated with a light powder, brightening it just enough to draw attention away from her clothing. At least the reasoning for her attire was clear, the shirt she selected was unbuttoned as low as possible creating a cleavage line from just above her belly button which curled up around her chest revealing just about everything from her neck down, aside from her nipples of course; not that the thin material did a great job of masking those . . .

The officer by the door startled me as he broke in, "WELCOME TO THE SEX TORTURE DUNGON!!"

As I glanced over my left shoulder to face him, "Sorry . . . Wh . . . What?" slipped from my unconscious.

He asked again, "Can I see your driver's license and the ticket you're holding there?" as he gestured toward my coffee cup. So I offered him the ticket and started to dig through my back pocket for an ID as he continued, "You must be Jake then?"

"Yep . . ."

"Good, everyone's here" he plucked the ID out of my hand and glanced down at it, and before returning it he made a check mark on his note pad, "We can get started."

On any other day I probably would have been at her feet like a loyal dog begging for bacon (she did a decent job of dolling herself up), but through that form of communication . . . and well . . . considering the time frame, I was about to hurl. So I went up to the front of the room as far away from her as possible. My mind rang like an automated bell as I sat down and glanced to my left. A gorgeous blonde coated in a white/cream'ish cashmere shirt and tan pants glanced over, her back muscles tensed up and torso curled back ever so slightly. Her face brightened and eyes widened as she gestured toward the back room and spouted, "Aren't you . . . ?" she paused, "Or?" and just barely gestured toward herself.

My brain was doing that thing where every synapse inside starts firing at once. So the edges of my mouth curled down on their own and I glared back up front.

The officer looked surprised as I glanced about the room, and he mumbled, "We'll ain't that depressing . . ."

It was . . . confusing, to say the least. I wanted to clarify; I wanted to explain it . . . I wanted to know who/what was operating behind my back . . . But I wanted to hide. I wanted to run, and cower on the other side of a desert. It's just not . . . normal.

He started in again, "So . . . let's discuss what this class is first. The Stop class was originally founded back in 1983 when a group of citizens lobbied for a program allowing drivers a second chance." My mind was elsewhere, it was just too . . . "After a bunch of debates and what not, they created a system based on three tiers, each for different severities of offences, this class is for minor offences like speeding up to fifteen miles an hour over and turning into the wrong lane." I glanced to my left, and the blonde locked eyes with me again, her ankle angled upward and her torso did that backwards curly thing again. "The idea was to give people a break on first offences, as we are all only human right?" She actually looked excited to see me, a complete opposite of the night before, "So if you are here don't beat yourself up too much, everybody makes a mistake every now and then."

He had this little clicker and poked along to the next page of his power point, as I glanced over his eyebrows shifted unevenly and his mouth curled down, "First off, as we should all know the proper order for right of way at a four way stop is as follows." The screen displayed a little diagram of three cars at an intersection, the one on the far right moved first and the rest in a clock wise succession. "While this is proper procedure, it doesn't always happen this way." He showed another in which the one on the right drove first and then the one across the street drove as well, so they both crossed the intersection at the same time. The last blocky car to move was the one turning or interfering with another's path the one at risk of damaging another's property. Before continuing he glanced toward me and locked eyes, "As long as everyone follows through with the intentions they communicate." Before he paused and glanced back to the screen, "Everything will go smoothly, that is why we put blinkers on cars in the first place."

Curiosity got the best of me and I glanced back at the voyeur again, the moment I did her eyes drooped like a dog being scolded. She really was cute. She must have taken a long time to curl her hair, it wasn't fluffy, it was hung like the weight of it kept it as straight as possible.

I couldn't though, it was just too wrong. The medium of communication was always consistent, but there wasn't a plausible explanation for the preemptive appearance. Nearly every time I go somewhere, someone I've never met before already seems to know where I am. Every time I come home, someone posts up there describing the last painting I was sitting under, or the last shop I was at. I wanted to puke, I couldn't let it get to me. It felt too much like an arranged marriage, and I was the specimen they selected.

The officer started in on descriptions of different road and weather hazards; naturally the next step was how to deal with these hazards . . . I glazed over it as my mind tried again to calculate just what to do.

I may have got the ticket on my own, but I felt like a rag doll in someone else's fantasy. She already had the ticket, I didn't know how well I could explain she was there for something else. If I didn't do as she pleased I'd be the nut job. I'd be the one disturbing the peace by taking an opportunity for redemption away from someone else.

I could only look the other way, let her dismiss her ticket, and hide. I didn't want to hide. I wanted to buy a gun, but still to defunct from a civil way of life isn't exactly in my nature. I'm too stubborn to give up everything my ancestors have worked for.

It was almost too disgusting to register, I still couldn't believe it. I glanced back a third time, and my mind rang like a macro, "dear god did she really oil herself!?" her skin was as shiny as a freshly waxed car; I could almost see my own reflection in it.

I had to focus though, I had to focus on a way she'd never find me again. Throughout the rest of class the girl to my left kept trying to get my attention, always smiling and perking up every time I'd look away from the screen. I couldn't tell if she intended to get the ticket as well, only that my stomach turned every time she smiled. She too would have been adorably attractive, if only I had met her in another situation, something just felt wrong about it. I glanced back toward at one point and she tried to start a conversation, "Isn't this shit corny?" but I was too pensive to respond, I just went right back to the screen.

Eventually it displayed a bottle of wine. It was the typical drinking and driving deal'y bob. It's all crap I've heard a hundred times before, the only thing going through my mind was that I wanted to reach through the screen and drink the bottle, someone else in the room wanted to ask a question though, "What's the worst experience you've had with a drunk driver!?"

The officer looked as if he was actually surprised and took another break to catch his breath. As I refocused on the dealer I realize that the tangent was probably intentional. She was my The Stench's niece.

"Well there was this one lady who crashed into a police cruiser, after the officers on the scene refused to let her go back to her car so she could smoke a cigarette while she'd wait, she got really huffy and peed on the front of the cruiser we had her cuffed to . . ."

"Oh my god!? She actually peed on the front of the cruiser!? What did she think she'd get off if she distracts you!?"

His eyes widened and dropped toward the ground as he chuckled a little more, "I really don't know, sometimes logic just goes out the window when we interact with DUI suspects. She ended up getting a one thousand dollar fine to repaint the cruiser and about a hundred thousand in damages."

"Did you get a tape of her doing that!?" the voyeur was speaking this time. As I glanced her way again she took the opportunity to wink at me . . . . That oil may as well been dripping off of her . . .

His eyes practically receded into the back of his head, "Yeah, we had to review it all in court too . . ." He actually looked mystified as he shook his head and finished his statement, "She just bent over, pulled her panties down, and peed right on the front of the police cruiser, the dash cam was aimed right at her."

Some guy filling a baseball cap two rows behind me pitched, "I'd think it'd be a lot heftier than a hundred thousand after medical and everything for the officer in the cruiser?"

"Well her dad bailed her out as soon as she arrived to the station, so she wouldn't cause any more trouble inside. And they hired a really aggressive lawyer . . ." he looked at the ground again and shook his head, "We had to review everything."

I glanced back and Stench's niece had this horrified look on her face before she voiced exactly what I was thinking, "Wow! People are crazy!"

Luckily enough we didn't have to take a test though. At the end everyone gathered round the instructor and the cream covered voyeur started staring at me without a word. As uncomfortable as I was I almost felt bad for her, she just started batting her eyes at me, and they began to glisten like she was on the verge of weeping . . . Until the officer called my name, and handed me the waiver.

When I got home the air was filled with sound waves, my father was playing The Carpenters' "Rainy days and Mondays" about as loud as a passenger jet's turbine. I could only see his ass as he was bent over inside the fridge. It was wiggling back and forth, there was this pop and waddle to it as he undulated up and down . . . from side to side as he cried aloud, "Funny but it seems that it's the only thing to do, run and find the one who loves me." I think he was trying to dance . . . .

His voice crackled and screeched as he plucked chocolate syrup, strawberries, and whipped cream out of the fridge. When I reached the top of the staircase he started to spin around to the left and slide back toward the center island, the strawberries took a different route and slipped out of his hands though.

I only made it half way down the hall way before the music dropped twenty decibel levels, he quickly chased me down the hall and called for me, "Back so soon!?" So I turned to face him. He was massaging his left hand which was sitting vertically in his right, and the horrified grimace splattered across his face indicated that something was up.

He kept pinching and massaging his left hand as I barked, "Yeah? Why?"

I didn't even tell him where I was but, with eyes bright as the sun his head shifted back and expelled the words, "Oh, no . . . no reason" like he'd seen a ghost. After glancing from the wall back toward me and then down like he didn't want to make eye contact he spouted again, "Ok!? Moms going to be home soon so be ready for dinner!"

He turned around and went the other way so I disregarded it and flopped into my bed with my laptop. It's rare he won't push an issue but he must have had something more important to attend to. A flurry of noise spawned from the kitchen as he put everything away . . . .

My first impulse was to pull up ZeitNews as I cooled off, they always seems to provide something rather entertaining. Maybe an article on social psychology, maybe materials engineering, but my father's footsteps rang through the house like a thunderstorm . . . From one end of the kitchen, then back to the other, from one end back to the other, then out to the living room and back, eventually he went down stairs and started screaming. The conversation was muffled by the walls between us but soon enough he burst through the basement door and up the steps. It is surprising that door is still intact, as it slams quite often.

He ripped the fridge door open, sloshing the jars of sauce and butter around like beads inside a maraca shaker and stormed back into the living room. The couch squealed as he flopped back into his special seat on the far end of the couch and turned the TV on, in seconds the volume went from zero to sixty. Gunshots and explosions rang through the guitar on my wall and it started to hum its own tune. ZeitNews was stoking this article about an electrically conductive gel . . . apparently it has been a difficult task in the past, but with the correct catalysts and some polymer as a base it was finally stable enough to sustain several amps without degrading or separating.

Maybe ten minutes later, the garage popped open, and my mother rolled in. After storming up the stairs she started screaming too, "Why is Jake's car outside?! he's supposed to be at dinner!"

"I don't know, maybe they had a fight again!?"

"Did you check the router, didn't he read it?"

"He did, did you see what was up there after that?"

"No, what was it?"

"There was another post; it kept saying that she needs to stay away from him. Whining that he can't get away?"

"He's the idiot that started this though!"

"That's what it said."

"He can't just keep changing his story on her, if he says he's going to take her to dinner he needs to be at dinner."

"We can't make him do it though . . ."

"The hell we can't, he's not putting the family name through this! I'm going to find out where she is, I'll drive him myself." She stomped down the stairs and back up to the top, "Change of plans, you make sure he stays here, and I'll come back ok!?"

I'd heard enough, and the thought of being drug somewhere to be raped by a freakin braless voyeur was making me ill again. I grabbed my book bag, laptop, tablet, and a couple of papers before frantically jamming them in my backpack so I'd have something to do and the garage door started opening. Figuring I'd get mauled if I tried to jet while the two of them were still here, I stopped with my nose to the door. He was outside on the couch still. I could hear the springs screech and moan as he rambled to himself, "No! We don't see the Stepnicks anymore!? The dumb fuck'in kid has to make her cry!" a short pause as he rocked back and forth shaking the house, "Ya little fucker, I oughta stick a needle in you!" I waited for another moment, I wanted to give my mother enough time to make it down the street before I crept out of the door and down the hall.

He was silent until I made it to the stair well, instantaneously he glanced to his left and belched, "Where are you off to!?" I got the door open and he hollered again, "Hey you little ingrate!!"

I couldn't make it through the threshold fast enough, so I barked over my shoulder, "Coffee-Shop!" as I shut the door behind me and made a break for it. As I made my way down the street I plucked the keys out of my pocket as swift as possible and hopped in to ping the engine, rounded our circle as quickly as possible, and gunned it down the street as well. Luckily enough he wasn't out in the lawn screaming and yelling like the last time.

Once I made it down a few blocks and around the corner I pulled over to figure out what I wanted, where to go, anything but back there. My answer was pretty sporatic, A burrito. So I drove west for a while and stopped at this local joint, normally the place is about as quiet as a library. Their drive through gets more action than the lobby.

After the kind gent taking orders brought my burrito out I pulled out my laptop, thinking I'd tinker around for a bit, and mow over just what I was going to do . . . It was too good to be true however, not but an hour later this slender blonde came waltzing in and ordered a plate.

Ya know how some books can be so engrossing that the world around, everything else, starts to disappear? Well I wasn't paying attention at first . . . She didn't demand any attention; she was barely a blip on the radar. The door swung open and some stick figures stormed the counter in my peripheral vision; the food there is orgasmic so that is entirely normal.

I was only able to pluck through a couple of pages before she started in on me again, "This place is a lot better!" I recognized her voice. "Seriously, you aren't going to do it!?" I started to shake again as she curled over her food like Golum devouring a live fish, "After all that!?" a little debris even flew across the table at the stiff that came with her.

"Sure ya little fucker just a ghost right!?" I didn't know what else to do, so I clicked along to the next page. "Not even when I'm going to buy then? You fucking creep!" I couldn't hide from her any more, I had to glance up from the pixels. "You're in ass hole, get off of your ass!"

I still don't know her legal name, she goes by four of them . . . "Sure just lead her on ass hole?" Apparently the blonde was Katie's posy . . . they were sitting at different tables. I had to go somewhere else, I dashed up to the counter to ask for a to-go box before she started again, "Are your ears ok!" I started walking back, "Maybe if you nerds wouldn't spend so much on head phones they wouldn't hurt your ear dumbs!" I started boxing up my food and she started bellowing again, "You could just tell the truth ass hole!" The guy didn't say a word, she on the other hand didn't know how to stop, "Casper the friendly ghost hurr . . . just be a baby why-doOncha." She was really at it this time, "Can't get it up little guy!? You're right! This is a shout out!"

After closing the lid on my Styrofoam, I started to let the marbles roll around my head a bit and flopped back down in the booth. The banshee continued hollering as always, "Awww! Are you too shy!?" and I glanced over toward them. They were still wearing the same tan cashmere.

She had a little bit of lettuce stuck to her chin as she screamed again, almost uncontrollably, but she kept staring straight across the table in between bites. "It's just a relationship you coward!" She'd bend over, curling around the burrito in her hands with her forehead just about knocking into the table. As she snorted and inhaled some more of the burrito she spat some back, "poor guy!? Can't figure it out? I've made it so fucking hard to get in my pants!"

The stiff across from her started to snarl; he was bulky, tall, and he had this real poorly groomed goatee. I thought he was a mute at first but he finally spoke up, "He has his phone out."

Without so much as a glance she cast her scraps down, slammed the lid and dashed for the door. He didn't seem to be quite as rushed, as he picked up her drink and trailed behind out the door.

I still couldn't get over it, I took the long way, no one was behind me. No one knew where to find me.

13: Yeah, like they'd stop . . .

It was proving to be rather difficult to find somewhere to live when my salary was neither extravagant nor consistent. Sure, even if I continued working with The Stench I'd make enough to buy a couple of toys and maybe a dinner or two every month. He never had consistent enough work for me to add it in as income though. So with rent, food, and gas I'd be saving just fifty dollars every month at most apartments I could find.

It was discouraging after an hour so I picked up my psychology book. I don't like falling behind my classes. But even with Pandora playing through my head phones I had to keep turning up the volume to block out my parents' TV. I was able to survive that for about an hour without losing my mind. I was able to finish the assigned chapter, but they started to discuss which movie to watch.

Naturally my father turned a couple of them down because they were merely stupid chick flicks. A couple of minutes went by, and explosions and gunfire started echoing down the hall, then it got a little louder, "Oh!! I gotta hear that again!!!" and louder. Eventually I just get a little tired, and leave.

While I was driving north I flipped on the radio, hopping for a good story.

"Seriously!?"

"What?"

"I just fucking hate that!"

"What?"

"When guys string a girl on and don't even give them a chance."

"Well yeah, it's bad for their egos right?"

"How would it make you feel if someone constantly threw you between denial and acceptance? It's like throwing someone in the trash."

"Rejection hurts man."

"It's demoralizing, she keeps going back for more and every time he rejects her."

"Who?"

"My daughter, I think this asshole is going to destroy herself image."

"What's he doing?"

"He keeps inviting her for coffee, shows up, and all he does is sit on the other side of the room and act like he's reading."

I thought I was going insane and mumbled to myself, "What the fuck?" as they sounded exactly like the last chapter I was reading.

But they continued, "Huh?"

"It's just a horrible way to reject someone, and let them just figure it out while you waste their time."

"Does he even realize it?"

"Oh yeah I'm sure he doesn't realize it. That little prick is there like clockwork."

"How do you know he's doing it on purpose?"

"He'll only talk to her over the internet."

"He's facebook'in her?"

"No. Worse, some forum."

"Bet that's great for her self-image."

"It's horrible, he's just trash'in her every fucking time."

"Are you sure it's the same guy."

"Positive, he acts like he doesn't even realize it but he is going to give in."

"What are you going to strap him down to a chair?"

"No! Of course not." Tigger took a moment to sort out his next statement. "I'm just saying if he actually took a few minute to listen he might want to."

"I don't know about that one bud. It doesn't seem like he really wants to listen if he keeps doing the same thing."

"He will."

"Really? You think so do you?"

He sounded rather self-assured, "Yep, He'll hear her out."

"What's that supposed to mean?"

"Nothing, I'm just positive he'll hear her out."

"Well does he have a choice?"

"He can do whatever he wants."

"Huh . . . I don't know what to make of that one bud."

I felt like a mental patient, but I scoffed aloud, "He probably wants nothing to do with the deranged word of some sex obsessed stalker."

Their voices exploded not but a couple of seconds later. "You have got to be kidding me! Guys have no manners these days, just call a lady anything they want." I thought it was just part of some show I hadn't heard the lot of but he continued. "Deranged, Seriously!? Deranged!?."

"I told you he didn't want to."

"Sex is the best part of a relationship. He will hear her out." Tigger's voice deepened like a bellowing ogre, "He invited her in. He can't just turn back like that without so much as an explanation."

"I guess she's already emotionally invested?"

Another exuberant cry echoed through the radio, "It's been killing her! She hasn't been the same since she met the guy!"

"If he doesn't want to he doesn't want to."

"He keeps going back there though; He's like the freakin asylum stalker. Seriously! Every time he says he wants to chat, and he just sits on the other side of the room."

"Hehehe, actions speak louder than words you know. Go fuck your self."

That's right about the time I rolled into Caffinated Nightmare's parking lot, he cried over the radio again, "Exactly! He needs to take a leap of faith and go talk to her!"

So I pulled out and turned around, "Oh and this guy wants to run."

"I don't think he wants to pay his child support."

"Go in!"

It was just too weird. I even felt like a nut crying aloud to myself, "Fuck that! Strictly submissive Aye?"

It just kept coming back through the radio, "So what! Throughout history the man has been dominant, he's been the bread winner."

And like an idiot I responded, "Nah, I'd rather have a strong woman by my side. If hello is so difficult that she's going to coach me and tell me I have to get my nut up and come talk to her I'd rather start anew with someone else."

But the radio did it again, "All of them are strong, do you have any idea how difficult it is to raise a child?"

"I love it when they submit too, uhh! It hurts so good."

"I don't get why they like it either."

"I don't get it either, but I'm glad they do."

It took a couple of seconds for my radio to make any noise again, "Seriously don't be a jack ass, just turn around for ten minutes."

So I got mouthy, "Oh ok big ole radio man, I'll hop right the fuck to that."

"I know what he has to do. He has to stop texting."

"Yeah it's that phone."

I got a little fidgety and plucked the battery from my phone before reaching for the radio, "Oh well that's not cool." slipped through before I managed to turn it off though.

Obviously I had to find somewhere else to go. I considered grabbing a burger at some fast food joint, but they're too common, too greasy . . . I could have grabbed a sandwich, but most sandwich shops close between eight and ten. Finally after bouncing it around in my head I decided to go down to The Stock Bottle, where the Big D works.

When I arrived I the waitress, Chelsea, greeted me. She directed me to a seat over in the area she was serving and left a menu with me before going back to the center bar. I had to glance around the room before I'd even consider ordering. After taking an inventory of faces I decided it was fine to chill and prop my laptop open atop the table.

I didn't really care about what I'd be eating, so when she came back to the table I picked something by sliding my finger down the menu and taking the first thing in front of it.

Soon after she brought over my food, two suits walked in and sat just across the room by the back door. Neither seemed to be recognizable, so I plucked up the burger and started munching. I didn't get much time, after just a couple of paragraphs The Big D came over to chat.

He barked rather abruptly, "So what brings you here!?", and startled me from exactly what Tigger had claimed I'd done wrong in the past. "We don't have coffee here, what's the point?"

"Well you keep bragging about your hockey puck burgers, so I figured eating a little ash wouldn't kill me if it'd make you feel good about yourself."

He chuckled a little bit and pulled out the chair in front of me to have a seat. "Try the onion rings" he barked with his finger toward my plate, "we slice um up and bread them ourselves."

"Great what do you use for seasoning, the cockroaches from under the grill?" as I picked one up with only two fingers I let it hang down like a dirty diaper I didn't want to touch. I instantly started complaining, "It's ripe and steamy!? Like baby poo!" but it burned the tips of my fingers a little and I let it drop back to the plate.

He started chuckling again, "Fresh out the oil!! We use about a pound of butter in every fryer, it gives the oil flavor." and flopped back in the chair beneath him, "The batters fresh too, it's just a mix of eggs, oil, flour, and a little milk."

It took a moment for me to decide to trust him, but I finally took a bite and complimented his handy work, "They're definitely a lot better than the pre-stamped onion pulp you get in a fast food baggie."

"Yep! Them are real onions."

"You actually have time mix up everything here eh?"

He nodded emphatically as he answered me, "Mornings are pretty slow around these parts, only the rich drunks who don't have a job to go to make it in."

His brother decided to tag team my study break and pulled up a third chair, "What are you two up to? Just going to leave me at the grill while you sneak out back to fornicate?"

The big D must have thought it was a pretty good idea as he perked up, "Actually I was just gonna ask if this idiot wanted to come out back for a cigarette."

I figured I'd point at D and build his ego a tad, "I was just complementing his French follicles, every time he lets it grow out his hair line starts retreating"

Little D doesn't laugh much, he just called me a dog, "This mutt isn't going to ruin it for us and leave a pile back there is he?"

So the big one supported me for once, "Nah . . . I've got him house broken."

I prompted lil D again. "What'd he poison you too!?"

"Nah I don't like um, taste like bolts."

It was a little below zero though so I made an excuse, "Well if ya wanna, I gotta go grab a jacket first"

"Ok" he gestured with both hands down toward the table, "leave your stuff here though"

I looked around the bar while my admittedly grandiose trust issues boiled to the surface and I snatched my laptop up, barked, "Can't do that . . ." and made for the front door.

I only found my leather jacket in my car, so I plucked it from the trunk and made my way back. I don't wear it quite as often but I left the house in a hurry, it'd have to do.

They were already on their way for the back door as I caught up to them, and lil D called for me, "So why do you bring your laptop everywhere you go?"

I braced the door with the back side of my wrist so I'd keep from knocking my netbook against it. "I just started working on a novel."

"What's it about?" he prompted

Big D handed me a lighter and a cig as I tried to develop a sales pitch, "The sexual harassment I had to endure at the hands of a crazy bitch. After finding her on the side of the highway she asked for a ride to go get a gas can. Just a week later she found some way to follow me to a coffee shop in the middle of Omaha and started stalking me throughout the city." As Big D stared up at the sky and exhaled like a chimney I continued, "Same one this baboon usually chills at."

As he inquired further the door in the lower level swung open and crashed against something metallic, "What do you mean by sexual harassment?"

He frowned a little and I went on, "Oh, I think it's a longer story than I even realize. She kept coming back while I was doing homework to ask her friends why I didn't recognize her, and made a big fuss about how some guy driving a golden chariot wouldn't ask her out. After a while she started hollering across the store about the last web page I'd been on and I got a little curious. As far as I can tell she either hired a programmer or bugged my computer personally, no one should have been talking about the first methods for insulating copper wires. It's just not that common."

In the middle of his next sentence some woman on the lower level growled like Marge from The Simpsons, "Damien have you seen this?"

"I've only been there sporadically while he was."

I filled in, "And you were out north at school for while she started in on me, I doubt you saw everything."

"So how does her following you turn into motivation for a book?"

"I really don't know how else to explain it, I'm pretty sure she started contacting me over CraigsList to antagonize me further. She likes to tell me to man up and flirt with her. I'm just not sure how that explanation is going to take without proof . . ."

The door on the lower level slammed again but he prompted like nothing'd happened, "So what of it was true . . . .?"

So I lied, "Well . . . . The car chase didn't happen . . ." and paused for a little bit . . . "I'm hoping that when I'm done I can go back to school and nudge my way into the right field, I want to tinker with alternative fuel sources like radiant receivers or all electric vehicles."

"What are these receivers?"

"Basically a really tall electrode that utilizes the static energy in the atmosphere, what you typically see as lightning is pretty much always present but when there isn't a collision between two bodies of air which have a large enough temperature differential the charge created isn't strong enough to discharge to the ground."

"You can't just make one of them? And use that to go to school"

"Without building a really tall tower I can't get much static out of the air. And if I'm going to tinker around with the circuitry at lower altitudes I'd need to use really high fidelity switches. Either way it'll cost more money than I can make at some burger factory. I'm trying to make due with what I have at my fingertips."

"Books are pretty easy to do?"

"Yeah, you should toy around with your own, it's virtually impossible to hurt anything while you're tinkering around with a word document. And if you get a big enough file just look at the bottom of Amazon's page, they have all kinds of stuff for publishing. If you want, you can find a publisher that'll help out with editing and whatever else you need too . . ."

It's rare the Big D is the first to start whining, but he snuffed his cancer stick and propped open the door "Ight I'm cold"

I was shivering anyways so we both followed, and the moment we crossed the threshold Chelsea beckoned for them, "We just got two orders, they're up on the ledge."

Lil D was the first to awnser, "Ight, we'll hop to it!"

I only got a couple of sentences down before her shrill voice echoed across the room, "OK! Your in!!" If it weren't for the fact I recognized the voice, I never would have looked. But the moment I glanced over she started in again, "Oh you are going to be a big boy now!?"

I'd love to say I was excited, but I chose to glance back toward my computer, which pissed her off even more. She hollered again, "Yeah . . . I know what that is, it's your tAAZEEr" as emphatically as possible.

I've never actually had to use it to defend myself, so normally it sits in my car like any other toy. When I first walked in I assumed it'd be there, but reviewed my steps anyways. The last time I'd held it was when I was walking my dog around the lake. It was fresh out of the package so I was trying to lite my cigarettes with it, I tried burning a couple of leaves, and managed to shock a couple of flies by switching its light on and off until they'd fly into it. I'm a child like that, and shocking my-self was painful enough the first time it didn't appeal to me anymore.

I was wearing the same jacket that night so I decided to fake stretching and nudge my front pocket with my heel. I couldn't feel anything so at risk of being caught I kicked my crocks up a little to expose my heel and nudged it again, the discovery rang through my spine like a shock wave.

Somehow she always knows what I'm not paying attention to, it's more than just a little uncomfortable. I was afraid to move, afraid she had something else up her sleeve, afraid I'd never escape her death grip . . . The thing about someone like that though, they don't stop for anything, "I don't care! He'll never use it, he's a freakin teddy bear." Her voice was barely audible, "Just make sure you grab his keys when he finishes it . . ."

The guy next to her whispered, "you didn't . . . . did you!?"

And another finished up, "I thought you were going to take that at the party on Saturday."

"What!? He's cute." Some more mumbling and, "Just make sure you grab them, I don't want anything happening to him." I couldn't hear but a bunch of mumbling after that, but apparently it sent her into a frenzy. "What!? He aint driving like that!"

I didn't quite know how to piece it together, it just didn't seem normal. She didn't seem normal. I had to know I wasn't hallucinating though, so I glanced over, making sure not to turn my head so she wouldn't flip out any more. If I could have avoided it entirely I would have. I stared back at my computer and tried to ignore her.

Chelsea walked up and startled me though, "Is everything ok?" as she gestured toward the plate.

"Just fucking dandy." I glanced back at my cup; there was only half an inch of coke left in it.

"I'm sorry?"

She was either playing, or dumb. So I stuck my thumb out, "Never mind . . . Do you know the slut over at that table?"

"Umm, it's really not nice to call someone that."

"I'm not trying to be nice, do you know her?"

She frowned and glanced back at her, "Yeah, she probably comes in about once a week."

"So she's a regular?"

"Yeah, I'd say so."

I didn't actually want her to hear me anymore so I mumbled, "Maybe I'm on her territory."

"I'm sorry what."

"Nothing. I'm just rambling to myself."

"Ok . . . Do you want to send her a drink or something?"

"Aww hell no. She doesn't have any DUI's or assaults on her record does she?"

Chelsea started to scowl and glanced back again, "Last I checked she was actually a pretty nice person."

"I guess we all have our own opinions."

The subject must have been bothering her, she tried to change it, "Can I getcha anything else, dessert maybe!?"

So I nodded, "The check." As she turned around I changed my mind, "Chelsea!" and propped my drink up in the air, "Can I get a refill first."

"Sure."

I glanced back at the glass, as far as I'd known or heard rufilin would leave some sort of trace behind . . . . Maybe some filler from the powder used to hold the pills together, there wasn't any oil droplets floating on the top, no discoloration, nothing . . . Nor do I have access to a lab so I figured I'd just prevent the unthinkable, "Can you dump out what's left in there before you fill it? I don't like my soda real thin."

So she took the glass, "Not a problem."

Just the very sight of her makes me paranoid anymore. Whether it was coincidence or not, I chose to watch Chelsea fill my cup before she brought it back. And like clock work my tail started hollering again, "What do you mean you're twenty!?" A little more mumbling and, "Ok!! You're in!!!" she started screaming while her hands flailed. "Seriously, now this . . . . . You're boring!! It's because you're boring!!"

Chelsea came back again to set the check on the end of the table. "Here ya go."

Again I tried not to let my voice tremble as I responded "Cool, thanks!"

She turned around and headed back to the bar, "Take Care!"

The bill was only for eleven twenty three so I figured I'd pay cash. I whipped out my wallet, plucked out thirteen dollars, dug a quarter out of my pocket, and tossed it up on the table with the bills.

"Why isn't he . . ." my tail moaned again and glanced at the baseball cap next to her. "Fix him!" She went on after I wolfed down my drink and shut my laptop "Seriously!? You're in you idiot!?" as I lurched out of my chair and threw my jacket around me. Yet again as I made for the door, "And now this!! Why do you always screw me over!? I just want to talk!?" Some guys at the tables adjacent to the door finally started cracking up, I couldn't open the door fast enough.

When I got out to the car I flopped down in the driver's seat and pinged the engine. I was about to fiddle around with the cassette deck and spin some tunes, but the radio kicked in the moment I engaged the accessory switch.

"She LiKes you, heheheheh . . ."

A second voice started howling along like jackals "Hehehehehe."

"I'm tellin ya, she's willing to go to great lengths for this guy."

"What's so special about this one? Normally that girl bags um and drops em."

"You know how love is, I don't really know but she'll never forgive me unless I befriend the guy."

"It'd be nice if he just came to wouldn't it?"

"Yes, yes that would be nice. A conversation with a guy like that's gotta be good."

"I wonder if he's listening to the radio right now."

"Of course he is, IT ROCKS! Hehehehe"

Three of them broke into a song of laughter yet again. "heheheheh!"

"Oh, that's good stuff."

"Yeah, I can't believe he didn't even say hello. What DID he do?"

"Says right here. He sat down to play with his laptop like a pre-pubescent little nerd, and proceeded to make oogly eyes across the bar. She noticed him staring and tried to coax him over, but he ran away like a pussy."

She walked out of the bar and lit a cigarette as Tanya finished up, "Why does she even like him if he can't even talk to her?"

She decided to scream after pulling out her phone, "I'm right here! Just get it over with and come talk to me like a big boy!"

"All she'll tell me is that actions speak louder than words."

"ReAlly? What kinda action's she lookin for."

"Hehehe! I really doubt she'll mind the stretch."

"Hehehe wow hehe hehehe heh You are a horrible father."

"WwHhaaat, if a guy does something like that I'd expect to walk her down the aisle."

"Yeah like you haven't looked at about a million naked women."

"Oh heheehe, get a load of this. She actually stood outside and waved at the guy."

"Where was he?"

"In his car."

"What!?"

"Get out of the car!"

"Grow a pair dude!"

"Seriously don't make this any harder than it has to be."

It was the kind of ostentatious display you'd expect from a psychotic. He didn't seem to understand how unnerving it was from the other end of the stick . . . Especially considering what they've said before.

"Really I thought he was over this by now?"

"Nope, she says he just flipped his lights on and honked at her."

"What a douche bag."

"Opp, now he's driving away."

"Stopp!!"

"Turn around"

"No!!"

"Oh god! Don't do it!"

I was, I was driving away. How else was I supposed to respond? Should congress pass a bill requiring all Americans to have a GPS chip embedded in their skin? Would a husband like having his wife ask about every place he's ever been? Could I lash out? Could I lash out and remain a free man? Would a judge believe me if I said I was hearing voices over the radio?

I couldn't come up with a solution other than turning off the radio and playing something else. Just before I could reach the button Tigger's voice leaked through once more, "I guess we're just going to have to run a special promotion in the morning." So I found some tunes, went out to my favorite lake and took a stroll. Unfortunately my radio and car were in perfect order the moment I returned. I even made sure to park on camera.

When I finally made it home I set my alarm, changed the station, and curled up in a ball.

In the morning the alarm started blaring, "Good morning sunshine"

They broke into another song of laughter before starting up again, "We're running a little contest for all our early birds."

"Yep, it's a game of where's Waldo."

"At about eleven we'll send our very own to a bar somewhere in the metro, and it's your job to find her by noon."

"Whoever wins, gets to eat for free and spend their lunch with Janet."

"She'll even take you to get drinks some other time if you're dandy."

"Who wouldn't love that, free drinks and free babes."

"Yeah, who wouldn't love to have lunch with a beautiful woman?"

"If you don't, you're nuts."

"So if you think you know which bar, HEhehheHe show up and claim your reward."

"Hehehe, your reward."

"You know what I mean."

"Don't just sit idly by and act like you don't know again."

"Yeah he knows which bar."

After yet another song of laughter they decided to continue with the day, "Until then, lets put it together for another solid block of rock, on the empire."

I was doing that deer in the headlights thing for a moment, I'd set the alarm to play a different station and didn't have a clue how I was hearing their voice. They started playing some Metalica track before I came to and turned it off.

Not but fifteen minutes later it went off again, "hehe, hi there."

"Seriously a million bucks for one date."

I almost fell out of my bed as I jumped up to smack the off button, "Aww don't be like that."

But I decided it would be better to reach for the power cord, as only one of the alarms was set. Unfortunately one of their voices slipped through again, "Don't unplug it."

I laid about and stared at the ceiling for a couple of minutes, turned on my computer and started searching for another file to tinker with . . . Suddenly the garage door opened and my mom rushed up the stairs and thrust the fridge door open, then the phone rang, and she stomped over to the table, I could only hear one side of the conversation . . .

"Hello!?" . . . . "Oh my god, that's too funny!" . . . . "Really he could make how much?" . . . . "Just to go up there?" . . . . "I don't know, he isn't even out of bed yet." . . . "I'm not sure he wants to, every time he goes to that coffee shop he brings a backpack full of junk" . . . . I could hear a bunch of laughter before I turned on Pandora to escape from the back ground noise. She screamed over it the moment I did, "oh common he's going to do this too her again." She paused, "I know, every time he decides to do something he falls through on it!!"

The phone slammed against its wall mount and she started back down the stairs, "She's waiting up there for you!" the door slammed, garage opened, and the car backed out of the garage.

I turned the music up as loud as I possibly could and started looking for another file to toy around with, another place to start . . . . After thirty minutes or so of sifting through files and files looking for another point for insertion I heard something coming through Pandora. "Common little guy, don't stand her up again."

"Be a big boy for once."

"You'll feel like a million bucks afterward, I promise."

"Yeah, her ex even told me she's pretty easy to get in the sack."

"Common she's a nice girl."

"You'll want to marry her I swear."

I turned the audio feed off and sat for a few minutes. The room was dead silent. So I turned it back on, "I told you he'd figure it out."

"Yes we can play with your audio feed." The sound started pulsating from speaker to speaker again.

"Just go already."

14: New Neighbors
Late June 2012

My older brother drives this crappy old minivan that's been in the family ever since I can remember, so it's kind of decrepit at this point. He'd been having issues with the braking system, so he showed up one morning in search of assistance. He started shaking my shoulder to rustle me from my slumber, "Hey Jake" he paused for a moment and shook me again, "Jake get up!"

I slowly rose from my pillow a glared at him, "What!?"

He dove in, "The van has been acting up, can you come look at it?"

So I prompted, "What's it been doing?"

And he rambled on, "The brakes are locking up, common I need help!" as he motioned toward the door.

"Fine! Atleast start some coffee then . . ." I grunted back toward him as I'd flopped back into the pillow and finally he stumbled out of the room.

I didn't want to get up. So I laid there for another moment and stared back into the pillow, wishing the clock'd stop moving and I could sleep until noon, but that wasn't going to happen. He screamed from the kitchen, "Common ass hole get up!" and I finally rolled off the bed and flopped to the floor to search for some pants and a grease worthy shirt.

Whence I'd finally crept back into the kitchen I found him at the table on his laptop, "What are you doing . . .?" I mumbled as I pawed at my face and let loose a yawn.

"Looking for reasons it'd be doing this!"

I glanced over toward the coffee pot and discovered there was nothing started, so I stumbled forward to grab the hot pot and fill it at the sink, "What exactly is it doing?" Normally when I think of braking issues I envision situations like cut brake lines and screechy brake pads. Possibly even a runaway vehicle like in the Simpsons when someone cut Homer's brake lines.

He cut me away from my little day dream, "The brakes keep locking up, by the time I get to work or here. When it happens there is a bunch of smoke coming from the driver's side and the wheel gets really hot."

I started pouring some coffee grounds into the French press and mumbled back, "Huh, that must be great for your gas milage . . ."

"Yeah and the last time I showed up at work there was a bunch of oil spewing all over the engine!" he thrust his chest back toward the back rest and gestured forward like he'd flip off the computer screen. "I'm not finding much, what the hell could cause that?"

"Well, it's just the passenger side right?"

"Driver's side!"

"I don't know, there's a chance that a bunch of rust'll build up in the line, it is some fifteen years old. If we try swapping out the caliper it may help."

He shouted again as he scoffed at me, "Ok! Can you hurry up, I have to be at work by four!?"

"Late start today?"

"Kinda, I didn't exactly plan on dealing with this today."

So I offered to hasten things as I started pouring the coffee into a to go cup. "You can look up a couple of parts stores and check the stock, we might have trouble finding such an old part just walking in . . . ."

He started taping away at the key board and I walked over with my hand out toward him so he could bark again, "What!?"

"Keys please . . . . I want to see what it feels like in case there's something else we can do."

He scowled again as he dug through his pockets and bent over to check his coat which was on the ground to rifle through that, finally he popped back up and tossed them across the table. They bounced off of a box my father left there and slid off the table. "Make it quick, I want to go get the part sooner than later!"

After bending over to pick them up I turned toward the door and grunted, "ok." The van was sitting right out in the drive way so I hopped in and pinged the engine, it sounded the same. I flipped it into reverse and made my way out of the drive way, it still felt normal . . . . A little sluggish but the van always was a gas hog . . . .

I took it down the hill and around the corner toward the park with no change, made my way up toward our old junior high and to Giles. It even crested the hill onto Giles just fine so I took a left back toward the house. Finally after getting about three quarters of a mile round it started cutting back, pretty drastically actually. By the time I'd made it round and started up our hill, I could jam the accelerator to the floor and I'd just barely creep along. It felt like I was trying to push a freight liner.

He met me at the end of the driveway, so I asked him straight away. "This piece of scrap metal even get you to work and back?"

"Luckily, I don't live too far from work. Look at the wheel, I wonder if it's smoking yet."

So I hopped onto the concrete and peered over at the rubber. "Nah it aint."

"Stick your hand next to it." It felt like the burner on a stove.

"You could probably cook an egg on that thing."

I wanted to check the engine for cracks and oil and popped the hood. He was in a hurry and inquired immediately. "What-cha up to?"

"I want to see if the engine is fine, you said it was spewing oil."

He propped the hood open for me and started pointing it out, "The oil fill cap here blew off and was sitting on top of this plastic piece." As I scoped around the engine bay for anything else which may be faulty, there was only a little tar dribbling down the side of the engine though. "They said that part is only fifteen after the core so we can go up there and get it whenever."

"Ok, well it doesn't look like the casing is fractured, hopefully this part will be all we need.

He started again. "What is a core anyways?"

"Basically it's just the value of the scrap metal that's on your car now, they charge you an extra fifty or some odd dollars and when you bring back the old part they'll refurbish it."

"Oh, so we don't even have to dispose of it?"

"Nope . . ." I couldn't help but to chuckle as I'd antagonize him. "So you're driving right?"

He was already exasperated, "Jake the car won't even roll, do you REaLLY think it's going to make it up there?"

I'd already been digging in my pocket for the keys; mine was blocked in so I started walking toward our parents' car and he followed behind me. "So which one has the part?"

"They have one just up the street at the store on seventy second."

I flopped down into the driver's seat and sipped on my coffee as he plopped in next to me. "So how is this thing running since you did the head gasket?"

I swung a right at the bottom of the hill and made toward the store, "Well it rolls don't it?"

"Yeah I guess it does . . ." he mumbled. "Why did you have to replace that again?"

"Oh . . . . When they crack antifreeze will flow through the catalytic converter and it reacts. That melts over the honey combs inside and plugs up the exhaust."

"Dad said it ran fine when he drove it home from the parking lot you left it in!?"

"I told him to take it down an interstate for a while but you know how he is . . ."

"I just hope you weren't making him spend money on that for nothing, I'd hate to think you were taking advantage of my parents!?"

"I fixed it for free . . ."

"Uh huh, I think you were faking it" he bellowed again as we pulled into the parking lot, and he stared at me for a second more. "Aren't you coming in?"

So I plucked up my coffee cup and grunted, "I think I'ma sit and sip on my coffee, you know what you're getting right?"

"Yeah just the caliper right?"

"For starters, we might need some brake fluid as well, you didn't give me much time to look it up but it might help."

He leaped out the door like his ass was on fire and slammed it before stomping off into the store.

After a couple minutes of staring off into the brick wall my brother came out with a bag and hopped in next to me. "The guy at the counter said that sometimes it can be a collapsed line as well!"

"In all honesty, if there were something wrong with the line it's more likely it'd be clogged with rust or some other debris . . . ."

"He said it happens all of the time, plus they're only like 3 bucks I'm goanna try it."

"You do know that a braking system is pressure driven right? It's more likely you'd have a ruptured line if they'd weakened enough . . . When you stick your foot on the pedal it pressurizes the lines and squeezes the calipers together . . ."

"Jake! He sells this kind of stuff, if he said he's seen collapsed lines obviously a couple of customers have had that problem in the past!"

his brows cocked up on the edges of his face and his nose curled as he spouted off again, "Just drive!"

I pinged the engine and drove back home; he didn't say a word the whole time.

When we got back I parked on the side of the street and started making my way up the hill. Once I heard his door slam I started poking at the key fob to lock the doors.

"So what do we need to do this anyways!?" he hollered

"Just a lug wrench, my socket set and maybe a crescent wrench for the bleeder valve . . . If you want you can go grab the jack, it's up under the work bench."

He ran up ahead to open the garage door and scurried toward the work bench as I stumbled up to my room to grab my tool bag and socket set. When I made it back down stairs he was crouched by the front of the car, one hand on the jack and the other under the car to feel around and find a place to brace the jack . . . "Where should I put this!?"

I mumbled just loud enough for him to hear, "Just use one of the chassis leafs near the wheel you want to raise . . ." and pointed toward the bottom of the passenger side . . . "Don't raise it all the way though, you'll want to use the weight of the car to keep the wheel in place as you break the lug nuts free." He started jacking the car up and when the circumference on the bottom side of the tire just barely started to take form again I broke in, "Stop there, loosen the lug nuts." And I handed him the lug nut wrench.

As he started loosening them I walked back over to the tool bench to grab a jack stand and flopped down in front of the car with my legs crossed and coffee in hand. "Once you've broke them all free so they'll turn by hand let me know."

After fumbling around for a minute or so he perked up and let me know, "Ok they're all loose."

I started jacking the car up again until the tire was an inch into the air and jammed the jack stand under the car as he inquired, "What's that for?"

"Just a safety measure, hydraulic jacks have been known to loose pressure or give out every once and a while, if it does it'll be resting on this. Knowing Dad this is probably a pretty cheap one too, so you defiantly want the stand under there." I smiled and nodded at him, hoping to scare him a little bit since he'd already been a dick.

"So if it does drop it'll still jerk around a bunch won't it? What if it hits my head?" his eyes widened just a tad.

"Better than getting squished" as I chuckled and pointed toward the car I offered a little more reassurance, "If this thing does drop I can't guarantee I'll be able ta lift it" and told him to stop whining, "Just finish taking off the tire!"

He loosened the bolts as a white sedan pulled up into the neighboring drive way, three people emerged and went straight inside before he needed more attention. He was pulling on the tire, "It won't come off!?"

So I glanced back over toward him, "Bolts are all off?"

"Duh!?"

"Kick it." He kicked the tire right in the center where all of the bolts are, "No at the top, so you wrench it out of there, the axle will act like the fulcrum." Finally he kicked it at the top and the tire broke free, dropped to the ground, and bounced a bit as I explained my uncle's reasoning. "In operation sometimes water'll get between them and the rotors and rust weld themselves together . . ."

He prompted as I handed him a crescent wrench for the brake line, "Huh, that's kind of freaky . . . Why don't they make some sort of coating to keep it from doing that?"

"I wouldn't doubt they do on high end models, but if every bolt on this thing were coated it take so long to manufacture the car'd be worth its weight in gold . . ."

He chuckled, "What's next?"

"Detach the brake line from the caliper and then unscrew it from the copper line so you can put your new one on there." After peering around into the wheel well I flopped back onto the ground.

The people next to our house rushed out of the front door and to the side the one in a suit started pointing up toward the chimney, there were a bunch of holes in it and the paint was peeling like mad on one side, obviously it needed repaired.

In the meantime my brother was trying to yank out the hose and he was jerking around the solid lines that leads back to the other wheels, "Here" I offered a 10mm socket and wrench, "Loosen the clip from the inner wall and take the clip off when you have it loose."

They hopped back in the car without a word and drove off as he plucked out the old line and tossed it to the side. The caliper came off next after a little disassembly and we started piecing it back together. After he tried attaching the new caliper he brandished it up in the air to show me that the brake line wouldn't fit together with the new caliper because it had this rounded lip on it and the new line had a bulky square fitting.

He whined and complained a little, claiming that he was going to be late if we have to go back up to the store and fetch a new one. But after staring at it for a second I walked back into the garage and grabbed the grinder and an extension cord so we could just cut off the rounded nubbin and piece it together again.

When we finally had it together he scurried off to work, only to start texting me when he'd arrived.

"I think we need to replace the other one now, the passenger side started smoking this time."

I replied after doing a little research and finding a diagram of the braking system. "We might actually need to replace the master cylinder, that's what regulates how much fluid/pressure goes to each side, there may be less gunk in the left now so the right will bind but it'll still do it afterwards."

There are three main components in a braking system, the two calipers and the master cylinder. The rest is just a bunch of solid tubes full of brake fluid. When the master cylinder operates properly, it'll compress when you push on the pedal and suck fluid back into the chamber when ya let off. When it malfunctions it'll compress just fine, but the clogged up valve won't let any fluid back into the chamber.

"Mom wants us to go over to grandma and grandpa's tomorrow anyways. We need to clean their gutters."

"I thought Stevin helped them do that already."

"Apparently one of them was over flowing last night."

"Ok when do you want to meet there? I'll bring what we need to replace your cylinder."

"Be there by eleven, should give us enough time to do everything."

"Ok, pick up the part on your way."

The next day he started texting me again, "Hey, get up, are you going to be there on time?"

"No, I think I'll show up at ten."

"Ok well I'm on my way so head over there already."

I flopped back into my bed like always, and waited ten minutes or so to get up. My clock said it was only nine forty so I figured I we had some time. I stumbled out into the kitchen to find some coffee first.

After boiling some water and sitting down at the table I plucked another paper from the stash I'd found on Google. Nikola was using a double walled pot to melt plastic or rubber before running a wire through it in order to insulate the wires he was using. The addition of water between the melting pot and the one in direct contact with the burner apparently dispersed enough heat more evenly so the rubber would melt without burning, just like one would use to melt chocolate for coating pretzels.

I got bored of that, they're always worded exactly like a text book, and plucked a web page from zeit-news for reading between swigs before he started texting me again. "Hey are you coming? We have to clean the gutters."

"I'll make ya a deal, clean the gutters, I'll fix your car." And I went back to zeitnews, a team of engineers created this thing dubbed a "multicopter" they strapped an electric pack to an inflatable fitness ball with four branches stemming from the pack. Each of the branches had four motors with chopper blades on them. Finally at about 10:30 I figured I'd leave.

When I got there my brother met me at the edge of the drive way, "You're finally here!? I already got the gutters cleaned out, and I picked up the other caliper and the line from the store!"

"I thought we needed a master cylinder?"

"Well the other side stopped doing it!? Now if we fix this one it should stop locking up!"

I tried to reason with him, "Yes, a fresh caliper helped one side, but the cylinder is still malfunctioning. It is pushing fluid into the calipers but it won't suck it back out. The passenger side is probably doing it now because the line is older, and it has more corrosion built up inside. Making the tube smaller."

"A smaller tube is going to fill first eh?"

"The cylinder will push the same amount of fluid into each, but the smaller one will seize first."

He scowled again and raised his voice to prove a point, "Jake!! The guys at the shop even said that if replacing one makes the other faulty then replacing this one should fix it!! Plus I already have the caliper, let's just put it on and it will work!"

"I can put it on, that part's not a problem, but you'll still need a master cylinder."

"Fine just put the damn caliper on!" he scowled again and finished up without admitting he was wrong, "If it doesn't work I'll believe you."

So after he handed me the bag, I immediately glanced down to make sure the hose and caliper would mesh up just fine. They did so we got to work, we jacked it up plucked apart the right side and pieced it back together, just like the other one. When it was finally together I asked my brother, "Can you hop in the driver's seat and start pumping the brakes?"

"Yeah, how much do you need me to pump it?"

"Just keep poking at it until I tell you to stop, we need to get fluid moving through the lines."

He started to complain the moment I cracked the bleeder valve, "How long is this going to take!? You know I have to go to work right!?"

So I barked back, "Not long just keep poking at it!" and walked over to the reservoir to dump some more brake fluid in.

A couple of minutes later my phone started buzzing; once, twice, three times . . . . It was my mother "You need to give your brother the keys to the car. He needs to get to work on time! You can drive the van home and trade again tomorrow!"

I stood up and glanced over at my brother, "Really?"

"You're the one that said you could fix it and didn't!" he paused for another moment, "I need to go to work on time!" he screamed again as he thrust his leg to the side and arms up.

"Just pump the brakes Jason."

My mother texted me again, "When you say you'll fix something you need to actually fix it!" and the next one buzzed again, "Give your brother the keys! You can drive the van home!"

"Yeah Jake, give me the keys and you can drive the van!"

"What do you expect me to replace the cylinder while you are gone?"

He didn't seem to care though, he just hopped out of the car slammed the door and stormed around the to the side door befoe he plucked out his back pack tossed it around him and snatched a plastic bag. After turning toward me he glared at me with another scowl on his face, "Give me the keys!"

"You'll pay me for the cylinder tomorrow?"

"Fine!"

My mother texted me again, "Give him the keys now, if you don't you need to find another place to live!"

So I looked back up toward him, "When?"

"I'll come by around noon!" his nose curled up and he shouted, "I'm going to be late! Just give me the keys!"

After I plucked the keys out of my pocket and dangled them by the key fob as he ripped them out of my hand with a quick swipe. He shouted again, "The keys are in the dash!" as a little bit of spit landed on my nose, and he proceeded to turn around and storm off to the sedan.

All I could do was turn to my grandpa who was standing by, "Any chance you'd pump the brakes? It's kind of hard to shut it off before fluid dribbles out if I have to lay a brick down and run all the way around . . ."

He chuckled and sipped on the beer in his hand, "You've had to do that before?"

"Yeah . . . When I replaced the brakes in my Elantra no one would help me so I had to cut a two by four jam it in place and run around to cap it off . . . The brakes were a little spongy though; I had a friend help me fix it a couple of days later . . ." As I wiped a little grease off my hand with a rag he crept up into the driver's seat and started to pump. After only a couple of minutes he started to gasp and his mouth dropped nearly to the floor every time he pushed the pedal to the floor. Sometimes I feel bad for him, this time I decided to pick on him, "Tired already!?"

He chuckled and glanced back toward me, "This is hard work!?" with a grin on his face (a phrase they tell me over and over I spawned in reference to maintaining a purring kitten on my lap when I was four)

When the stream spewing out of the bleeder valve was finally steady I barked back, "Ok this time push it in and hold it down!" when it stopped squirting I tightened the valve and stood up to thank him.

After packing up we had to sweep up a little debris and sit down for a couple of minutes. They fed me some soda and a couple of stories before I decided I had to head out.

I took the long way home just to reassure I'd have an issue, or to test the possibility I was wrong. Naturally the brakes bound up so bad I couldn't even roll forward and had to pull over onto the shoulder of the highway. Of course I wasn't exactly ecstatic to be stuck on the side of a highway so it took me a couple of minutes to figure out just what to do, I went rooting around in the tool bag and plucked out a number ten socket and wrench, crouched under the van and broke the bleeders free, the fluid squirted all over my hand and I closed them back up. Soon it rolled free and I was able to take it up to the same shop we got the calipers from.

I would have done it in the parking lot but I couldn't find an extension that'd allow me to get into the little crevice I had to work the master cylinder out of. I started rooting around my impact accessories, found a quarter inch drive extension and made my way back to the van by the time another car pulled up next door. When two people emerged from it I about had my first heart attack at 20, she'd been a regular at Nightmares. I've probably seen her face a couple dozen times. They stormed straight up to the door without a word, and went inside.

So I tidied up the master cylinder in a couple of minutes, and did the same. It is a top level repair, about as easy as replacing a belt. After tinkering around on the computer for a couple of minutes I could hear something crushing wood and the sound of a reciprocating saw.

The lady that used to live there was actually pretty nice most of the time, she used to have a day care running inside and the kids would always run around out back to play tag or climb the apple trees. We hadn't conversed much in the past two years however, she and my mother got into an argument and she'd stay inside the house. These people did pretty much the same thing, when they'd leave they went straight out and down the street, when they came in they would go right inside.

After a couple of days apparently they started to open up a little, but I hadn't the chance to speak to them, I'd always be inside staring at a word document. A week or so later the sound of power saws and swinging axes became a little more frequent and my mother came in to talk to me, so I poked CTRL.ALT.DLT and glanced over, "Hey, have you talked to the new neighbors yet?"

"Uhh . . . no why." Recognizing one of them made me a little reluctant.

"Well I haven't met the girl yet, but Thomas said they just came from Utah. Apparently they had a pretty big construction company out there; you should ask them if they need any help."

"I might, but I still want to focus on polishing this document."

"I wasn't asking you Jake."

"What do you mean you aren't asking me?"

"Jake! If you are going to live here you need to have a stable job, how are you going to put gas in the car if you don't have money?!" she scowled just the same way my brother does and flung her hand to the side.

"I've been working for quite a while, I think I can survive for a little while so long as I don't try and buy a house or something."

"No! You need to have a real job!!"

"I am working, at the burger factory!"

"No! Doing something that consists of actual work! Something hard like a plumber or an electrician!"

"I've been working with The Stench when he needs help."

"That isn't work though! That's a couple of extra bucks on the side of your other job."

"There! You said it! My other job."

"No." she just stared at me and shook her head. "You don't get it, that isn't a career, that isn't something meaningful which you can do for the rest of your life."

"That's why I'm going to school woman."

"I don't need your sass god damnit! I already know you are going to school!"

"Then why are you so worried about my so called job?"

She took more than just a moment to concoct an awnser, "You are going over there Jake."

"Why?"

Her voice even bellowed over mine, "You are going to be friends with these people Jake!"

"I'm sure I'll get to know them eventually mom."

"No, now."

"What do you mean now?"

"Go over there now."

"I'm in the middle of something."

She screamed and pointed at my monitor, "This isn't a job! There is no way you'll ever make anything off of this stupid story so get off of your ass and go talk to him!" She stormed out of the door and slammed it behind her.

I still didn't want to get out of bed, nor did I want to stop typing, so I poked the button that says resume and went back to my word document. After poking at a couple more keys my mother screamed from the kitchen, "Today Jake!!" so I plugged my ear buds back into my canals and opened a window for Pandora.

It didn't take long before she was in my room screaming again, "Jake, its already ten O-clock, get the fuck out of bed and go over there!" as she jabbed my shoulder and gestured over hers with her thumb.

"I have to work at four mom."

"I don't care, you work mornings with The Stench all of the time."

"And when do I have time for my own crap?"

"GET UP JAKE!!"

"Fine" I finally disregarded her and continued toying around with my document again.

She didn't seem to care though, "No I said now!! Get you lilly white ass out of this bed and go over there!!" and she ripped the keyboard out from under my hands leaving a stream of "lkwner;lansfpo" before she continued, "You can have this back when you are done working over there! They need help doing the plumbing for the bathroom!!"

Without a word I leaned over to my laptop to click save and she reached for that too, "I said right this instant!" and I pushed my shoulder in the way so she couldn't muck anything else up.

"I have to work at four woman."

"No! You have to work now!"

"I just want to save it before I leave mom, I'll go if it really means that much to you."

She started screaming louder, "Who said you get to save anything, I told you to get out of bed and go over there right now!!!" apparently she was holding the back space button down as the cursor was moving farther and farther back on the screen, so I unplugged the dongle I had in the USB port and clicked undo a couple of times with the touch pad, "Are your ears ok!?" I clicked save and started typing in a file name as she started tugging at my left elbow, "God damn-it I said now!!" Luckily it doesn't take long to save on a flash drive so I yanked it out and shut the lid on my laptop.

As I backed off of my bed to face her I spoke again, "Ok I'm going now, happy?"

"No, give me that!" she started pointing down toward my pocket, "Give me that two!"

"Why, It's my flash drive."

"I don't care, you are being insubordinate, I'm taking something!!"

"I was doing homework."

She scowled and paused for a moment, "Give it to me right this instant!!" and she stepped toward me with her face merely an inch from mine.

I didn't want to get sent away for defending myself, or get smacked around again so I reached in my pocket and plucked out the USB dongle I snuck in there with my drive and handed it to her. "Can I at least put some pants on first?"

She screamed again with her head cocked to the side and her mouth half open on one side, "Yes, you can put some pants on first!" and made her way down the hall, "What do you want them to think we're white trash, if you weren't going there to help them renovate you'd be wearing your good cloths!!"

After sliding my laptop into its bag and tucking it beside my dresser in the closet I tossed on some pants and made my way out the door with her beckoning behind me, "Don't say anything stupid!! You aren't putting the family name through that!!"

Just closing the door behind me gave me the chills, as I crossed the yard I noticed two women sitting out on their patio, one an elderly woman, the other a regular from caffeinated nightmares. So I reluctantly offered her my hand, "Hi, I'm Jake . . . ." As she grasped my hand and shook it she shifted up in her seat cocked her head down a little bit with widened eyes and looked down toward my feet and back up to my eyes.

Her toes curled just barely enough to start bending her flip flops, "I'm Katie!"

Speaking my mind has gotten me in arguments a little too often in the past so I figured I'd go through the motions and find out how far they'd go. "So are you moving in here with Thomas or . . . ."

She immediately changed pace and her eyes widened, "Oh . . . umm . . ." and paused for a second . . . "NO! That's . . ." her eyes darted to the side for a second and back to me, "Thomas a . . . and Cassie!" and her head vibrated ever so slightly as if she was trying not to nod.

"Yeah . . . my mom said that Thomas and ya'll were in Colorado before coming here?" she started to open her mouth and almost stuttered for a moment.

Her face was pale as a ghost as she replied, "Yeah, his dad had a flooring company they were running out there." And she paused for a moment before continuing, "Wh . . . Why are you the plumber she was talking about?" as she gestured toward my house.

"Yeah I've been working with a master plumber for almost a year now, my mom told me to come over here because you might need some help with the house?"

She slowly cast her thumb over her shoulder, "Uh.mm yeah Thomas is in the garage if you want to go talk to him." And her eyes started to droop like a dog begging for attention . . .

She was in the way of the stairs so I went around the railing to the drive way and toward the garage to find four men standing around with beers in their hands, and asked "Hi? Are you Thomas?"

So Sawyer emerged from the crowd, "That's me! Why what brings ya by?"

"My mother told me to come by." After glancing back toward my house I prompted, "She said you might need some help around the house?"

"OH, You must be the plumber then?" His face lite up and eyes widened like black holes, "Leaving so soon Katie!?"

I glanced over my shoulder and she had had her car door propped open, "Yeah I . . . I have to go pick up Jacqueline!" and she slammed the door behind her pinged the engine and squealed out of the driveway.

The four of them broke out into laughter like a crowd of jackals as another called aloud, "Bye!!"

So Thomas broke in again, "So you know how to set a tub right!?"

"I've done a couple of them . . ."

He started through the basement door and waved over his shoulder, "Let me show ya what we need done!?" as he lead the way into the laundry room he started in again, "These pipes here have been leaking, so if you can patch that it'd be nice, unless we have to replace the whole line. I'd like to have separate shutoffs in there for each room so we could put those in right away."

"Yeah it looks like your leak is just below the floor boards so if ya want we can put the valve in about eye level here and I'll just use that to patch the hole there."

"Ok! And you can do that on both hot and cold right!?" I nodded as he lead me back into the basement by the main. "This shut off here has been leaking every time we turn it off so I think we'll need to replace that one too."

"Unless you want to pay for rental of a tool I don't have we'll need to leave it off and put another up the line. It doesn't leak when its open does it?"

"No that'll work just fine" he cocked his head to the side, "how much do those tools cost?"

"Usually two hundred or so if ya buy um, I might be able to get ahold of one for less though. I'll have to check with The Stench."

"Who's that?"

"The guy I've been working with."

"Ok, Well let me show you what we need done up stairs!" as he started back toward the stairs he stopped for a second and I took a better look around, the whole place was torn apart. He pointed toward the box lying by the wall, "this is the tub we're going to put in."

I only glanced at it but it looked a little longer than the ones we usually put in a five by ten bathroom, "Ya got it measured to fit right?"

He gazed up at me with eyes wide again, "Umm . . . I think so, my girlfriends dad picked it out!?"

"Ok we'll have to see if it works, it looks a bit long though . . ."

"Ok, well we'll see . . ." he started walking up stairs, "Up here is where we have the most of our work cut out for us! There was a bunch of mold all over, apparently the house sat unattended for about a year!" as he pointed out toward the living room.

"Yeah the last owner was running a day care in here; I imagine it was pretty torn up . . ."

He started grinning as he nodded and turned toward the bathroom, "This is where we'll need the most help from you though; hopefully we can set the toilet first so we don't have to go somewhere and use the restroom."

The restroom and kitchen were flooded with bleach and nearly nothing was left on the walls except for the old tub and a plastic surround.

After a short discussion in the kitchen he wanted help tearing apart the center island and then we went to the dump to get rid of a load full of trash. After that we went to the hardware store to pick up some copper and valves.

When we finally made it back to their house he asked me to start with the valves so he could go upstairs and finish demo. As I was trying to solder the valves in place water kept seeping down from the floor boards and all of a sudden I heard a bucket slosh and bleach came rushing down the pipes and splattered in my eyes. I buttoned up the pipes A.S.A.P. and packed up the tools I'd brought over.

When I finally crept out onto the patio the same five guys were standing around in a circle with beers in hand and Thomas propped his finger up at me to blurt out, "Hehe, look he's freakin soaked!!" before the group broke out like a crowd of jackals again.

About that time Katie drove up in to the drive way hopped out of her car. She propped her arms up onto the railing and set her chin down atop them to grin over toward me as the words, "Sex Jake!! Sex!!" replayed in my mind . . .

About the Author

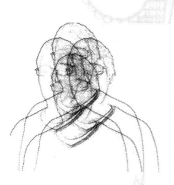

After graduating from high school in LaVista Nebraska, I felt it necessary to do some soul searching, I didn't want to go straight into college as I'd likely just party and build a debt for a degree I either can't use or don't care for. I wanted to know where I was going, I wanted to make sure that what I do with my time on this planet will matter. So I spent some time looking through different career options, medical degrees were my first inclination, operating an aircraft sounded like fun, and pyrotechnics degrees allowing me to design fireworks displays would make me feel like a kid in a candy store for the rest of my life. But most treatment processes are actually pretty effective and in all honesty I'm a lot better with machines than I am with people. Sure I could loaf around, set off some large explosives for a crowd and live the life but it just didn't seem like it'd do much . . .

I got a little hung up on our nation's current transportation systems for a while . . . Vehicles provide so many opportunities to those whom want to make a difference, a highly skilled Ph.D. no longer has to pump their own well water, taking a stroll down to walmart gives them more time to focus on keeping us alive . . . Almost all of our children are able to attend school and become all they can be and the localization of resources just makes life EASY. The gas suckers we use to get around these days are kind of fickle though, in that they need fuel.

The issue presented by "Peak Oil" is rather daunting . . . with a limited supply of oil on our planet it may not be the most enjoyable subject, but one which is difficult to avoid. Sure maybe this is a distant situation, the price of fuel will slowly climb past any reasonable threshold a minimum wage position can sustain (even at forty hours a week) and soon enough we'll have to take out mortgages we cannot pay just to get **to** *work. The cost of shipping would make staples like bread and milk so expensive only CEOs and highly paid officials can afford them, even a night out on the town may cost years of saving and foresight.*

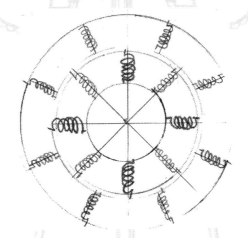

Yeah it's an exaggeration, but we've all seen movies which portray post apocalypse situations and barbaric free-for-alls at supermarkets . . . It's actually entirely possible this may come to pass if our planet doesn't plan ahead . . . When we run out of oil an electric motor (like the diagram I've drawn above) could very well be our only option (even hydrogen fuel cells use an electric motor to bear the actual work load).

Nikola Tesla was kind enough to give birth to the electromotive engine along with several useful versions way back in the nineteenth century, yet very few modifications have been made to it since. The word "engine" (or locomotive device as he'd call it) is quite an adaptive little creature . . . it'll spin a fan, run your air conditioning system, spin your hard drive, move your car, compact some trash, drive a RC toy, it'll pick up dust for you after the switch on a vacuum is flipped, cool your computer, or even pump water out of a flood zone. So yeah, one can find it almost anywhere, yet it still consumes a specific amount of energy per revolution against a particular load . . .

When the cost of transportation effects everything from the price of milk to the sporting goods on the other side of our supermarkets, it seems our economy will crumble if we run out of oil too soon, as even the best electric vehicles on the planet only travel some three hundred and some miles on an eight hour charge. That fact puts this little guy, the electric engine, under a lot of pressure.

Improving the engine and how it is used is my life's goal. It may take some time to polish, but I will do my best to ensure that future generations have as few road blocks as possible; doctors, lawyers, military personnel, and everyone alike shouldn't have to walk across the country when earlier generations could fly. I aim to help all those who want to save lives, protect human rights, and defend our country do exactly that which is in their hearts.